MADE OF STONE

CHARLIE WILLIAMS

MADE OF STONE

THOMAS & MERCER

The characters and events portrayed in this book are fictitious. Any similarity to real persons, living or dead, is coincidental and not intended by the author.

Published by Thomas & Mercer
P.O. Box 400818
Las Vegas, NV 89140

ISBN-13: 9781611098051
ISBN-10: 161109805X
Library of Congress Control Number: 2012917081

MAN DIES IN CLUB ROOF FALL

A 22-year-old man fell from the roof of Rockefellers nightclub last night in what police believe to be an alcohol-related incident. Ambulances were called to the club in Frotfield Way, but the man, named locally as Scott McCrae, of Canal Street, Mangel, was pronounced dead on arrival at the infirmary.

"We're not treating this as suspicious," said Inspector Stephen Jones of the Mangel Constabulary. "Here is yet another incident where a young man has lost his life due to alcohol. I want this to be a warning to all, especially the young—if you drink too much, you're setting yourself up for a fall. Here was a young local man who had his whole life before him, just stepping out into the world of work via his dad's mobile burger van business, and he threw it all away. He drank too much, and he took a fall that killed him."

1

Things seemed different when I woke that morning, which later turned out to be the day when it all kicked off.

A bit of sun were slicing between the curtains like a massive light saber, stretching bright and yellow across the dusty and farty emptiness and hitting the wall opposite, illuminating a bit of wallpaper the shape of a squashed diamond. And that don't mean much, taken like so and in the tepid light of day. But that morning, with me swede clambering out of a barmy dream and my muscles flexing and my cock standing proud like a tent pole, I seen the light. Meaning the light on the wall, which were vibrating a bit like an alarm clock. *Wake up!* it were shouting. *Wake the fuck up!*

I stared at it for a bit, that vibrating diamond of light, wondering what it meant. Cos I knowed it meant summat. It were telling us to change me ways, try and find the old Royston Blake way of doing things and stop fucking about with that other, the one I'd fell into. And the more I lay and looked at it and thought about it, the more I realised it were saying three things in particular:

1. Lay off the bad stuff.
2. Go on a nice holiday.
3. Summat else.

That number three there were an odd one, but I knowed it would come clear soon enough. And it did, about one day later, after the shite had hit the spinner good and proper and I'd sailed past the point of no backing out. You'll find out about all that in a bit, long as you keeps your gob shut and your ears peeled. But first I had the other business to sort. I'm talking about going on holiday. And by that I don't mean camping in Hurk Wood—I mean a proper, fucking expensive holiday.

In a caravan.

2

I knowed where I could get one.

A caravan.

Nice white one it were, only one previous owner so far as I knew and he were still owning it at the time. What's more, he were always out all day during the week, and I knowed how to pick the type of padlock he had on the gate, meaning I didn't even have to pay for it. All I needed were summat to pull it with, and everyone knows the best motor for pulling caravans, don't they? That's right—your 1983 Ford Granada Mk. III hearse. And it just so happened I knowed where they had one of them and all.

Best time to rob a motor in Mangel is about five a.m. Only ones who gets up that early is milkmen, but you don't have to fret over them seeing you, cos most folks believe em to be thieves anyhow. So I set me alarm for half four and had a little kip. It's always important to get a good kip before a robbery so your nerves are sharp, like them of a fox or a badger. Or Rambo, when he's out in the woods in *First Blood*, and he's stitching his arm up with one eye and watching out for cunts with the other. But I couldn't manage to prize meself out of me pit at half four and ended up rolling onto the carpet at about eleven. That's still quite early, mind, so

I felt alright as I walked downtown with me robbing gear in a placcy bag.

To the untrained eye, it don't look much like robbing gear. To him—the person with the eye he ain't trained—your classic robbing getup is a black top and strides, pair of black leather gloves, and black mask or summat. I tried that meself once, as a younger man, but I found that folks notice you and start screaming. Especially when you're in their house and dying for a shit, cos of the kebab you had last night from Alvin's, and your trolleys is already round your ankles as you shoulder into the bathroom and the person is in the bath. And she is a bird. And it's broad fucking daylight. After that, and with the screams still ringing in me lugs, I started looking for a new approach to robbing gear. That's when I stumbled upon what I now call the Uniform.

I stopped in the alley behind the place where they kept the hearse and put the Uniform on. It's more of a disguise than a uniform, but it is a uniform as well, being as you're disguised as a milkman. Only problem were that the hat didn't fit right. When I'd first acquired the Uniform, I'd done a bit of research and located what I thought to be the largest milkman in Mangel, but when I jumped him and twocked him and pulled the togs careful-like off his deckwise shape, I realised that milkmen is a different breed, and that they're pinheaded streaks of piss. Mind you, if you pulls hard enough you can get anything on. I proved that the time when I was pressurised into using a rubber johnny, and I went on to prove it again in the alley behind the hearse place, but with the milkman's hat this time. And on me swede, not me knob.

Then I walked right in the back door.

That is the thing about daytime theft—you can just waltz right in. Not that I can actually waltz. I tried it once with a bird I really fancied, going to a ballroom dancing lesson and everything, but when I bust her ankle, I realised I were onto a loser here—no way were I getting in the pit with a bird in a plaster cast. Them things have a certain hum about em that reminds me of hospitals, which I fucking hate. And do you know what? My nostrils picked up a bit of that selfsame whiff as I stepped inside the place where the hearse were kept. It were a fucking ozzie smell, I swears it. But summat else and all. Summat a bit sweet that made you wanna spill your kebab. Not that I'd had a kebab the night prior. I'd had a few Pot Noodles, same as most nights around that time. But I still wanted to spill the fuckers.

I bent double to do just that, fighting against it cos my honking is fucking noisy and some cunt were bound to hear it and rumble us, meaning I'd have to twock them or clear off, thereby kissing a sweet and tender goodbye to my expensive caravan holiday.

That's when Count Dracula walked in.

3

When I says Count Dracula, I'm talking about a bloke who looks like Dracula. I ain't thick, you know, and I realise it weren't really him.

The real Dracula lives in Transylvania, so far as I knows, which is in Scotland. Only Jock I ever knowed in Mangel were the one used to have the burger van in Frotfield Way. Jock his name were. But this one here, this bloke who had just waltzed into the place where they had the hearse, he didn't half look like Dracula. That's all I'm trying to say, for fuck sake.

"What the hell are you doing in here?" he says, stopping dead when he clocked us. And when I say dead, I mean he looked like a dead man. So much so that he had me reconsidering all I just said about Dracula and Scotland, but not the bit about Jock the burger man. (And if you're wondering why the fuck I keep going on about him, it's cos he comes into it in a bit. So keep your fucking hair on.)

The feller were looking at me, eyes all glassy and skin that way and all, waiting for an answer. But I couldn't come up with one, no matter how hard I racked me swede. "What's the fuckin' question again?" I says.

"I said what are you doing here? This is a private area. Do you have a deceased here?"

I had an answer now. "Disease?" I says, feeling the hackles rise. "You sayin' I got diseases?"

"I'm asking if you—"

I cut him off.

One thing I cannot stand, being a person who has gone through some shite to do with his swede and ended up in a mental hospital for a spell, is people thinking I'm a lesser man for it. Like this one here, suggesting I got a mental illness on account of the scars I bear. In a certain light they shows up prominent, I've noticed, making it look like I got a thin silver band around me swede, stretching across the forehead and just above the lugs, and this were one of them lights here. And it is true: they did pop my lid off in that ozzie and have a rummage around, looking for fuck-knowed-what and not finding it. But it don't mean I'm barmy, right? And it don't mean I let cunts like Dracula here cast asparaguses about my intelligence. Which is why I cut him off. With my hand.

He went down.

I were surprised at that and none too happy, sensing a minor bit of scrumping ramping up into summat more major, but I forgot all about it when I turned around and located the hearse.

I were in a sort of a workshop area, with saws and bits of wood and workbenches and wossnames all around. And that had throwed the fuck out of us at first, making us think I were in some kind of carpenter's shop instead of a place they keeps the hearse. And then Drac had come in and insulted us before I'd had time to look through that door there in the corner, which I were doing now. And finding the hearse there. Polished up and shining and basically using all her charms to lure me inside her and give her one. I went and tried her driver-side handle.

It opened.

As did the up-and-over door that gave her access to the yard out back and the streets of Mangel.

"I said this is a priv…What are you doing?"

It were Drac again, coming to in the workshop area. I had a glance through and saw him sitting up. His mouth were all mashed, and blood were streaking his chin and neck. It showed up like black against his skin, which were white and leathery like a handbag our Sal used to have, bless her rotting carcass that is buried deep under Hurk Wood. Actually, not that deep at all, but the varmints will have ate her by now, like as not. Drac put a paw to his lips and parted them wide, wincing and flashing a bit of gnasher where it don't have no right to flash, being as it extended about an inch clear of his gums. And I gotta tell you right now…

I sort of shat meself.

Not proper like, but a little bit. Almost. Cos there and then, as I jumped in the hearse and hared off on me hols, admiring the walnut dashboard and savouring the surprising amount of torque the 2.8 V6 ticker delivered, despite the hearse being so long and with the big load I'd glimpsed in the back, I realised that vampires truly do exist.

4

I loves driving.

Ever since I were old enough to drive—aged nine—I always appreciated that special magic that is created when man gets behind wheel. There's only two other things I can compare it to: shagging and having a dump. But it sets itself apart from them two.

It's pure, driving is.

You don't have to wipe your arse afterwards, and you don't have to fart and roll over, then wake up a few hours later with your cock dried to the sheet. With driving it's man and machine in total harmony, teaching the world to sing. You're in a different world when you're bombing along like that, one hand on the wheel and the other behind the passenger headrest, fag in mouth, pushing sixty up the Wall Road and not a fucking fret in the world. For that brief moment, I swear you comes a bit closer to heaven. Then some cunt in a van pulls into the fast lane, and you plough right into the fucking back of him.

A while ago I were telling you about Jock the burger man, him who used to flip and flog bits of gristle out the side of a van in Frotfield Way. You can guess what I'm gonna say next, can't you, you being a clever fucker? That's right—the bloke I'd just slammed backwise into weren't Jock but some other fucker entirely. In fact, now I came to get out of my hearse and puff my massive chest out as I went up to exchange insurance details, I realised that it were Alvin.

Of Kebab Shop & Chippy fame. But, right, he were in Jock's burger van.

"Alright, Alv," I says, opening his door for him.

He were rubbing his neck and not turning it in my direction. "I got whiplash," he says.

"You pull a stunt like that again, hauling in front of me at thirty mile an hour on the Wall Road, I'll give you fuckin' *arse-lash*."

"But it's a thirty-mile-an-hour zone, Blakey."

"Exactly. You're meant to go a bit over, not stick to it like a fuckin' granny in a wheelchair."

"But you was doin'—"

"More to the fuckin' point, Alv, what the fuck is you doing in Jock's burger van?"

"I got a new line o' work, ain't I?"

"Since when?"

"Since I beat Jock at cards last night. You know that arselash you was on about? Tell you what, I reckon I got a bit already. This seat's shet."

"Jock's a big lad."

"Erm, I'd describe him more as big boned and—"

"Bollocks, he's a fat fuckin' bastard who eats more burgers than he flogs. Tell you what, I seen him once flip a burger in the air and catch the fuckin' thing in his gob, swallering it whole. He's like Jabba the fuckin' Hutt with glasses on. Even his glasses is fat. You seen them lenses? Fuckin' two-inch thick, they is."

"Erm…" Alvin didn't seem to know what to say, preferring to hoick a thumb behind him and cover his face.

I leaned over to see where he'd been hoicking to. "Oh, alright Jabba?" I says, noticing him there. "I mean, Jock."

He didn't reply. Always were a quiet one, Jock. I think it's cos of him being foreign.

Sight of Jock and Alvin in the same place had brung a sudden and violent hunger to me guts like I'd never known. "Listen, lads," I says, backing out and thinking of the chippy round the corner, "I'd love to stay and have a natter with yers, but—"

"Hang oan," says Jock. I think that's what he said anyhow. "Whit are yis doing in that funeral car there?"

I looked at his fat face for a bit, thinking hard about it, then says to Alvin, "Do you know what the fuck he's saying?"

"Yis fill will fuckin' ken whit am sayin' tae yis, Royston. Yis have just crashed a filly laden hearse intae ma van. Yis have spilt the fuckin' coafin, yis daft wee preck."

After a bit of silence I nudged Alvin. "Did he just swear at me?"

"I reckon we should just go and have a look, Blakey."

"I ain't having cunts swearin' at me, Alv. Not even in foreign."

Alvin were already getting out of the van, taking a wide berth around me and pottering off towards my hearse. I found it embarrassing to be in a one-to-one situation with Jock and no interpreter, so I gave him a thumbs-up and went off to join Alvin, who were peering into the back of my new motor. I were more interested in the front, meself. Grill were hanging off and one beam gone, and the hood had popped up and wouldn't latch down proper. "For fuck's fuckin' sake," I says.

"Can I just ask why you've got this?" says Alv, looking like he'd rather be deep-frying his own cock than having this conversation. "I mean, are you working for them now, or what?"

"This ain't work, Alv, this here is for my holiday. I'm off on an expensive caravan holiday."

He glanced behind the hearse, maybe wondering where the caravan were. He could be thick sometimes, Alv could. "Fair enough," he says, "but, I mean, where'd you get it from? Were it the Sweet Dreams Funeral Ho—"

"Fuck sake, Alv...do it matter? I got her from a place up on Barkettle Road. Fuckin' creepy place, as it turns out, but I'll tell you about that in a mo. Anyways, I've had me eye on her a while now, seeing her going in and out of there a few times over the years. Tell you what, she's going to waste there. Every time I seen her, she's going about ten mile an hour. Do you realise what this engine here is capable of?"

"Erm..." I felt that Alvin were ignoring us, quite frankly, but I let it pass, considering what happened next. "There's a coffin back here, Blakey. And it's...well, it's fell over a bit, and the lid's come off and..."

I weren't harking him no longer. I didn't have to, cos I were clocking it for meself, seeing a leg hanging out and a size ten patent leather shoe on the end of it, ankle stiff like a mannequin. "Shite," I says. "Fuckin', fuckin' shite."

"Look, Blakey, it's alright. We'll just pop him back in and take the hearse back to—"

"That ain't the problem, Alv. You dunno the half of it. See, back at the place where I got this hearse, well, I sort of had a little scrap with...And I swear I fuckin' never noticed this fuckin' coffin when I climbed aboard. Do you really reckon I'd have drove off in her, knowing there's a...Ah, shite. *Shite.*"

"Blakey, woss you tryin' to say?"

I looked at Alv. It were the most serious look I'd ever gave anyone, cos right here I had a problem like no other I'd ever had, and I were being forced to share it with him. "That ain't no normal corpse, Alv, " I says. "It's a fuckin' vampire."

5

"Look, Blakey," Alvin were saying, eyes looking every direction but Blakewards, "I don't want you to take this the wrong way, right? I mean, I reckon it's a common mistake."

The main problem with having a shunt on the Wall Road is that it is a busy road, and if it's daytime, like this were, you're in for a traffic jam. As in fifty-odd motors nosing the arse of your hearse, which has got a vampire in it.

"Fuck you on about?" I says, trying to stare out fifty irate drivers.

"I'm just sayin'…well, I reckon you got a slight gap in your, erm…"

"Alv, spit him out or you'll be feeling the back of my hand. Plus the front and sides of it. And the front of my head."

"Alright, well, can I just ask you a simple question? Without you taking offense to it, I mean?"

"When have I ever took offense to summat? I'm a fuckin' *head doorman*, fuck sake. High-ranking security staff. It is vital that we looks at things subjective like."

"What, in your opinion, is an 'earse for?"

"Eh?"

"A hearse, Blakey. Type of vehicle you've crashed here, what is it used for? Bread vans is for carrying bread, post vans is for carrying letters and that…What's a hearse for?"

Fuck knows why he'd been fretting over me hitting him. I were more *worried* about him than lairy at him. I mean, were he going senile or summat?

"Alv," I says, all gentle and like I were talking to a small youngun, one who can't tie his own laces yet and has got snot running out of both nostrils, the dirty fucking bastard. "Alv, hearses is taxis. They'm just posh taxis with a bit o' space in the back, for posh folks, like. There's no great mystery, my little friend." I reached out to ruffle his hair. He tried flinching away, but I grabbed an ear and reeled him in, then done the ruffling. "You dozy fuckin' twat," I says all affectionate.

"Alright," he says when I let him go, "so, the place you got this hearse from—what do they do there, in your opinion?"

"Posh taxi firm, ennit?" I says, shrugging.

I were more interested in them backed-up motors, realising that they made things a bit difficult here. If it were dark it would have been alright, but it were blazing fucking midday sun, give or take a couple of hours, and it were like I were under the spotlight and they was my audience. A fucking pissed-off audience, going by some of their faces. I stepped towards em, watching fifty drivers shrink back in horror. Fucking chickens the lot.

"It's a funeral parlour, Blakey," says Alvin, his voice getting fainter and somehow more distant. "And hearses is like taxis in a way, but for deadfolk. For ferrying em to funerals and that."

Taxis for deadfolk? Things was worse than I'd thought, regarding Alvin and his swede problems. If I'd had a moment to think on it I'd have said he'd been swigging petrol. I'd seen a few go down that route over the years, and Alvin were exhibiting all the signs. It's a fucking mug's game, petrol is, and you'll end up penniless and in the gutter. Save your money and get some creosote instead—it's way fucking cheaper. But like I suggested, I had other matters going on. Like fifty motors turning into seventy.

"This ain't so good," I says, rubbing me chin. "I'll be honest with you, Alv, and tell you that I dunno what the fuck to do next. So if you got any suggestions, short of just pegging it, I'm all ears."

I thought about that a moment. "Actually, shall we just…Alv? Alv, where the…" I peered up the other way, clocking his white kebab-man coat flapping around his legs as he hared round the bend up there into Clench Road.

Haring into Clench Road—another classic sign of petrol-induced dementia.

Right about then, as these advanced trains of thought was tearing around me swede like Orient Expresses bombing full tilt towards wherever the Orient is (Wales, I think), Jabba the Hutt were prizing himself out the crumpled rear of his van. Meaning Jock the burger man.

I went to catch him as he gained his footage and let go the van door. That's the former doorman in me coming into play, the highly refined lifesaving reflexes that can spot a paralytic drunk at fifty yard and step in just before he keels over and slams skull on dance floor, then drag him out and kick him into the gutter, angling him so he lands facewise and gets a bit of gravel rash to take the edge off his hangover. But Jock weren't like that. He like as not were drunk, stinking of Bell's like he done, but when I grabbed his arm, he seemed more steady even than the Igor Statue, which stands proud to one end of the High Street, representing all the values summed up by some local cunt from olden times named Igor. "Get yis fuckin' paw oaf us," he says.

For fuck sake, I thought. Is it gonna be like this now? Cos I didn't have an interpreter no more, did I?

"Look," I says, "I ain't got the first fuckin' bit of a clue what yer sayin', Jock." Cos you cannot beat around the bush with these people. "Can you talk more slower, like? And with more English words in it?"

In response he did summat with his arm, shaking it free of my grip and sending us backwards a bit. But not so far like it were pushing me. I mean, fucking come on—we're talking about Royston Blake here versus a fat Scottish cunt who came about up to my armpit...and who were climbing into my hearse just then. I got up and went over, brushing the dust off my arse.

"I want you to understand summat, Jock," I says, leaning in. He were in the driver seat, fucking around with my cruise control buttons. I think that's what they was anyhow. "First off, I am the hardest pound-for-pound former doorman in Mangel, which means you do not fuckin' do summat with yer arm that makes us fall over. Not in front of eighty-odd punters, like we got here, and not even in front of no punters at all. Second off, stop fuckin' around with the controls and get out my fuckin'—"

"Thus is a fuckin' raight-oaf, " he says.

I thought about that, watching him toy with the key in the ignition. "I gotta say, Jock, that is a fuckin' odd thing to say. The controls of my hearse is right oafs? Eh?"

"Ye wee fuckin'...I should leave youse to yis ain devices, is what ah should dae. But ah'm a compassionate man, Royston. Ah'll tell yis the truth here—when I look at youse, I dinnae see the typical breed o' cunt yis see aroond here. Yis are a cunt, true enough, but no through yis ain doing. Yis are a product ae yis environment is what yis are."

"The fuck is this *yis* bollocks? " I says. Cos it seemed to be an important word in his language.

I started wondering if he weren't getting at summat deep, and that I'd be missing a trick here if I didn't start catching his drift. Lot of them foreigners can be quite spiritual, after all. Like Demis Roussos.

"Do you mean like ying and yang?" I says. Cos I'd read about that once. It means where you get two things that look like sperms, one black and one white, one upside down and the other the right way up. If that ain't deep, fuck knows what is. "Are you trying to say *yis* and yang, Jock? Like a version of ying and yang but slightly different, with one of the sperms having a longer tail, perhaps?"

"Do youse even realise the problem yis have got here?" he says, totally ignoring what I'd just said. "Him in the coafin back there, do yis ken who that is?"

I were starting to understand him a bit better now. *Yis* meant "you," for example. It's amazing how good I were with languages. Put us in front of a fucking Chinaman and I'll have him worked out in half an hour. Mind you, it's much harder with your Scotch-men.

"Look," I says, "if yer gonna give us the spiel about funerals and shite, I've just heard it, mate. Here, have you and Alv been supping petrol in the back of that—"

"Shut yer stupid face a minute, will yis?" he says, reaching into his anorak and rummaging amongst the folds of flesh he had in there. Couple of seconds later he pulls out some sort of stick. One end were sharpened and looked quite dangerous, actually. "Him in that coafin, he's a fuckin' vampire."

ROOF DEATH NOW
SUSPICIOUS—POLICE

Mangel police are now treating the recent death of Scott McCrae as suspicious. McCrae, 22, died when he fell from the roof of Rockefellers while the club was open for business last Saturday night. A postmortem examination revealed traces of the hallucinogenic drug Plasma in McCrae's bloodstream.

"No," said Inspector Stephen Jones when asked if these results had given them reason to look again at the case. "It was the dead body we found at McCrae's house in Canal Street. We didn't notice it on our first look around because it was well hidden, but on a further visit we spotted it, laid out behind the sofa in the living room. We thought that was suspicious, and that it might be connected with McCrae's death in some way."

Asked how the illegal drug link affects Chief Cadwallader's bold claim two years ago that the authorities had won the drug battle in Mangel, Jones said: "From what we can see, here is an isolated incident where a young man has lost his life due to drugs. But we want to stress the isolated part of this—one incident does not constitute a drug problem in this town. Clearly the McCrae lad obtained his drugs from a source outside our tight-knit community, and we've a pretty good idea where to look. We'll be following it up, don't you worry."

Jones refused to name the dead man.

6

"Did yis get that?"

"Aye."

"*Did* yis, though? Ye cannae fuck this up, Royston."

"Nah, I'm alright, Jock, just a bit…Why'd you want us to do this, again?"

"I need youse to create a distraction. Over there, away from this hearse. Youse do that and I'll take care o' Mr. Fuckin' Vampire here. So go oan. I'll meet yis roond the back and pick yis up. OK?"

"Aye, aye…and you'll get my hearse started, right? I need this hearse, Jock. I'm off on holiday, see. Thought I'd go to—"

"I'll get yis fuckin' hearse started. Now go oan."

"Right you is, Jock. Erm…"

I were still in a bit of a daze, truth be telled. About everything Jock had just telled us, like. I'd only picked up the odd word here and there, but it had been enough. Enough to know I'd been right all along about that place where they kept the hearse being a bit odd, and the bloke in it who I'd decked being a vampire. Enough to know I weren't alone. Enough to know I had to put me own wossnames aside for the minute and do exactly like he'd said, down to the fucking letter. Which in this case is a big *S*.

Cos Jock were ahead of the game, vampirewise. He were so far ahead of the game I reckon he'd lapped it a couple of times.

I says a big S there, but I gotta admit I weren't convinced. If I'd heard it right, it were a fucking top idea in terms of creating a distraction. So top that I couldn't believe I hadn't thought of it before. Mind you, I'd best see if it worked first. And to that end, as I went round the front of the grid and onto the pavement, I started getting ready, loosening my top shirt buttons and humming the first couple of bars.

While I'm doing that I might as well bring you up to wossname on what Jock had told us about the secret life he'd been leading these past few years. See, while everyone thought he were just doing the burgers, he were actually keeping Mangel safe from creatures of the night. And I'm on about vampires, not badgers, though they can also be a menace. Apparently, right, *5 percent* of Mangel's population is vampires right now, though you wouldn't know it if you just went about your daily life and stayed home nights. But if you keep unsociable hours, like Jock with his van parked up Frotfield Way to cater for all the ravers coming out of Rockefellers, you got the full picture. And Jock had seen it—right down to his very own son getting snatched from out of his van by a giant vampire bat, who carried him up to the roof of Rockefellers and turned back into human form, then feasted upon the poor youngun's blood. Ever since that moment Jock had dedicated his life to getting revenge, learning all about how they operate, what their weaknesses is and where they doss during the day.

I think that's what he said, anyhow.

Who could blame the poor cunt, though? I'd be doing same if my Little Royston had got snatched by some evil cunts who can turn into bats. Hey, maybe that were what happened to him? All

I knowed is Little Royston had gone missing a few years back, presumed snatched by an evil witch who wanted to bring him up as her own. Who's to say it weren't a vampire what got him? And the more I thought about it, the more I could see how it had to be the case. I mean, *50 fucking percent* of the Mangel population, Jock had said. That's about *a quarter* of the people in town. With them kinds of odds staring you in the face, you just know. Do you know what I mean? I knew what I meant anyhow, even if you don't, you thick cunt. And right there and then, as I stepped up onto the wall of the youth centre and removed my final garment, which were my trolleys, I swore a solemn oath that I'd rid Mangel of all creatures of the night. Except badgers.

And hedgehogs.

"*When I said...I neeeeded you...*"

Personally I ain't got a problem with nudity. Not in meself and not in others, so long as them others is birds. When it's meself getting togless, like I were now, I look at it as a great opportunity to show birds what I got, and how much better I am than other fellers. They don't like it, other blokes don't, cos it makes them look bad and opens their birdfolk's eyes to what they could be getting if they had a man like me. But that ain't my problem. My problem, as set by Jock the vampire hunter just now, were to create a distraction using the S-word—namely *stripping*. He'd also suggested singing "You Don't Have to Say You Love Me" by Elvis Presley at the top of my voice, which I thought were a nice touch.

"*You said you...would aaaalways stay...*"

And I'll tell you summat—it were working like a fucking dream. Not only did I have every set of eyes in that traffic jam turned Blakeward just then, enabling Jock to get on with his vampire-hunting business in peace, but I were also quite enjoying meself. And my audience were as well. They was taking photos and getting out of their motors and cheering and whistling and everything.

"*It weren't me...who chaaaanged, but you...and—*"

"Oi, Pee-wee Herman!" one of em shouted. I think it were Michael Ballot from the hairy factory.

"Herman who?" I shouted back. He were alright, Michael Ballot. Bit of a cunt, mind.

"I says Pee-wee Herman! You, with yer fuckin' pee-wee out!"

"Eh? Fuck d'you mean by that?"

"Blake." This one were more nearer, one of the motors on the gutter side who had the best view. Also it were a bird's voice. And sort of whispered in a loud way. "*Blake,*" it went again.

I still hadn't let Michael Ballot off the hook, but I did a quick scan of the motors nearest us, latching onto one that had a bird leaning out of it showing a bit of cleavage. I felt meself stirring down there and went to cover meself up, then noticed who it were.

"Alright, Rache?" I says, going over and not bothering to cover meself up no more. I'd always felt at ease with Rache.

7

"Blake," says Rache, "what the hell are you playin' at?"

"I'm just creating a…I mean, I'm just singing 'You Don't Have to Say You Love Me,' by Elvis Presley."

"But why are you?…Are you drunk or summat? It's Dusty Springfield, by the way."

"It's fuckin' Elvis, Rache. I got it at home on one of me Elvis tapes."

"Yeah, but it was originally…" She stopped there, cos I'd just opened the passenger door, and she had to lean back onto her side while I climbed in. "Um, Blake, I didn't really mean for you to get—"

"Smart motor, this," I says, testing the wipers. They worked alright. "What is it?"

"Eh? Oh, it's just an old Mitsubishi. Blake, you need to—"

"Good cars, them. You can't go wrong with German motors." I tried the fag lighter, and that worked as well. Not as fast as the one in the hearse, mind. "Got a fag, Rache?"

"Oi, Pee-wee!" came another shout from outside. "Where's you gone, Pee-wee Herman?"

"I'll fuckin'…" I went for the handle, still deciding what I'd fucking do to Michael Ballot when I got him. But Rache got my arm and held it.

She were strong for a good-looking lass with quite big tits.

"Leave it, Blake," she says in that same calming tone she always had, except when she were having a pop at us. "Just look at me. Listen to me."

"Who the *fuck's* this Herman feller, Rache?"

"Never mind about him. Tell me what's been going on."

I found myself spilling the beans about it all, right down to Jock and his lad being killed by a vampire. I left out the bit about Alvin and his petrol habit, mind. Rache loved her kebabs, and I wouldn't want her fretting that they wasn't available no more with Alvin going off the rails. All the while I stared down at me lap, watching meself go from stirring to not so stirring. By the time I'd got to the bit about Little Royston being a victim of the vampires and all, I could hardly see my cock at all. I rummaged around between me thighs and found it again.

"Oh, Blakey," she says, touching my cheek and gazing at us with eyes that was moist and tender, like pickled eggs. "When are you gonna see the big picture?"

I weren't entirely sure what she meant by that, but I had an idea it were about me finally giving her one, the big picture being her with her kit off and ready to go. In short, she were putting herself on a plate for us, and you got to grab moments like them when they arises. I grabbed her hand from my cheek and brung it down to groin level, winking at her.

"Um, do you want summat to wear?" Rache says, breaking free and reaching for the backseat.

"Eh? I thought you—"

"You really ought to wear summat."

"I'm alright, Rache. I left me gear over there, and—"

"I think you'll find it's gone now."

I looked over by the youth centre wall and, true enough, gone was my strides and trolleys and other garments. "The thieving fuckin'—"

"Here, put this on. " She dumped some sort of pink anorak in me lap. "It's better than nothing."

I picked it up, trying to find the words to tell her I'd rather scalp meself than wear a garment that is pink. That's when I heard the sirens. Behind us, in front, and to all sides, by the sounds of em.

I opened the door and jumped out.

"Blake!" she yells after us, like as not disappointed that yet another chance to get shagged by Royston Blake had gone begging. But she'd have to wait—I had business to attend to.

The first blue flashing lights hoved into view up ahead as I vaulted the wall, near crushing me knackers but only sustaining some minor scrotum laceration in the event. I shouldered through the entrance doors of the youth centre, ignoring screams and shouts, running up stairs and kicking doors down and getting a bit lost, quite frankly. Right about the time I heard the walkie-talkies somewhere downstairs I found a window that opened. I stuck my head out, and there were a nice drainpipe leading you down to an Astroturf pitch, or summat. Taking it nice and careful, I climbed out and got a good grip of the pipe, then let go the window ledge. Straight away the pipe gave way, and I went down, landing arsewise on the pitch with a load of guttering shrapnel raining down on us. Stung like a bastard my arse did on that Astroturf, and I had to rub both cheeks for fully half a minute while I jogged out the back and down the road there.

It were getting dark now and lights was coming on, but there weren't many of em on this street. Up ahead I could see a hunchback bridge that took you over the canal. I needed to hide for a bit and get me swede straight, and under that bridge seemed like a good spot. Rain were starting to spit as well, and I could shelter down there. I seemed to have brung Rache's pink anorak along. Fuck knows how I hadn't dropped it in all that turmoil in the youth centre, but here it were, clenched in my sweaty paw like a keepsake from better times. I found it comforting, having that anorak with us. I pulled it on, savouring the hint of perfume and stale fag smoke.

"Och, that suits you, Royston," says Jock, stepping out from behind a Fiesta up on bricks.

"You cheeky cunt," I says, going to pull off the anorak but not. It were getting well parky. "Fuck's you doing down here? Was you spying on us?"

"Didnae mean tae make yis jump—my apologies." He got a half-bottle of Bell's from his pocket and swigged from it. "I said I'd pick yis up roond the back, though, reet?"

"You never made us jump, I just…"

But he were off, down an alley behind the Fiesta and past some manky allotments and the backs of houses I hadn't clocked nor thought about in donkeys. Pretty soon we was in a road I didn't recognise, though the moon were bright and gibbous and washing everything in a silver light that made you wonder if you was in a dream. One side were terraced houses, half of them condemned by the looks of em, and with windows boarded up and warning signs. Other side were lockups and a vacant forecourt with weeds growing up out of it. Jock's burger van were parked in the corner.

"Where's my hearse? " I says. "You said you'd get her started and—"

"It's no yours anyhoo. Belongs to them vampires."

"But—"

"Shut yis mooth and get in here." He unlocked the van door and climbed in, then leaned out again. "Ah've sumthin tae show yis."

He smiled. I didn't like that smile. Made us want to walk away, pulling Rache's anorak tighter around us and sinking into her warmth and comforting smells. But I had to go on. I had to follow the path, though it were dark and rubble-strewn and had strange things lurking in dingy corners. I had to find out if that path led to Little Royston. Or the cunts who had swiped him.

I climbed aboard.

To one side of the van interior were a bench, about six long and two wide. The dead one from the coffin in my hearse were stretched out upon it, legs and arms stiff, and face grey. Jock's sharpened stick from earlier were planted six inches deep in his chest.

"This one here ain't wakin' up the neet," says Jock, locking the door behind us.

8

"I don't reckon you understand, Jock," I says, staring at the corpse.

It were quite interesting, because no blood were coming out of where he'd rammed the stake. I knowed it were dead quite a while now, and the blood dried up or replaced by special vampire blood or summat, but it were still a strange sight to behold.

"It's youse who disnae understand, Royston," says Jock, sharpening another stake. "Youse and all the other cunts aroond here. I'm giving you a chance, here. If yis come in with me noo, and help me do what must be done, yis will be a hero. The world will praise the name o' Royston Blake, who wis the assistant of James McCrae, the great vampire eradicator."

"No, I'm on about the hearse, Jock. I don't think you understand how much I needs it. It ain't just the pulling power them hearses have got, I could also do with the space in the back. When I goes on holiday, I takes a lot o' gear, know what I mean? Who's this James McCrae, by the way?"

Jock took the half-bottle of Bell's out again, uncapped it, and took a swig. He held it out to us, spilling a bit. "Yis'll need this."

I frowned at it. "Don't take this the wrong way, Jock, but I'm gonna say no this time. I got refined taste buds, see, and you can damage em if you drinks cheap shite like this. I drink Famous Grouse or fuck all."

"It's no for yis taste buds, ye wee fuckin' bampot—it's to line yis blood. Vampires cannae drink blood that is lined with Bell's whisky, which is a holy spirit."

I took it and had a closer gander. "Is that what they mean, then, when they're on about holy spirits in prayers and that?"

"Aye, it's what they mean. It's a coded message—they're tryin' tae send us a public warning aboot protection from vampires. They dinnae want us tae know the full facts, Royston. But ah found them. And do yis ken what? I'm no standin' for it. Nor are yis."

I sniffed the whisky, wondering who the fuck Ken was. Seemed to be a lot of folks I didn't know tied up in this. "Cos when they says the holy spirit," I says, getting back to the subject of prayers, "I always pictured a massive ghost with a big white sheet and—"

"Drink up, will yis!"

I necked some whisky. I'll be frank with you and say that Jock were making me a bit nervous. But he didn't half know a lot, didn't he? I found it amazing how he'd worked all this shite out on his tod. And him foreign. "This Bell's ain't so bad, Jock, once you gets used to it. Got any more?"

"Aye, I got more. I got these wee fuckers."

He were sat on a small chest of drawers, and he reached down and pulled the top drawer right out and dumped it on the floor. Inside was about a dozen wooden stakes like the ones I'd seen so far. He pulled the other two drawers out and they was full of em too.

"These are the tools o' battle, Royston, " he says, picking one up and holding it aloft, like he wanted it blessed by the striplight he had up there. "With these, and the Bell's, there's no stopping us. The evil ones widnae stand a fuckin' chance. No even the fountainheed ae the entire brood. Yis and me will deal wi' that cunt last, by the way. Eradicate the fountainheed and the entire evil hoose o' cards will collapse for good. But let's no get aheed ae oorselves. First we've a few drones tae eradicate."

He grabbed the bags, now stuffed with about eight stakes apiece, unlocked the door, and peered out, looking left and right and up towards the sky, which were now black like I couldn't recall ever seeing it. He handed me one of the bags. "Take these," he says. "Yis drive the fucker under the rib cage, angling it like so. Reet? Then stand well back and watch him turn tae dust before yis very eyes."

I looked over me shoulder at the one stretched out on the bench. "So, erm, how come that one there never…"

But Jock had bailed out, leaving the door swinging behind him. I followed.

"You got a map or summat?" I says, catching up with him. He were crossing the road, heading back the way we'd come. "I mean, say we get split up, we gotta know where the other drones—"

"The other drones are all in the one place. You dinnae need a fuckin' map."

"Aye, but we still might get split up. The coppers'll be…erm, Jock?"

He'd turned off the road into the frontage of one of them condemned houses with the boarded-up windows. I got closer and saw it were only the front window that were boarded, the rest being unsmashed glass. And it weren't a warning sign out front but a blue-and-white notice saying POLICE.

"From now oan, shut yis mooth," Jock hissed, sweeping through the crime scene tape. "Reet?" He picked up a half brick and smashed the window of the side door with it then stuck his arm through and let himself in, holding a stake high.

YOUTH AWARENESS PROGRAM

A press conference was held today at Mangel Police Station announcing a new initiative aimed at the town's youth. "Humans Cannot Fly," spearheaded by Sergeant Lee Plim, will focus on the dangers of drug-induced hallucinations and was inspired by the tragic recent death of Scott McCrae, who fell from the roof of Rockefellers.

"First off, I want to make it clear that we have no drug problem in this town," said Plim in front of a packed auditorium. "This campaign is just a safety thing, in case a young person should chance upon some drugs or a drug problem should arise in the community. But it won't, because we've stamped out drugs for good in this town."

On the focus of the campaign, Plim said: "It is not just about humans believing they can fly. We'll be talking about other things that drugs can make you believe, such as being superhuman. A human cannot be superhuman. The only people who can be superhumans are superheroes, such as Superman and the Hulk, and they almost certainly don't exist in real life."

Asked to expand on that, Plim said: "Well, look at Superman—a flying man who wears his underpants on the outside and rescues people from villains. Is such a thing likely? For a start, no person could wear his pants on the outside without getting laughed at by everyone, so we know he can't be real. Then there's the Hulk, who is green and is said to have obtained his super-powers from gamma rays. Now, we know that green people do exist, so this is more likely, but gamma rays? Are we expected to believe that gamma rays exist? Come off it."

Questioned further on the subject of green people, Plim became evasive. "It's a touchy area. Some people don't like to think about it, because it opens up a whole can of worms, but the fact is that there have been documented reports of green people at large in our world. Some believe them to be a different species of humanity that has evolved in tandem with us, hiding away in tunnels. My personal belief is that they are aliens."

9

I do love knickers.

Soon as I sees a pair—even still wrapped up and hanging off a shelf in a togs shop—I can't help but think about what goes inside em. You're meant to, ain't you? Fellers is programmed since caveman times to get a hard-on at the sight of knickers and bras and that, and to want to pull them off and shag her. And I don't reckon I'm being sexist or whatever neither—it's just the way men is built. If it weren't, and blokes didn't give a toss about knickers, none of us would ever have been borned. I wouldn't have been here now, picking up a pair of them in the hall of a cordoned-off house in a shite street in a forgotten part of Mangel, glancing up to see if Jock were looking at us, so I could have a quick sniff. Jock wouldn't be there neither, going up the stairs and not looking at us, and thereby allowing us that crafty sniff. Not even Rocky Balboa would exist, and none of the fights he'd been involved in over the years would ever have took place. And where would we all be then? Where would Ivan Drago be, for example? Heavyweight World Champion, like as not, cos Rocky were the only one capable of getting past him.

"Erm, Jock?" I says, looking at the knickers.

He ignored us, carrying on up the stair, all but his boots and the bottoms of his dirty jeans now visible to the naked peeper.

"Jock," I says again, louder.

"Och…what?"

"It's just these here knickers. There's summat up with em."

His boots and jeans stopped a moment then trudged down a few steps. "I'm on an eradicating mission here. Do youse think ah've got time tae sniff knickers?"

"Nah, I weren't—"

"Put them in yis pocket and sniff them later, ye wee fuckin' pervert."

"Jock, these knickers is fresh. Like someone's just took em off, know what I mean? And it's defo a bird."

Jock let that swirl around his swede for a bit, then gripped his stake even tighter and went on up, saying, "Youse perform a thorough search at groond level. Reet?"

"But Jock," I says, pocketing the knickers, "when I says fresh, I mean they'm still warm. Ain't vampires meant to be dead? Dead-folk ain't warm, Jock."

"Warm knickers are a classic sign o' vampire activity. In fact, it's yis female vampire on heat, which means, erm…they're oan the cusp of spawning new vampires. We've no time tae squander here, Royston."

He were gone now. I could hear his feet on the landing floor-boards, creaking and cautious. I shrugged and started performing a thorough search at groond level. I mean ground level. It's amazing how I picks up foreign lingo without even trying. I swear I'm a fucking natural. I went through a door.

It were the living room. Not a bad one, truth be telled, with a couple of sofas with flash blankets draped over em and a big poster of Bob Marley on the wall. The overall effect were one of making you want to set your arse down and have a quick kip, despite the dirty mugs and wossnames on the coffee table, and the bust wood chair in front of the telly, and I were on the point of choosing one of the sofas and doing just that. Then I noticed the fag smoke lingering in the air, like someone had been here not so long back. Plus the telly were still warm when I touched it. It were odd, this whole setup with the police cordon and the telly and the knickers, and I might have been curious on a normal day. But this day I seemed to be traipsing around after a Scottish vampire eradicator on a mission, and it were making us well nervous. Truth be telled, I quite fancied clearing off and leaving him to it. I knows I said all that about vampires swiping my Little Royston and me getting revenge for him, but it just didn't seem so likely now, in the cold dark of early evening. I mean, come on, fucking *vampires*? Vampires is from fairy tales, ain't they? Nah, I had to be realistic and accept that the evil witch had snatched him and took him to her house in the woods. I had some ideas about that, actually, and I were tossing them over as I went through the kitchen, headed for the door we'd come in through. Then I opened the fridge, out of habit, like, and there it were.

The thing I most wanted at that moment, although I never knowed it until now.

As pies went, it were a fucking beautiful one. From the outside you couldn't tell if he were a sweet one or a not sweet one, and that is the landmark of a fine pie, in my opinion. It's all about surprise, see—you bites into one and you dunno if you'll be getting dinner or pud. I picked it up and had a nibble. While I were still trying to work things out, prolonging the mystery and thereby my enjoyment of the pie, someone stepped up behind and bit us on the neck.

I put the pie careful back in the fridge and stuck me paws in the air, wondering if that's what you're meant to do when you gets bit by a vampire. Actually, I weren't wondering it at all, just doing it. I plain hadn't ever considered this as a thing that might happen in my life, and I didn't have a response for it. So hands up it were. "I surrender," I says. "And that."

I could smell it. I'm on about the vampire. It were defo a she, not an it, and quite a nice she and all going by that smell. Not only were it a fragrance I knowed and loved, it were the one from the knickers just now...meaning this one here were like as not naked, or at least not wearing no knickers. I felt meself stirring.

"Any last requests before I suck the life out of your cholesterol-clogged veins?" she purrs into me ear. I could smell fags on her breath. It struck us as a mite odd, that did, but I suppose it weren't. Just cos a bird turns into a vampire don't mean she has to give up the finer things in life, like fags.

"Well, have you?" she says all quiet.

"Have I what?"

"Last requests."

"Well, I'd quite like to know what's in this here pie."

"Do you realise how close you are to oblivion?"

I thought about it. "Not very close at all, I don't reckon."

"What?"

"I'm pretty sure that's in Scotland."

"I could destroy you in a split second," she whispers. "But I might not. I might give you a chance to carry on living your pathetic life, even though my entire being yearns to consume you, and Nature herself begs for you to be culled."

I weren't sure what she were on about, and to be honest, my thoughts was drifting back to the pie, which were still right there afore us, its aroma overpowering all others by now and begging us to consume it with my entire soul, or summat. It got so chronic that me guts was whinging about it and moaning like I hadn't ate fuck all that day, which I had. Half a dozen eggs I'd had that morning, plus a few ripe snags and half a bag of crisps I'd found under me pillow. And then I realised that it weren't complaining of hunger at all, but summat else entirely. Them fucking snags, like as not. I knowed I should have left em. But they looked alright once I'd scraped the growth off.

"Oh my God, what is that...*Eeeuurgh*..."

"Yeah, soz about that," I says. I'd just farted. As in a rancid one, reflecting the state of my insides just then. I always tries not to do that in front of birds, cos it affects the way they think of you, I once heard. One whiff and they forever smell that fart when they ganders your mug or harks your voice, apparently, and I didn't want that. Not when I ain't even shagged em yet. "Look," I says, turning about to face her. "Is there any way you could try to eradicate that smell from your swede? Only...hold up a min..."

"Swede? Oh...*bleurgh*."

She bent over and started upchucking, right there on the expensive-looking kitchen lino. But that weren't my primary concern. More interesting just then were the fact she didn't look to me like a vampire. I mean, do vampires have normal gnashers where they're meant to have big long sharp ones? Plus she had on not only knickers but a complete set of togs. Mind you, could be she weren't wearing nothing under them jeans. Like as not she were, though. A man can tell. I felt meself stirring no longer. Atop all that, she looked familiar. And I ain't just saying that.

"Erm," I says, trying to find the words so she didn't reckon I were chatting her up. Cos I weren't. I got high standards, and I don't chat up puking birds. Not unless they're truly exceptional, with big tits and blonde hair and an alright face. "Do I know you?" I says, choosing me words delicate. "I mean, do you come here often? No, no...I meant..."

I stopped there, cos Jock burst into the kitchen, stake held aloft and the intense look of a Scottish vampire eradicator on his face.

10

"Erm…Jock," I says, trying to get his attention.

It were hard, cos the female had just shoed him in the spuds. "Jock," I says again, "I reckon we ought to hold up for a min and have a think about this, mate. Jock?"

He'd fell backwards onto the sink area, upsetting a drying board and a couple of mugs thereupon. One of em went floor-wards and smashed, no fucker noticing except me. They could fuck off if they thought I were clearing it up, mind.

"Jock, I ain't positive this bird is a vampire. We gotta stop a minute and…ah, shite."

He'd launched himself at her again, pushing off the side and using his bulk to send her into a cupboard. The door came off as she hit it. Jock fell atop her and raised a paw high but didn't have the stake in it no more. In all the excitement and lairyness he must have dropped it. He spun his head around looking for it, holding an arm out to staunch her flurry of small fists.

"For fuck's fuckin' sake, Jock," I says, also doing a quick scan of the lino, "this one ain't even got fangs."

"The vampire can retract its…its fangs when they want tae fool someone. She's…och, ye wee fuckin' *bitch*…she's fooling yis, Royston. Be strong."

"But you can't just—"

"I can and I will, soon as ah find ma fuckin'…where is it noo?"

But he couldn't and he wouldn't. Not with me standing by with my dooring skills. In a situation where one person is trying to cark another who might not be a vampire, you can't get better than a doorman for breaking it up and putting a stop to the carking. Actually, you can get better: a head doorman. In Royston Blake, you're looking at the most highly revolved example of head doormanship known to man, although he were unemployed at that time.

Jock finally located the stake and made a grab for it. It were about three foot behind his arse, which were like two space hoppers full up of lard and wrapped in filthy denim. I went to kick the stake out of his reach, but I tagged that arse by mistake and he went sideways.

"Oi you, yis fuckin'…" he says, scrabbling back up a bit and making a play for my ankle. I snatched my leg out of reach at the last moment, but for some reason me toe connected with his swede and he went down.

"Fuck," I says. Cos I hadn't meant to do that. "Jock, are you…"

"Get him off me!" the bird were shouting. Jock had slumped atop her, and his face were up against her, like he were trying to get his oats but had fallen akip. Didn't half look funny. "Will you stop laughin' and get him off me?"

"Alright, keep yer fuckin' rug on. Just looks like you and him is havin' a little cuddle, and…"

"Help!" she screams.

I hauled him off, shoving his dead weight sideways and leaving it facedown, arse up. Last thing I wanted were coppers getting called and me having to explain what were up here. Most Mangel coppers is thick twats whose only concerns is scoffing biscuits, poking prozzies, and trying to put Royston Blake inside for summat he never even committed—or had a fucking good excuse for. And then you got the shite ones. She went to scream again, but I got a paw to her gob in time.

"Shut yer fuckin' trap or I'll bust it," I says, all gentle like. "You ain't got a right to scream, right? Who saved whose fuckin' life here? Eh?"

"I saved yours."

"That's right, and you'd best fuckin' believe it. You saved my life here, and...erm...No, no, it's *me* who saved *your* life, you cheeky fuckin'—"

"Yeah, that's what I said."

"Did yer?"

"Yep."

"Oh. Soz."

"No problem."

She were an odd one, this one. And she seemed to be able to talk even though I had a paw to her gob. I took it off. "I got some questions for you," I says. "First off, why the fuck did you bite my neck just now?"

She weren't answering. Maybe she could only speak with my paw to her gob. I went to put it back.

"Please don't do that," she says, flinching away. "You dunno where it's been."

I looked at my hand, wondering about all the places it had been. "Far as I knows, this paw ain't been nowhere I ain't been," I says. "I can vouch for that." Mind you, you just dunno, does you? I mean, how do you know what's happening when you're akip, for example? I had another look at the paw. The more you looked at it, the more you started wondering if it had a life of its own. The lass made a break for it.

She were a fast one, but I grabbed her ankle and reeled her in. "What's you fuckin' playin' at?" I says. "I'm the goody here. I'm a fuckin' community pillar."

"I'm scared," she says, surrendering a bit but still trying to get her leg free.

"Why's you scaredy o' me? I'm Royston Blake, ain't I? I'm—"

"I know who you are! That's why I'm scared. I'm being held against my will by a notorious local psychopath wearing nothing but a pink anorak. Wouldn't you be scared if you were me?"

"Oh yeah," I says, looking down at meself. "I forgot about that. See, it ain't *my* anorak, and…" I noticed that me tadger and bollocks was in full view of her, so I pulled down the anorak a bit, covering up most of em. It made us feel uncomfortable, her looking at us like that, like she were taking advantage of us. Plus I'd just hauled Jock off her and booted him in the face by accident. All that swinging of me legs, she were bound to have clocked my arse. I felt naked of a sudden. I wanted to hide away from her and the rest of the world and perhaps put some togs on. "Look," I says, "can you stop looking at my tadger? It makes us feel…" But she weren't there no more.

I looked round and she weren't there neither. Jock were, mind. And he were still out cold.

A door slamming brung us to me senses a bit, and I hared towards where the slamming had come from. Front door were swinging open, letting all the cold and darkness in from outside. I had a look out and didn't see no one. Maybe she were hiding behind that bush over yonder, or Jock's van, but I couldn't be arsed to look. I had to get control of things here. I felt like I'd been on drugs or summat and I were just coming to and realising I'd been marching to the tune of a fucking spanner, him being Jock. And now look at the shite I'd landed meself in. Mind you, it weren't that bad. So far as I knowed, no one had got killed yet, and folks getting carked is the landmark of proper bad shite. So I were in some fairly decent shite at the minute. I shut the door and went in.

Walking back to the kitchen, I thought about how folks kept disappearing every time you turned arse on them. Alvin, this bird here, and like as not half a dozen other ones I couldn't recall just then. I were hoping Jock would be the next one, but I knowed it weren't to be. The ones you want to stay, they fucks off…and vicey versa. It's the way of all life, and I'd been getting used to it in recent years, especially from watching Rocky films and seeing first Mickey, then Apollo, and then the robot from *Rocky IV* do a runner on him (cos it had mysteriously disappeared by *Rocky V*, even though Paulie were meant to be going out with it). But Jock were still there, lying where I'd felled him by accident and in the same arse-up position and everything, but now with the notable difference of having some blood leaking from his swede onto the white lino.

"Shite," I says.

I'd been saying that word a lot of late, and I said it again as I ferried Jock back to his burger van and banged his arse on the door. I couldn't leave him, could I? All them cunts back on the Wall Road had seen us with him, and the coppers'd be swooping down on my house like crows to roadkill once they found his carcass. Cos carcass it were, no doubt about it. I've seen a few deadfolk in my time and this were one of em, for fucking surely.

"Fuckin' shite," I says again, but with a *fuckin'* at the start this time. Cos I had to fish around in Jock's lardy pockets for the key, and it weren't a pleasant thing to do. For a goodly minute or so I seemed to find everything under the sun apart from that key, including one of his gonads under the pocket material. It were way out to the side compared to mine, but then you got to consider that the sack grows with age, so they says, and Jock had a few years on me. I put it to the side and had a further rummage, finally locating the key along with a couple of quid, which were a bonus. Then I fired up the van, pocketing the bonus and humming a pleasant tune by Elvis Presley. I always done that when I scored a bonus. But the tune didn't last.

I were in fuck, weren't I? Fuel on empty, a fucking dead Scottish bloke with a massive scrotum in the back, and no place to go. No matter how hard you tries to make it not so, things always seem to come around to this, every fucking time. But there is always summat around the corner, and in this case it were Alvin, pootling along in his little miniature van. This were all his fault, weren't it, when you looked at it? If he hadn't have fucked off back there on the Wall Road, Jock wouldn't have done whatever, and I wouldn't have done my bit, although I couldn't recall what it had been just now. And I'd still have me togs on. So I went after him.

I dunno if he had mirrors on that van. If he did, maybe he would have seen us. And maybe he wouldn't have led us to the place he did, pulling into the car park and slotting her next to a silver Vauxhall Carlton. Then again, maybe he did clock us and he done it on purpose, thinking I wouldn't follow.

I waited out in the street, watching him get out and go in. Then I scratched me swede and did a few sums and thought fuck it, life's too short. And I never were that good at sums anyhow. I got out.

And followed him into the Paul Pry.

11

"I'll grant you a tab but there's an upper limit of five pound, which you've now reached. You wants further service from this here bar, you pays cash."

I'd been in the Paul Pry a while now, maybe ten minutes. Once upon a time I'd have told you all about going in that place and breaking the ice with Nathan the barman and what other punters is in there and all that shite, but I can't be arsed. Nathan ain't worth the breath, in my opinion. And neither is the Paul Pry, which were getting to be a dump lately. For starters, it smelt of earth. And I don't mean earth as in the planet, I mean the stuff you gets in the ground when you digs it. Far as knowed, the planet just smelt of manure, and this weren't that. Then there was the new rules.

"I've reached me limit?" I says, necking half of the pint he'd just put afore us. "This is only me fuckin' second. How can I reach a five fuckin' quid limit after two fuckin' pints?"

"Mind yer language," says Nathan, "ladies being—"

"Fuck my fuckin' language—I'm talkin' about human fuckin' *rights* here. How much is a pint? And I don't see no ladies, by the fuckin' way."

"Don't mean they ain't present. One pint o' lager comes to two pound."

"Two fuckin'....For fuck sake, Nathe, no wonder you got no ladies in here. No wonder you got no decent punters at all down here."

I looked around at what punters there was. You had old Mr. Fillery, Gromer (the miserable cunt from the offie down Cutler Road), Margaret Hurge (who were looking a bit like a bloke these days and easily mistaken to be one, I thought) and some cunt I didn't recognise, although he didn't look no more decent than the ones I already mentioned. I didn't see Alvin nowhere. He'd be in the bogs, like as not, hiding from us. I'd go for a piss in a minute and give him the slap he had coming.

"You're free to go elsewhere," says Nathan. "Far as I knows, we're still the most reasonable place in town fer lager. And we're second on peanuts, after the Volley."

I weren't harking him now. I were doing some sums, counting me fingers and finding there to be ten of em, including the fat ones on the end. But I don't think that's what I were meant to be adding up.

"Four pound is your answer," says Nathan, polishing a tankard. "Two pints cometh to four pound, leaving you with one pound. I can do you a half, if you must."

"I ain't drinkin' halves."

"Thass your prerogative."

"I don't give a toss what you calls it, I just ain't drinkin' em. They'm fuckin' tiny." I rummaged in me pocket, finding the two-quid bonus from Jock and putting em on the bar top. "Right," I says, fixing Nathan with a look that told him he were dealing with a different breed of businessman here, "how much can I get now?"

"One and half."

"Fuck sake…" I looked at me fingers again, but I didn't have no half ones, so there were no point. "Alright," I says, draining me drink, "giz one and half pints o' lager. But I wants it in the one glass, right?"

Nathan matched my stare for a few seconds, then reached under the bar and pulled out an unusually large glass. "You never came in here to quibble on beer prices," he says, filling her up. "I'd wager you never even came here in pursuit of Alvin, although that were your front. No, I reckon you had another thing on your mind when you broke yer exile after all these months and came back in my pub."

He put the full glass before me. I picked it up and went to down it in one but got stuck about two-thirds down for some reason. "Fuck's you on about?" I says, my words chased out by a massive burp.

"What I'm on about, Royston Blake, is that van you've parked in my car park up there. And the outsider inside it."

I'd forgot about that. Nathan knowing every fucking thing that came to pass in the Mangel area, I mean. You might have gathered that it had been a while since I'd been down the Paul Pry, and things slip your mind when they ain't under your hooter every day. Especially things you don't want to think about, like Nathan and his ways. "Aye, alright," I says, draining the dregs, "so I got a dead Scottish bloke up there, and I'm lending his motor off him for the minute. So fuckin' what? No one's perfect, is they?"

"How'd you know he's dead?"

I shook me swede slow, like I were a schoolteacher and he were a young lad who didn't know the ways of the world yet, although he had a dense tash and very hairy arms. "Nathe, I think I'd know, don't you? I mean, for fuck—"

"The name's Nathan," he says. "And I'd encourage you to go up there and check his pulse, cos I do believe he's still drawin' puff."

"But how—"

"Cos I can hear his heart beatin'."

I scratched me swede.

"I find it deafening, Blakey. It's all I can hear just now, the thumpin' of that outsider's heart and the madness that propels it. It will bring chaos to this town, that man's heart will. He will worry at the roots of our tree until all the leaves dries up and falls off. He is the one of which they spake, Royston. One from outside will come into our midst and do all this, they said. And no one will be able to stop him, because he is invested with a power that none of us can equal. Only one man, perhaps. If the stars is lined up right, and the wind blows a direct west, and the moon rises gibbous over the Deblin Hills, perhaps that man might be able to do summat. But there can be only one."

It were odd, the next bit. It were like I fell akip and got dreaming, traipsing through a misty land and not recognising it, although I could see the hills over there in the distance where they was meant to be. But then I noticed that them hills was right next to us, and that they was miniature versions of the actual Deblin ones.

And then I looked down, and I saw.

It were Mangel, the whole town like it had always been, right down to the prison over here and them factories down there, and the River Clunge slicing through the middle of it all, like a weeping blister. Plus you had new bits like the Porter Centre, which looked quite nice from the sky, I had to say. Cos I were a giant, weren't I? I were like that one in *Gulliver's Travels*, although I can't recall his name just now. But then it all disappeared, and I found meself in the car park behind the Paul Pry not knowing how I'd got there. Fucking typical—the very moment you realises what's going on in a dream, and you're about to plant your massive boot down in the middle of town and crush hundreds of little bastards like ants, it all ends.

But I weren't empty-handed.

Or empty-sweded, I should say. I had summat up there that I hadn't had before, a bit of info that changed everything and made the future look rosy and exciting. It were from what Nathan had said, I think, but my time up in the clouds had made it come clear. I opened the door of the burger van.

Jock were sat up holding a rag to his forehead and smoking a fag. He did seem to be alive, just like Nathan had suggested. But he couldn't *not* be, could he? Not with the thing I'd found out about him.

"Jock," I says, hardly able to keep the excitement off me face. "I just found summat out and it's—"

"Was this you, yis wee cunt?" he says, holding the bloody rag out to me. "Did youse cut mah heed?"

"Don't worry about your fuckin' cut," I says. Cos he were immortal, weren't he? No amount of cuts to the heed could cark him.

There can be only one.

"I ain't a hundred percent pos, right," I says, "but I'm pretty fuckin' sure you're the Highlander."

DEATH HOUSE BODY
IDENTIFIED

The dead body discovered in the house of murder victim Scott McCrae has been identified. Thirty-four-year-old Martynas Gustas, an Estravian asylum seeker, died of a single stab wound to the chest.

"We are not treating this as suspicious," said Inspector Stephen Jones, heading the case.

Asked if he considered it an accident or a case of suicide, Jones said: "No, obviously he was stabbed by someone, but it's justified homicide, isn't it? Quite clearly this man was caught in the act of burglarising one of our citizens, and that citizen—the poor lad McCrae in this case—took reasonable steps to defend his property, grabbing a kitchen knife or whatever came to hand. It's open and shut. We've even got the drug angle cleared up now—McCrae must have found them on the immigrant's person and ingested them, thinking it was aspirin or something."

Pressed on what evidence of burglary police had found, Jones said: "Look, here was an asylum seeker. What else was he doing in the McCrae household? Are you telling me that McCrae let him in voluntarily? Pull the other one. The only tragedy here is that the lad then became racked by guilt and took his own life. That I find unacceptable, but we can't prosecute a dead man, can we? So the asylum seeker gets away with that. It boils my blood, thinking about the things they get away with."

12

"But why the fuck wid yis dae that?"

I couldn't get Jock concentrating on the matter in hand, which were about him being the Highlander. All he seemed to give a shite about were his swede damage, which amounted to a minor scratch, if you asks me. Alright, so the blood weren't stopping, and a flap of skin and meat about an inch wide were hanging off, but he'd fucking survive, wouldn't he? And it weren't like I'd bust his skull nor nothing. I knowed I hadn't cos I could see a bit of it, glistening white and pinkish there behind the flap and not even a scratch on the fucker.

"I told you, Highlander, it were a fuckin' accident," I says, pulling into the road. Jock's van handled quite well, actually. "Every cunt has accidents from time to time, you know. Not that I'm a cunt, mind. But I does have the odd accident, just like cunts."

"I'm no on about the cut oan mah heed, Royston. It's mah fuckin' troosers. Why are yis weering mah fuckin' troosers?"

I looked down at em and frowned. I gotta tell you, I weren't happy about it—they stank, had dried bits of fuck knows what all over em, and the front were stiff as cardboard, like he'd spunked in em and it had dried up, the dirty cunt. They was just about the worst strides I'd ever wore (except for some orange flares I used to have as a youngun), but Nathan had refused to serve us when I'd gone in with me nuts hanging free. Them fucking new rules again.

"I thought you was dead," I says, slipping into second up the Wall Road. I wanted to see if my hearse were still there. "Dead uns don't need strides."

"Well, I'm no deed, am I?"

"Aye, but you was."

"Well, ah'm no."

"Aye, but…shite."

I pulled up, encountering the back markers of a jam. It were the same one from earlier, stretching not so far back now with maybe forty motors in it. Then it started moving a bit. I looked up ahead and saw that they had a roadblock set up, and they was diverting the traffic into Carl Street. Beyond the roadblock you could see the high tail end of my hearse, coppers crawling all over it and blue flashing lights hither and thither. Mostly thither. But I ain't mentioned the worst bit yet.

"What the…Royston, what are yis doin'?"

"They'm stoppin' everyone," I says. "I can't get involved."

"But…for fuck's sake, Royston, yis cannae traverse the central reservation like that. The suspension cannae take it."

"I knows what I'm doin', Jock. I drove a 2.8i Capri for years. Gold, she were, with a black vinyl roof. Fuckin' classic motor."

"What the fuck's that got to dae wi' it?"

"Look, Jock, just fuckin' shut yer face and trust us, right?"

"I dinnae see why we cannae go through. The polis will no connect us with that hearse, if that's yer worry. Ah'll dae the talkin'."

He were almost right about that suspension, as it turned out. I could hear it making awful noises as I rocked to and fro, trying to get some momentum to mount the kerb, which were fucking high. And when I finally achieved that, I could hear it scraping fuck out of the undercarriage, which set me bollocks aquiver. I mean, what if I got stuck here? The coppers'd stroll down at their leisure and have a good old gander around, finding Highlander, a bunch of wooden stakes, and summat else incriminating (although I couldn't recall what just then). But it were alright, cos I got over in the end and scooted off down the other side, ignoring the blares of horns behind us as I glanced in the rearview and clocked the belly plate falling off. "You got shite clearance on this thing," I says.

I got no answer from Jock, and when I looked over he were in a bit of a daze, stretching himself flat on the bench there. It were like as not for the best, I thought, swinging into Strake Hill and sparking a fag. I hadn't seen the film *Highlander* in a while, but I had an idea they regenerated themselves when they gets injured, like Doctor Who. Give it five minutes and his forehead would be good as branny. I drove and smoked and thought about that, not knowing where I were going just then but knowing I were doing alright, that things was as good as they could be at the min. Maybe I'd head up to Hurk Wood and bathe him in a stream or summat. Then again, the water in them streams up there is all brown and full up of poisons and shite from dead sheep, so I hears.

Every now and then I'd glance over at Jock and see how his regeneration were coming along. It were going alright, actually, and you could see he were about halfway to sorted after three or four minutes. I tried staring for upwards of ten seconds, seeing if I could catch the actual regeneration in progress, like one of them nature programs where they films a sheep rotting for a couple of weeks and then speeds it up. I could have fucking swore I seen the flap start to shift back into place, but I clipped a Mini coming the other way and had to swerve a bit, dislodging Jock from his regeneration bed. I also dislodged summat in me swede. It were the thing I'd not been able to recall just now.

The incriminating summat.

"Jock," I says, pulling over. He were still fucking around on the floor, trying to get on his paws and knees. Looked a bit like an upturned tortoise, and I wanted to have a laugh about that, but I wanted to take care of business more. "*Jock!*" I yells, taking care of business.

"Wha…wid yis give us a hand, here?"

"Where's the fuckin' corpse?"

"Corpse? What corpse?"

"You knows what corpse." We was on the Barkettle Road, up by Beaver Lane. Weren't a good place to stop, this. Especially with the clipped Mini upside down in someone's front lawn back the way a bit. No one were coming out of house nor motor yet, though, so we was alright. "The fuckin' vampire corpse who were laid out right there. Where the fuckin' shite is he?"

"Och, him? He turned tae dust, Royston, just like ah told yis he would."

"Like fuck did he—spill the fuckin' beans, Jock. I ain't having corpses going AWOL no more. I had that before, and it's a fuckin' pain."

"I swear to yis—the fuckin' thing turned tae—"

"*Jock.*"

"*Alreet*, alreet…A wee man came in and took him when you wis in the pub."

"A wee man? What fuckin' wee man? You mean he stank of piss? What?"

"He wis a wee man. A wee man in a mask. Margaret Thatcher ah believe the mask wis meant tae resemble, aye."

"Margaret Thatcher? Who the fuck wears a mask of that old slag?"

"This wee man did, I assure yis. Yis cannae mistake the blonde hair, which is akin tae vanilla ice cream. Me, ah've always had a soft spot for that woman."

"She's a fuckin' old dragon."

"Aye, but it could be that yis opinion of her as a woman has been tainted by her actions."

"She were in some fuckin' shite films, I gotta admit."

"What are yis on aboot, Royston? Margaret Thatcher wasnae an actress."

"Weren't she? I must be thinkin' of someone else. Who's the other one?"

"Sheena Easton."

"Aye, her."

"She's too thin."

"I don't like em too thin."

"Too thin for her ain good. It's no healthy."

"They ain't got such big tits neither when they'm thin. Mind you, you do get some where they'm thin *and* got big tits. That's the fuckin' jackpot, ennit?"

"A woman needs a bit o' padding tae be healthy and fertile."

I felt meself stirring. "For fuck sake, Jock, can we change the subject? What else were this piss bloke wearin'?"

"Ah didnae notice much. A wee apron, I think."

"That were fuckin' Alvin, you twat. No other cunt wears an apron."

"Ah tend tae wear one mahself, Royston. Yis must observe proper health and safety regulations."

"So yer sayin' what? Yer sayin' you walked in and asked yerself if you can rob a dead vampire off yerself?"

"Och, no. But it wis the best thing, honest it wis. See, if the eradicated vampire disnae turn intae dust for some unknown reason, there's only one surefire way tae dispose of it. And do yis ken what? The wee man happened to be proposing that anyhoo. So I let him."

Lights was coming on all over now and folks coming out, aiming to have a gawp at the poor fucker in the Mini, like as not. People can be bloodthirsty cunts at times, I fucking swear. Mind you, ambulance and coppers'd be there in a minute, and I'd only get under their feet, so I pulled away and carried on northwards.

"You don't even have to say it," I says, I couldn't bear to so much as look at Jock now. He were fucking mental, weren't he? How the fuck had I got meself tangled up with a mental Scottish bloke? I swear, the only thing stopping me from punting him out on the roadside were cos he were the Highlander, and there can be only one of em, annoying cunts though they can be. "You don't have to say it, cos I can guess it. I can read you like a fuckin' newspaper, Jock. Some random twat walks in and suggests doing summat or other with the dead un, and you goes along with it. You lets him get on with it cos it fits in with your fuckin' bollocks fantasy about vampires and shite."

"I swear, Royston, that wis no what hap—"

"Alvin's gonna butcher him, ain't he?" I says, slotting her into fourth and crunching it a bit. She only had four gears, and I weren't used to that. "Alvin's gonna turn our fuckin' corpse into kebabs, ain't he?"

I could feel Jock looking at us like I were the mental one instead of him.

Just relax, Blakey. Calm down and try not to kick his fucking teeth in.

There can be only one.

Actually, I think he did have only one tooth, looking at his mouth.

"Kebabs? No…for fuck sake, Royston, that's barbaric. And it might carry a risk o' infecting the entire populace via his kebabs."

"Eh? But…"

"No, he only wants tae burn it."

"Alvin wants to burn our corpse?"

"Aye. In fact, what's that through these trees here? Is that a fire?"

13

"So yis think ah'm this Highlander just because ah come from Scotland? Is that it?"

I slammed the van door and handed Jock one of the two stakes I had. I weren't expecting to use em, but you had to protect yourself out here in Hurk Wood. Especially when barmy kebab men is burning human carcasses on bonfires. "Woss you being Scottish got to do with shite?"

"Well, tae start with there's the wee matter of Highlanders being from Scotland."

"Jock…" I says, looking at him with the patience of a dad telling his son that Father Christmas ain't real, and that the lad's a fucking twat if he thinks different. I had to find the right words here, cos I didn't want Jock believing himself to be a twat, like that lad. There can be only one Highlander, and he must not think he is a twat. "Jock, I hate to break it to you, mate, but Highlanders ain't from Scotland."

"What are yis oan about, Royston? If Highlanders are no from Scotland, where do yis think they're from?"

I looked at me watch: 10:00 p.m. Didn't seem five minutes ago I'd been lying in me pit and harking that vibrating diamond of light, hearing it tell us to go on holiday and lay off the bad stuff and summat else, summat I hadn't worked out yet but I will in a bit, if you'll just keep your fucking wig on. But the point here were that I'd started the day off so well, and now look at us—out in the sticks, wearing the filthiest trousers in history and teaching a Scottish nutter about geography. "Jock," I says, "the clue is in the title, mate. I mean, 'Highlander'—think about it."

I could see the cogs turning but fuck all happening. With some folks, you just have to spell things out for em.

"Highlanders is from *Highland*, for fuck sake," I says. "I thought you of all people would of knowed that, being one yerself. And by the fuckin' way—there's no such thing as 'Highlanders.' There can be only one of em."

"Highland? Royston, there's nae such place as Highland. There's the High—"

"Jock, look, it's a lot for yers to take in, I know. But you just gotta trust us here—Highland *exists*."

"Aye? And where do yis think this Highland is located?"

"It's...I think it's near, erm..."

"And wherever yis think it is, I'm no from there, Royston. I'm from Kilmarnock. So how can I be one ae these High—"

"For fuck sake, Jock, it ain't about wheres and whys, it's about *whats*, right? And what you is, right, is an 'Ighlander. Now shut yer fuckin' face and get shifting."

I did feel a bit bad for the way I'd handled things there. This were all new for Jock, and I ought to have been more gentle with him. Mind you, it were new for me as well. But I couldn't let Jock know that. I had to be like Sean Connery in the film, all deep and philosophical and wearing a stupid fucking hat.

"Can I just ask yis one more question?" he says.

"Aye, but it better be a good un. They been shite so far."

We was yomping now, following a track that took you into the woods and ran alongside a gulley so deep you couldn't see the bottom of it. Once or twice I'd kicked a stone in that direction and harked it go over the edge but never hit the bottom. I didn't like this end of Hurk Wood. It were a lot denser, and not many used it, so the branches and brambles and shite grew right into the path and snagged your togs as you went past. I had a torch though, so I were alright.

"*Aaagh!*" yells Jock behind us. "Fuck sake, what wis that?"

"Is that the best question you can come up with? I gotta say, Jock, I were expecting summat more—"

"I've caught mah arm in some briars here. Can yis no help?"

I rolled me eyes, booted a tree trunk and shouted a few choice words, but I did manage to hide my impatience. It were important, like I told you. "Jock, I'm on a fuckin' *mission* here. Can't you see? Do you truly reckon I got time to fuck around with you and your fuckin' brambles?"

"I cannae see anythin', Royston. Is theer no chance I could hold that wee torch?"

"*I'm* in front; *I* gets to hold it."

"Well, can I no go in front?"

"No, you can't."

"Why? Ah'm no good in the dark, Royston, and…"

I tuned out his whinging for a minute while some interesting thoughts popped into me swede, and I sat down in the little waiting area I got up there. As a deep thinker, I gets a lot of things occurring to us, and when you gets more than one at a time they starts shouting and having a pop at each other and trying to get in first. I couldn't have that, especially with me being a head doorman, which is where the waiting area came in. Mine were a top one, with nice brown sofas and a telly on the wall showing Rocky films, porn vids, or *Coronation Street*, depending on who were in at the minute. Best of all I had a secretary keeping it all calm and flirting with the blokes, within reason. If I had to describe her to you, I'd say she were exactly like Rache but with a short skirt, stilettos, and a tight blouse that showed off her tits. Actually, there were no flirting with the blokes. They tried it on with her alright, but she always put em in their place with a polite smile and a firm shake of the swede. She knowed who her boss were, our Rache did.

Anyhow, the main thought that had turned up just now were about *Highlander*, as in the film, namely the bit about halfway in where he's in the boat with Sean Connery, who is like his teacher of all matters Highlandish. Connery starts rocking the boat, and Highlander's moaning about it, saying he's gonna fall in, and he can't swim, so fucking pack it in, Connery. But Sean ain't having it and rocks even more. He rocks so hard that Highlander falls in. Not being a swimmer, he splashes around and starts screaming like a fucking girl.

And Connery ain't having none of that, neither. "Stop being a fuckin' ponce!" he shouts. I dunno if it's exactly them words, but it's near enough. "Highlanders can't die, you fuckin' twat, so you ain't gonna drown. Go on and sink to the bottom of this here lake and have a gander down there, then walk along, and I'll meet you over there on the shore. Bring a couple o' fish, eh. And some chips."

The thought I had in me swede, and had just come in from the waiting area and parked across the desk from us, were about me having the same situation here with Jock. He thought he couldn't see, and that he were getting fucked around by the wood with all its thorns and darkness and shite. But he *could* see. Actually, I dunno, cos he did have them fat glasses on, so his eyes were shite anyhow, but the point weren't about that—it were about Highlanders being indestructible. But they don't know it yet, and you have to force them to find out.

"Do you trust us?" I says to Jock, getting him by the arm.

"What?"

"Does yer? Do you trust us or what?"

"But why would yis ask—"

"Just *answer* the fuckin' *question*, fuck sake!" I shouts, leading him up to a gap in the undergrowth.

He gave it a moment's reflection. "Aye, ah do trust yis. Youse and me, ah believe that we are in a partnership here, and—"

I shoved him into the gulley.

INTEGRATION IS KEY

A new drive was announced today to encourage the integration of immigrants. The "Welcome to Mangel" campaign will be headed by Sergeant Lee Plim, who has been taken off the "Humans Cannot Fly" campaign, and will aim to raise mutual consideration and respect between locals and their foreign neighbours.

"It's about teaching them about the values we have in this town, the things you can and can't do, and the reasons for that. We have our ways of doing things, and yes, they have to take that onboard. But these people have traditions and customs of their own that they want to carry on, even though they're living here now. Cooking, for example. Foreigners like squid, and we should let them eat it and not make fun of them for that. Remember—if we'd turned a blind eye to foreigners and their ways regarding food, we'd never have discovered pizza. My personal favourite topping is anchovies, but I'm willing to try out any kind of seafood on a pizza—and that includes squid. I don't like pineapple, though. Pineapple is a pudding, and I don't think you should put pudding things on pizzas."

It was pointed out to Plim that this new campaign follows hard on the heels of the McCrae case in which two men—one local, and one an immigrant—died under suspicious circumstances.

"I don't know anything about that," he said, "but what I can say is that right there is a good case for them learning about our values and respecting them. And one of those values is that you don't kill people, pure and simple. Maybe it's alright to do it where they come from, but it's frowned upon in this country. We need to show them that. But in a considerate, respectful way."

Asked how that might be achieved, Plim said: "Well, we could start by just frowning upon them. When you hear of an immigrant breaking one of our laws, just frown. But it's no use only one man or lady doing it. I want everyone frowning. That's what this campaign is all about—the whole community pulling together as one big family, insiders and outsiders alike. We're all in Mangel now."

14

"I'll meet yers back there by the van, right?" I shouts after Jock, watching the cow parsley calm to a standstill after he'd crashed through it and stirred it up not ten seconds prior.

It were odd knowing that Jock were down there in the gulley. You wouldn't know it, everything being quiet and still again. He'd shouted and whinged a bit when I'd first pushed him, just like the Highlander in the film, but that soon stopped once he got his momentum. Then I heard that noise down the bottom, a sort of cross between a thud and a squelch. And a crunch. It weren't a nice sound, thinking about it now, but I knowed he'd be alright. Highlanders is immortal, and this were the only way for him to learn that.

"Bring us a couple o' fish, eh!" I yells, trying to cheer him up with a little joke. But my voice were a bit quieter now and less sure of itself. This were all new to me as well, after all. "And some chips."

I set off down the path again, stopping after a couple of steps to add summat to the order. "And a couple o' fishcakes," I bellows, hearing it echo deep down below. "And see if they got any saveloys. If they ain't, get a few battered sausages. And some mushy peas—three of them little cartons of it. Right?"

It seemed to echo louder and louder the more scran you ordered, and by the end of it I couldn't hardly hear me own voice for it coming back at us. And it took a long while to go quiet again, that last word lingering like a curry fart in church come Sunday morning. Then I noticed summat about it, just as it finally wafted away into silence: it weren't the same as the last word I'd shouted. I'd signed off with "Right," hadn't I? This weren't that. This were another word.

Which gives you the fucking creeps, don't it, no matter how hard and courageous you is? Mind you, it were like as not Jock, replying to us from down there in the gulley. I knowed he'd be alright.

The path came out into a clearing after a few twists and turns. I were still headed for the flickering flame we'd clocked from the road, far as I knowed, but as yet I'd found not a trace of it. Only a whiff of burning wood on the breeze, which put us in mind of bonfire nights as a youngun, when they used to burn a big guy down by the river at Ditchcroft. But there were summat off about that smell, summat a bit manky and damp, like the bathroom at the flat I were living in just then. I tramped around a bit, poking around here and there and wondering what were what and where that fucking fire were, when I chanced upon it. As in the fire.

But a fire it were no longer.

I were stood upon it, and the heat from it rose up through the soles of me boots and made us step aside and have a gander. I'd thought it a simple pile of wood at first, but it had been a bonfire alright, not ten minutes prior by the heat still coming off it and the embers round the edge. Someone had put it out, and the whiff were from the damp ash and half-burned bits of wood. And piss. There were a definite element of urine in the air, rancid and unmistakable, like the very rare occasion when you wakes up after a massive night on the pop to find you've pissed your bed.

I crouched down for a closer gander, marvelling at the sheer bladder capacity and accuracy of someone who could put out a bonfire just by slashing on it. Had to be some kind of giant, for fucking surely—no way could Alvin pull off such a feat of pissing. And there were no sign of corpses being burned here. Not even a tuft of hair, or some blackened bones, or a touch of barbecued meat alongside them other smells.

I stepped around a bit, noting the flattened grass and a couple of empty baked bean tins nearby, and one of them oblong, corned beef ones. This were a camp, pure and fucking simple. Some poor homeless cunt had been dossing here, and I'd scared him off, all thanks to Highlander back there and his cock-and-bollocks story about Alvin saying he were gonna burn that corpse, which were Dracula or summat. The more I thought about Highlander, the more I saw what a spinner of shite he were. I wouldn't have been surprised if he were laid out down in that gulley right now, mangled and bleeding and with his brains spilled from his swede like yolk from a cracked egg. That'd serve him right for claiming to be the Highlander. And then I saw the mask.

As in Margaret Thatcher.

I picked it up, wondering what it all meant. Did this mean it were Alvin after all, and that he did indeed have a massive bladder and had burned the corpse here? Or did it mean the one who'd snatched the corpse from the van weren't Alvin but some old dosser? Or were it Margaret Thatcher? And what about Sheena Easton—where the fuck did she come into all this? Did she have a massive bladder? Or were it massive tits? Nah, that's Dolly Parton with them. So did that mean Dolly Parton were involved? All I knowed is that I didn't know. My head felt like Hurk Wood—massive and dark and full up of nasty things—but I couldn't see none of em nor recall where they was nor even what they was.

I couldn't even see the trees.

I punched meself in the head a few times. It were his fault, weren't it? If I had a swede that worked right, I wouldn't have none of this. I'd know me Dollys from me Sheenas, tits from bladders.

I'd know what had came of Little Royston.

One thing I did know were that I were knackered and hungry. Actually, that's two things, which were bonus, but it didn't lift me spirits much. I just wanted to get home, rustle up a few Pot Noodles and crash out in me pit, safe in the knowledge that I must have done some good work today, even though I couldn't recall what. I tell yers, I dunno what this town would do without me. I were like all the members of the A-Team rolled into one—the brawn of Hannibal, the good looks of Murdock, the cigar of Clubber Lang, and whatever the other one had. I started whistling the theme tune to that program as I went back the way I'd come, picturing the burger van out by the roadside, and how I could make it look like the one from *The A-Team* with a lick of paint. But that thought flew right out of me swede when I heard the shout.

It were distant and echoing like before but more clear and most defo not the voice of Jock nor no one else I knowed. Then it came again, that selfsame word that had made us stop before and wonder what the fuck. I stood for a minute and harked, waiting for more.

Then I pegged it the fuck out of there.

15

I reckon you sussed already that I were living in rented.

I says rented. I never paid it meself. Only a cunt would pay actual wedge for the kind of septic tank with a window I had to live in. The council paid it, or someone, which explains it all, don't it? I mean, them lot is all cunts, right? Have you ever had to deal with one of em? A shirt and tie and a fucking posh job title and they reckons they'm Lord Shit. Which they ain't, I can tell you, cos I went to school with one or two of em, and it's more like Lord Bell-End.

So aye, I were living in a place out Muckfield way, although I only had a room in it. A bedsit, I'd heard someone call it, but I didn't understand that meself. Personally I were able to stretch out to me full length on the bed I had, and not just sit on it. Mind you, could be cos I had a bigger room than your average. For all I knowed, the cunts in the other rooms had to kip on their arses, on little square beds or summat. Served em right, though, didn't it? You makes your own way in this life and it's a dog-eat-dog world, although personally I hadn't ever seen one dog eating another. But I did hear they puts it in tins of dog food, so that's like as not where the saying comes from. And them cunts in the other rooms was all foreign anyhow, so it didn't matter.

I don't want you reckoning I'd hit hard times, mind. You think that and I'll *ping* you, right? I'll ping you so hard you won't even know about it, cos you'll be backwise on the deck with teeth spread around you like confetti. Royston Blake don't take sympathy off no cunt, especially not one of your ilk. And he don't take charity neither.

I were thinking about that as I went in the kitchen, looking for some bread to tax so I could make a Pot Noodle sarnie. One of the foreigners were in there, chopping up some squid or summat on the way to making one of the fucking abortions they call food where they comes from, which I think were Egypt. One of em always had bandages on anyhow, which were like a mummy. "Oi," I says to him, leaning into his face. You have to be direct with em, else they pretends like they can't understand you. "Oi, fuckin' Tutankhamun, can you bung us some bread or what?"

He tried leaning away and continuing what he were doing, pretending like I weren't there. He weren't even making eye contact with us. And if you knows about Royston Blake, you knows this ain't the way to behave when he's asking you for bread. I shoved him.

Just a gentle one.

He went back on one leg a bit but not down and didn't even break from what he were doing with the blade. I watched it slicing through all that wossname and coming so close to his fingers, yet not cutting em off. It were moving too fast—so fast it had to be magic or summat. Or martial arts. Either way, I didn't like it. I felt threatened by it and like I had to defend meself. And that got us pissed off, cos I were fucking knackered, and all I wanted to do were crash in me pit, like I says. And then summat were coming over us. I could feel it, a darkness lapping around us like I were floating on me back in a sea of black ink. It were an odd feeling and not that nice a one, and I'd felt it before and knowed that it never led to much good. But I couldn't help but embrace it and let it take over, like when you're copping off with an ugly bird.

Fuck knows how long it lasted. All I knows is I came to on the deck, a knee on each of the Egyptian's arms and my fist over his face, knuckles aching in a way that told us I'd been using em. The poor cunt's face also told us I'd been using em, judging by the blood and snot on it. And someone had a blade to me throat.

"You stand slow," this one were saying, pressing it into my Adam's apple so hard I didn't dare swallow.

"He were gonna knife us," I says, thinking back to the squid and the knife and the chopping. "I only asked him for some bread and he—"

"Shut face, OK? You stand slow and not move hands. They move, I use knife. OK?"

Seeing as he'd been so polite, asking if it were OK and that, I thought I'd oblige him. I planted one foot followed by the other then drove up from a crouching position, like I were doing squats down the gym. The blade stayed on my neck the whole while, easing up not a bit on the pressure and following my movements like it were strapped there, although I knowed it weren't. In the corner of me peeper I could see the hand that were holding it, brown and hairy and with a tattoo on it. Then I moved me arm. Just a bit, trying to get me balance.

He pushed in with the knife, yanking me swede back at the same time.

I ain't ever had me throat slit before. Most live people haven't, there being such permanent aftereffects, including blood spraying everywhere followed by death. But it weren't so bad as you'd expect, I gotta tell you. I could feel the blood coming down into me T-shirt and remember thinking how alright it felt, like getting in a nice hot shower. And I even felt the skin of me throat go, popping like when you puts a fork in a sausage straight out of the pan. But I didn't cark it. Far fucking from it, pal. I turned around to see who'd done this to me, dabbing my neck at the same time to see how much sap I'd leaked. Fucking loads.

"You move hand," he says, holding out his knife that now had a little droplet of red on the end. My red. "I say not move hand, OK? But you—"

"Hold up a min," I says, squinting at his face. There were only one bare light bulb in that kitchen, and it were dingy as fuck, but there were no mistaking what me eyes told us. "Ain't you..."

But it couldn't be, could it?

I mean, how the fuck can a corpse get up and walk again? Not only a corpse but one that has been dead a good few days, going by how stiff and grey it were when it had been in the back of my hearse just now. And also considering how Jock had rammed a fucking wooden stake in his chest. But maybe that weren't enough. Maybe the stake had missed his ticker.

I looked at the blood on my hands and T-shirt and the end of his knife, and I thought of how hard it is for people like him to resist it when they sees it and smells it. Cos they can't help themselves, can they, vampires? One whiff of the red stuff and they'm gagging for it. And I ain't talking about tommy ketchup. Mind you, I'm like that with tommy K meself. I pegged it upstairs.

Like billy-o.

CLUB FALL MAN NOW MURDER—FOREIGNERS ARRESTED

Evidence has surfaced that sheds new light on the case of Scott McCrae, who fell to his death from the roof of Rockefellers while high on drugs.

"We've arrested some Estravians for it," said Inspector Stephen Jones. "We've just got the four at the moment, but we know there are some others in the Mangel area somewhere. They can be identified by the following characteristics: swarthy, greasy haired, and foreign sounding. If anyone knows anyone like that, give us a ring at the station, and we'll round them up."

Jones became taciturn when pressed to reveal details of the new evidence. "I'm not becoming taciturn, I'm just keeping my cards close to my chest—there's a difference," he argued. "Last time out, you tricked me into revealing more than I should have. I won't be making that mistake twice, I can tell you."

Asked to name those arrested so far, Jones was equally evasive. "Look, I'm not being equally evasive either. Fact is, I don't have those details yet. If I gave you names, what difference would that make to you anyhow? These are asylum seekers. It's not like you know them."

This reporter pointed out that it would be of relevance if any of those taken into custody shared a family name with the dead man found in McCrae's house. Taking the initiative, this reporter also pointed out that there could be a possible drug link between McCrae and the Estravians—maybe this was a bungled drug deal, for example.

"Don't you people listen? There are no drugs in this town—we cleared up that problem long ago. What happened here is this foreigner breaks into the McCrae residence and gets his comeuppance in the form of a sharp instrument to the heart. McRae goes on a night out on the town, like any other young man on a Saturday night, but the dead burglar's associates get wind of what's happened. They track McCrae down, force him to take illegal drugs, which they have smuggled in from wherever it is they come from, then slaughter him like an innocent lamb. We've uncovered a murder here, ladies and gentlemen. Not only that but we've got the villains for it. And you mark my words—I will not rest until these so-called men, women, and children have spent their entire lives behind bars for it."

16

I couldn't even recall falling akip. But I must have, cos I woke up and the sky were shining bright onto me lids, turning my dreams red. Which they already was, in a way.

You'll not fall off your chair in shock if I tells you they contained vampires, my dreams did. Two of em. Massive hairy ones the size of blocks of flats, with swedes like hot-air balloons up in the clouds, holding huge swords the length and breadth of buses, only flat and sharp and made of shiny metal. But they weren't after us normal folk on the ground, these vampires weren't. They was hacking away at each other, fighting an epic battle that had the whole town out on the street and watching. Every time a sword swished through the sky over our heads it made a noise like a fighter jet, and when the vampires struck blades they sent off sparks of lightning that made the rest of the sky go dark for that moment. One of them lightning bolts forked downwards and hit the Igor Statue, smashing it into little bits. I laughed at that cos I fucking hated that statue. "Are the stars in the sky just pinholes in the curtain of night?" says someone stood next to us.

I looked, and it were Igor. Not the statue but the actual one. A bloke who looked like the feller in the statue anyhow, only flesh and blood and face turned up to the dark sky. He looked at us and smiled, and his teeth at the front was long and pointy and covered in blood. He started clacking em against the lower ones. The sound were more like bits of wood knocking together than gnasher on gnasher, and I couldn't bear it. I went to punch him in the face, but my hand passed through his swede.

I opened my eyes.

"Shite," I says, realising that I'd fallen akip arsewise on the bed, like them foreigners in their poxy bedsit rooms. "Shite," I says again, cos although the dream had finished, the wooden-fang clacking were continuing, ramming into me ears and through me guts and doing me fucking swede right in.

"*Open the door, Royston!*" someone were shouting out there in the corridor, making matters even worser. "Royston, if you don't open up I'll have to—"

"Fuck off!" I'm shouting back at him, covering me lugs. Cos I thought it might be Igor. You know how dreams can fuck with your swede, even after you wakes up from em? It were like that. I knowed it weren't Igor and that there hadn't been no actual giant vampires fighting over town, but it didn't make us feel no better. "Go on an' fuck off!" I yells again. "I got enough on me plate with this fucking clackin."

The clacking stopped and things fell silent. It were like everyone had harked what I'd said there about having enough on me plate and felt guilty about it, leaving poor Blakey on his lonesome and fucking off to sit in the corner, tail between bollocks. I opened me peepers and let paws fall from ears, feeling the weight took off me shoulders, which was aching a bit still from the exertions of yesterday. Then the door shattered and two blokes in green overalls came charging in, one of em crashing into my table and knocking the telly off, the cunt.

I got up and started casting about for summat to protect meself with. But one of em got us by the thigh, doing summat with it that had us nigh on screaming. He started yanking, but I'd got a grip of the headboard, and he weren't getting nowhere. Then the other one joined in, and I heard the wood splinter. Couple more yanks and I came free, headboard and all.

I landed facewise on the carpet, trying to get up straight away, but one of em got a knee on me back and pushed us down again, sitting atop us. The other one pulled me strides and trolleys down. I couldn't fight em off.

I never could.

"Shhhh," says one of em, sticking a syringe in my arse and filling us up with the bad stuff. "Shh, shh, shh."

I reached out for someone's hand to hold as I drifted out of consciousness, but there were no one.

17

In a way you could blame my recent run of shite luck on *Rocky III*.

I realise how that sounds. I'm as big a fan of that film as the next man, and I wouldn't ever say nothing bad about it nor insinuate that it ain't right up there in terms of all the films ever made. But there's one scene in it, and it came to us of a sudden about a year back, when I were playing pinball in the arcade. You know the bit near the start, where Paulie's in the pub and he gets arsey, cos the barman keeps going on about Rocky? After that, right, he's staggering down the street, pissed out of his fucking swede, and he sees an arcade and goes in it. Looks like a top arcade as well, with way more folks in it than you gets in the Mangel one. Mind you, in ours we got Fat Sandra, who is a built-in customer deterrent, unless they'm into walruses poured into glass boxes, which is what Sandra looks like in her shrapnel kiosk. But fuck that—I'm on about me and my episode, which is how come I got saddled with cunts on me back all the while, jabbing needles into my arse cheeks and giving us grief. More precisely, I'm on about *Rocky III*.

Cos there's *parallels*, see.

What happened in the film, right, is that Paulie's having a gander around this arcade in Philadelphia, which as well as being where Rocky comes from is where they make that fucking shite cheese that only fat birds eat. He's having a smile and a chuckle at most things, including one feller who's got a mullet like you ain't ever seen. I've always sported the cropped look meself but, I dunno, there's summat that appeals about this one in a way I can't put me pointer on, and if long hair of any sort on a male weren't considered a safety hazard in Mangel, I might give it a go. But that weren't what finally grabbed Paulie's attention, pissed as a cunt like he were and lairy in the head, despite his jovial wossnames. It were the Rocky pinball machine. Just like the one we got here in Mangel. And that I were playing a year ago, when all this came to us.

Everyone knows what happens next. It is a scene more famous even than the one in *First Blood* where Rambo chucks that rock at the helicopter and the bloke falls out. It is a scene that is full of shock and drama and pure horror. Not horror like zombies and Frankenstein and shite, but horror like when summat precious has just been destroyed. Cos that's what Paulie does, the fucking twat. He's jealous of Rocky and pissed off, cos Rocky buyed him a watch instead of a sports car, which is what he really wants (Escort Mk. II RS Mexico, I bet), and so he takes his whisky bottle and lobs the fucker at the pinball machine, smashing it and thereby setting the alarm off.

That scene just came to us, stood at the pinball like I were, full can of Strongbow Super in one hand and fag in the other. I were trying to get the ball in that hard bit up on the left and not getting no nearer, no matter how rough nor gentle I handled the flippers. I'd never got it in there, not in all the long hours I'd spent playing that fucking machine. And it weren't like it were fixed nor nothing, cos I'd stood by like a twat and watched while others had done it. Even a couple of birds, for fuck's fucking sake.

So why couldn't *I*? What's wrong with old Blakey?

And when you thought about it, it weren't just the pinball. It's every fucking hurdle life puts up, so far as old Blakey is concerned.

Every other cunt gets over them hurdles, running up and clearing em with nary a grunt nor a blink, but when it's Blakey's turn to make his run up, some fucker goes and makes the hurdle higher. So Blakey clatters into the thing, damaging it quite a lot but not getting past it. He's stuck the wrong side of it, watching all them other cunts making decent and respectable lives for emselves—getting wedded and having younguns and buying nice houses with ponds round the back and koi carp in em. Where was *my* koi carp? And why the *fuck* couldn't I get that ball in the hole up there?

Looking at all that, you can see why I suddenly realised how much like Paulie I were, so much so that I took the can of cider and lobbed him at Rocky Balboa's smug face, which didn't look nothing like him anyhow.

It were the coppers first. Six of em, headed up by Jonah in his stupid fucking bulletproof anorak. Someone else had a megaphone (Plim, I think), and he were out there on the street, blaring at us to throw down me fucking weapon and think about my family and friends. Family and friends? If they'd done a bit of asking about they'd know I didn't have no kin left (except Little Royston, who'd been snatched by that witch), and any mates I had was all cunts. And what fucking weapon anyhow? How could I throw down a weapon I didn't even have? Then I looked at me paws and clocked the monkey wrench, which I had poised just then above Fat San's swede, her having come out and had a pop at us about the pinball. She were giving us a fat smile, letting us know she didn't think I had it in us.

To be fair, I dunno if I did. Sandra were a bird, if you wanna be strictly technical about it, and I got a rule that I don't harm the fairer sex, not unless they'm trying to take my life, which meant that not many birds at all had felt the back of my hand nor been killed by me over the years. But Fat Sandra were hardly the fairer sex, were she? A fucking one-eyed mongrel with an external tumour is better looking than her. Plus she were asking for it. She represented every cunt who'd done their best to raise the bar just as I'm coming up to clear it. I raised the wrench just as summat hit my neck, like a big wasp were crash-landing stingwise into it. I went down. And stayed down.

And I hadn't got up since. Not when you thinks about it.

These was the reflections going through my swede as I lay on the floor of my room, still with me trolleys down and a mouthful of Axminster but not feeling the sting from the needle no more in my arse cheek. Or maybe I did feel it and just didn't give a toss. It were always the same, each time they pumped that shite into my bloodstream and fucked off until the next time. That's one of the three things that vibrating diamond of light had been saying yesterday morn, telling us to lay off the bad stuff. *Don't go to that clinic*, it were saying, as well as the holiday and the unidentified thing—the thing I'm gonna find out about in a minute. *Don't let em pump that shite into your veins no more. Get your head straight and true.*

And I'd tried, hadn't I? You seen how I failed to turn up at the clinic and got meself occupied with other shite and fought hard against them green overalls just now.

But I'd failed.

I were back to peg zero and pumped full of the bad stuff once again, further from going on holiday than a sheep is from leaping over the fucking gate. I craned my neck a bit, looking at that same bit of wall where the squashed diamond wossname had been only one day prior. No light there now. I think it were raining.

I listened to the big drops falling overhead, *plop-plop-plop*. Fucking massive raindrops, these was, and not many of em. Not very watery neither. More like a person doing a series of dumps from a great height onto the roof.

"Hello? Mr. Blake? Is there anyone home?"

That didn't sound much like rain neither. More like a human.

"Mr. Blake? I'm sure I can hear someone in there."

A female human, aye, with big tits and blonde hair and an alright face. Cos you can tell, can't you? All the important things about a person, you can tell it in their voice.

"Well, OK, maybe not. I'll be off, then."

"Hold up a min!" I shouts, staggering up and putting shoulder to wood. Them green overalls had slid my wardrobe where the door had been before they'd smashed it, and it were fucking heavy. I gave up trying to budge it and started shoeing the back panel, which were made of ply or summat and gave way sharpish. Then I stuck my swede out and saw her.

It were her from that house yesterday who'd bit us on the neck and chucked her guts and nearly got staked by Jock. Except she looked different now.

She were halfway down the first flight, turning back to us with a smile. At that selfsame moment the clouds cleared outside, and the sun came bursting in, filling everything with a warm, soft light like you gets when you stick your thumbs in your eyes and press hard for a few minutes. Or maybe it were still pissing down and grim outside, and all the light were in here, coming from that smile. Either way, it were in me now. I felt the bad stuff getting swept aside and flushed down the drain, replaced by that light. I felt meself stirring. Stirring so much I had to bend over a bit.

"They said you might know where my father-in-law is," she says.

She were the most beautiful woman I'd ever clocked.

"His name's James McCrae, but people call him Jock."

CORPSE OF
DEAD ESTRAVIAN STOLEN

The corpse of Martynas Gustas, an Estravian asylum seeker who was found dead in the home of tragic club fall man Scott McCrae, has been stolen from Sweet Dreams Funeral Home on Barkettle Road. The proprietor of the home, John Crepuscle, was injured in the robbery, suffering minor cuts and bruises. A large, white milkman aged approximately 40 is being sought in connection with the attack, during which a hearse was also taken.

"We've only got two men left on duty here," said Eric Clapton of Clapton & Sons Dairy. "One is Old Tom, who is aged 80 and of slight build. The other is me, and I am the owner of this dairy. What would I be doing robbing dead bodies from funeral homes? I've enough trouble keeping this place going. Everyone buys their milk at that supermarket these days."

Mr. Clapton suggested that the corpse thief might be someone from the immigrant community. "I mean, they eat all sorts in their national dishes, don't they? Meat is meat to them. That's all I'm saying."

When it was pointed out that the stolen dead man was himself an immigrant, Clapton said: "There you go—there's no such thing as a coincidence. I'd just like to notify readers that you can get two pints of gold top for one if you sign up for delivery before a week Friday. We also deliver eggs, orange juice, and a wide selection of vittles."

The hearse was later recovered from the Wall Road, where it had been abandoned after a collision with an unidentified vehicle and the corpse had been removed. Police have been unable to locate any witnesses to the accident or subsequent corpse removal.

18

Kerry her name were.

And she weren't blonde.

That's the first thing what hit us, after the earthquake had died down a bit and I felt meself getting control once again. Cos that's what it had been like—an earthquake. She weren't only the fittest bird I'd ever clapped peepers on, she were Number Three, the unidentified thing that vibrating diamond had been on about. It were the world's way of telling us I had a big one coming, a jolt so fucking major it's gonna set your teeth rattling and yet make you stronger and better in yourself than you ever felt. But she weren't blonde.

And her name were Kerry.

"He's been having some problems," she says, toying with a bottle of ketchup. "That's what it was all about, back at the house yesterday. He's got it into his head that I'm a...well, you know what he thinks I am."

We was in the caff. It weren't Burt's Caff no more but in the same place. And Burt were still in it, pottering around behind the partition there. His own business had gone the way of most others in Mangel of late, meaning it had sailed down the pan and been took over by a bunch of outsiders you never saw. They'd stripped out all the old shite and put new shite in, most of it shiny and a bit like a hospital, except a lot cleaner than the one in Mangel. Then they'd gave Burt his old job back, although he were restricted to making toast these days, so I'd heard. But at least he had a future. I had a future and all, now. That's how I truly felt, staring at Kerry's dark lashes and willing em to lift up and show us them green eyes behind em.

"What's that?" I says.

"Jock, my father-in-law. He's been…well, he's been back on the whisky. He's always liked a drop but he's gone overboard since—"

"Jock's your father-in-law?" I says, picturing em rumbling on the deck of that kitchen, him trying to stake her and her aiming a shoe at his spuds.

"Well, I call him father-in-law, but technically he's not. Me and Scott never married in the eyes of the law. But you don't need a piece of paper to say that you're meant for each other. You don't need a bloke in a dog collar to tell you that you're going to spend the rest of your lives together."

I squinted at her. This sounded well fucking dodgy, I gotta say. "Dog collar?" I says. "You're married to a bloke who wears a fuckin' dog collar?"

"No, I just meant—"

"Cos that's fuckin' sick, that is. Finney used to have this vid, and a bloke in that had a dog collar on. Dog Man his name were. He'd bark like a dog and all, and this fat bird wearing a strap-on dildo would—"

"Look, I'm not married to a dog man, OK? Forget the dog collar. I'm here about Jock and his problems. Since Scott died, he's lost control of his drinking."

I thought about that. No matter how beautiful she suddenly were, and however much I just wanted to look at her and ask her out and try and get off with her, I had to play things careful. I had to make her see that I'm an intelligent, professional person who is not brain damaged. And to do that I had to say the right things, ask the probing questions. "What d'you mean lost control of his drinking?" I says.

"Well," she says, shrugging. I loved it when she done that. It made the whole top half of her body move in a certain way. I could have sweared it never done that before. "He just never seems to let up on it. He's always knocking it back, no matter what time of day it is."

"Yeah, but in what way has he lost control of it? You mean he's spilling some down his chin or summat?" Cos I'd heard about that. Loss of motor skills, they calls it. The next stage is that the patient won't be able to drive his motor no more, which is where the condition gets its name from. Mind you, Jock didn't have to fret over that no more.

Shite.

I'd plain forgot about all that business of last night. I'd shoved him swede-first down that gulley, hadn't I? Didn't seem like such a good idea now, with the bad stuff inside us, and the professional part of my brain firing full cylinders. Had I really believed Jock to be the Highlander? People can be twats at times, I swear, and I'm including meself on that, not just yerself. Fuck it, though—can't be helped now.

I could help his daughter-in-law, mind.

I could comfort her.

"He's just…you know, he's just trying to escape reality, I suppose," she says. "With the drink, I mean. But he's going too far. I'm not worried about myself. Yesterday, I shouldn't have let that situation arise, him finding me at the canal house like that. I just needed to go there. Just for a bit, you know? I wanted to feel near

Scott. I only moved in with him a few months ago. Anyway, he's gone, and I guess I'll come to terms with it in time. But I still have Jock. He's like a father to me, and I don't like seeing him like this. I think he's gonna hurt himself."

"He were alright when I seed him," I says, reaching out and squeezing one of her delicate paws, trying to set her at ease. I noticed it had a fair bit of dirt under the nails, which is a good sign that she'll put out sooner rather than later. "I seed him put away at least a bottle and half, I reckon, and not spill a fuckin' drop of it."

She frowned and withdrew her paw. Maybe I were being a bit forward there. I budged around the table instead, going for some leg contact. Mind you, I wished I weren't still wearing Jock's trousers—they fucking reeked. Then again, she might find that reassuringly familiar, if he were like a dad to her underneath. But what the fuck were I playing at, not giving meself the once-over before stepping out with her? Change of strides and a clean shirt and I'd have been humping her by now, no fucking problem. I had to get me swede straight, truly I fucking did. And I'd already thought of how.

"Two Big Breakfasts?" the waitress were yelling from somewhere behind us.

I called her over, and she set em down in front of meself and Kerry, saying she'd be back with the teas. I rubbed me paws together and got stuck in, swallowing a streaky rasher whole.

"Erm, I don't think I can eat this," says Kerry, grimacing at the plate in front of her.

"Nah, I never ordered you one," I says, reaching over and getting that plate. I scraped it onto mine, giving me a nice pile of scran about four inches high. If that didn't get me swede straight, fuck knows what would. "Erm, was you hungry and all?" I says, noticing the empty space in front of her. "Fuck sake, my manners is shite, ain't they? Here we is, out together for the first time, and I ain't even ordered you no scran. Here, have a bit o' black pud."

"No, I don't really—"

"Go on. It's made of fresh pigs' blood. You can't go wrong with it, I fuckin' swear."

"Really, I…"

I put a bit on the spare plate and shoved it back in front of her. Kerry needed her head straightened and all, after all. I couldn't think of a bird who didn't, thinking about it.

"Look," she says, "we both know Jock's been living in a fantasy world lately. Since Scott died, he—"

"Hang on a min," I says, hushing her up with a hand, "who's—"

"Can you take your hand off my knee?"

"Is that my hand? Soz about that. I'm just wondering who this Scott is."

Cos I didn't know no one by that name in Mangel. Foreign name like that, I were wondering if he might be linked with Jock in some way. This is the way you have to think if you wanna do private investigating, like I were doing here. Kerry had come to us cos she'd seen some of my skills in that area, like as not, over at that house yesterday when I saved her life.

"Hang on, don't tell us the answer," I says, putting my fork down and pressing a finger to my temple, like clever folks does when they wanna get even more cleverer. I think there's a hidden button there or summat. Like the turbo boost button in *Knight Rider*. "This Scott, he's linked with Jock in some way. Aye, I'm getting strong feelings on that. Also I'm wondering if Jock ain't linked with this Scott as well. So it's a two-way kind of linkage. Aye, I truly feels that." I glanced at her, making sure she were keeping up with this.

"OK," she says, looking a bit disgusted. I don't think she liked her black pud. "Does the name Scott McCrae really mean nothing to you? I mean, do you not read the papers?"

I had a think. Only Scott I could come up with were the one out of *Neighbours*, that Irish telly program. "Is he famous?"

"Scott was Jock's son. He died…well, he had a drug-related fatal accident. They said afterwards that he was hallucinating on acid or something, and I suppose he thought he could fly. They always warn you about stuff like that, don't they? But my boyfriend was reckless. He was always doing crazy shit."

I ate a couple of bangers. "Your boyfriend?" I says, chewing. A bit of sausage flew out of my gob and stuck on her forehead, but I don't think she noticed. "How do he come into this, then? Did he know this Scott feller?"

She looked down and rubbed her pretty eyes, the pressure of it all coming down upon her. I wanted to clap a paw round her shoulder but I sensed this weren't the moment. I went for her knee again instead.

"Maybe I'm not explaining myself well," she says, batting it away. "I was in a long-term relationship with Scott, Jock's son. Scott died falling off the roof of Rockefellers. Do you get it now?"

"Ah, o' course," I says, casting me swede back to summat Jock had said about his son getting killed by vampires on the roof of that selfsame club. It all made sense now. All you had to do were tie up the wossnames, cross-reference your thingios, and you found the true picture. "So Jock had *two* sons, right? Bit of a fuckin' nightmare, ennit, both of em carking it on the same roof? Anyone'd go a bit barmy after that and spill some of their whisky. So which one were first, the druggy one or the vampire one?"

Kerry pushed her chair back and got up, flashing us a bit of creamy thigh before tugging down her skirt. At first I thought she were gonna give us a big hug, me being the first person to finally understand where she were coming from and know how she felt. Maybe she'd sit in my lap as well. Stick her tongue in me ear and waggle it around a bit. I don't half love it when they does that. But she never.

She pissed off outside.

"Hold up a min!" I yells, going after her. Some twat got in my way by the door, but I didn't have time to fuck around with that. This were a test, weren't it? Kerry were my vibrating light saber diamond, and I had to prove meself worthy. I caught up with her on the corner of Friar Street and grabbed her arm, not letting go when she struggled to get free. If that didn't show her how worthy I were, fuck knew what would.

"I made a mistake, OK?" she says, calming down. Some tears were coming down her cheeks, and I wanted to wipe em off. With me tongue. *No*, with a hanky or summat. Fucking calm down, Blakey. And I could finally get that bit of banger off her forehead while I were at it. Waste not, want not. "I thought you were a serious person," she says, getting all emotional now. "I thought you'd be able to help me. But now I can see that—"

"I *am* a serious person. I fuckin' swear I am, Kel. See that place over there? I used to be head doorman of it. And you can't get more serious than that."

"What place? The Porter Centre?"

"No…I mean, aye, but…Look, that place used to be Hoppers, Mangel's premier piss house, and it were me who done the doors there, letting in them who's welcome and knocking back them who ain't. I were a fuckin' community pillar, honest I were. Ah, you should of seen us back then, in me dickie bow and that. I'd of soon defrosted yer, I fuckin' swear. I mean—"

"I'll tell you what you are—you're worse than Jock. His brain's addled from the booze, but *you*, you're just nuts. You're off your head. Look at you—you're wearing a woman's raincoat, for fuck's sake!"

"No, you don't understand, I—"

"Go on then—what don't I understand?"

"See, you're the vibrating diamond and, erm…well, before that, I thought Jock were the Highlander, and that there could be only one of him, but, er…"

She walked off again. I didn't blame her. I were fucking it all up, weren't I? Here were the biggest chance of happiness Blakey's ever had, and he cocks it up by getting his swede all confused. I mean, fancy saying that about defrosting her? She were too classy for that kind of wossname, this one, even though she were a bit frigid in actual fact. I'd blown my chance, no doubt about it. But I knowed how I could pull it back. I had one card left to play. And it were the ace of fucking spades.

"I can take you to your father-in-law!" I shouts.

She stopped.

CLUB FALL MAN DID NOT KILL IMMIGRANT BURGLAR

New evidence has been uncovered proving that Scott McCrae, who died falling from the roof of Rockefellers night-club, did not kill the intruder whose body was later found in his home.

"This Gustas character died of a stab wound alright," said Inspector Stephen Jones, "but it wasn't with a knife. It wasn't with anything made of metal at all. Nor plastic. Nor glass, glass fibre, polycarbonate alloy, resin…"

Urged to get to the point, Jones said: "Wood. Our foreigner here was stabbed with a sharp bit of wood, plain and simple. And not only that—we can prove that it wasn't Scott McCrae who inflicted that fatal wound."

Jones then presented Walter Cathcart, of the Mangel Constabulary Forensics Division. "I've only got five minutes," said Cathcart, looking at his watch. "I do this part time, I hope you realise, and I'm already past my clock off for today. I'm meant to be playing bowls. We've got a match against Wanderers."

Cathcart shook his head and produced a clear plastic bag from which he withdrew an object of about a foot in length.

"This here is what you call a bit of wood," he said, holding up what looked like a piece of pine, two inches wide at the base and tapering to a sharp point. "We got it from Overwoods Timber Yard, who are doing a two-for-one offer on all interior doors at the moment, by the way. But the person who killed Gustas, the immigrant, categorically did not obtain the weapon from that place. See, we can tell it from the type of wood used. Overwoods, as we all know, only deals in a high grade of pine, fresh from the dense and fragrant forests of the North Pole. The traces of wood I found in that death wound were of a different grade. A much lower grade."

Members of the gathered press reminded Mr. Cathcart that he should come to the point, column inches being at stake here.

"This is by way of a preamble. You don't have to print it all, do you? In fact, what kind of fool reporter files a story that is a verbatim regurgitation of the press conference, warts and everything?"

Mr. Cathcart cleared his throat and produced another plastic bag. From this he pulled a severed human hand.

"Now, this is Scott McCrae's right hand, the one he would have used to stab with, him being right-handed. But this hand was used for no such task. See, the grade of wood and splintering patterns I detected from Gustas's wound leave me with no doubt that whoever killed him would have a lot of splintering in the palm of the hand. This one here contains no such splinters."

Responding to the suggestion that McCrae could have worn a glove, Jones stepped in with: "What was the motive here? A disturbed burglary? Homeowners don't put on gloves to protect themselves and their property against burglars. They grab the nearest thing that comes to hand."

But what if the motive is wrong? What if Gustas was murdered for other reasons? Romantic jealousy, perhaps? Or a bungled drug transaction?

"Like I told you already," said Jones, "there is no longer a drug problem in this town. And as for 'romantic jealousy,' are you saying that Gustas was seeing a female, and McCrae took exception to it? What local girl would get friendly with one of these asylum seekers? None is the answer to that. So forget it."

Asked what further steps the police will take to find the killer, Mr. Cathcart said: "I need another look at that Gustas corpse. I'd be rummaging around in it right now if some bright spark hadn't got ahead of himself and released it back to the family. And now someone has gone and robbed it."

"We've got some promising leads on that," said Jones. "Don't you worry."

"I do worry, Inspector. I'll be worrying right up until I get my hands on that cadaver. Now, if you don't mind, I've got a game of bowls to play."

19

My main problem were that I didn't have a motor.

I did have one, if you wanna get arsey about it, being as I still had Jock's burger van and the keys to it somewhere, but I couldn't hardly take the lovely Kerry out to Hurk Wood in that. Not without her getting suss about it, anyhow. She were a right little sparky one, weren't she? Did you see her when I grabbed hold of her arm? For fuck sake, I thought she were gonna yank herself free for a minute there. And she got even sparkier when they came out of the caff to have a go at us about knocking some bird over and not paying the bill. Mind you, it were good to see Burt having summat to do besides popping toast. Weren't so good to see him kicked in the knackers by Kerry, though. Actually, fuck that, it were good to see. In some ways she reminded us of Sal, former bird of mine and mother of Little Royston. Kerry and her both knowed how to swing a shoe when required, and they both had dark hair and the kind of pale skin you normally sees only on prostitutes. Also they was both in Hurk Wood at the minute—Sal buried a bit too shallow for my liking up in the north bit (though she'd be well rotted by now, or her flesh ate off her bones by foxes and rooks and that), Kerry stood beside yours fucking truly on the edge of the south bit.

"And you're sure you dropped him off here last night?" she says, squinting into the path through the undergrowth and not looking happy.

"Defo. Said he wanted to go for a walk in the woods, commute with nature or summat. I think he had matters on his swede."

"His swede?"

"Aye," I says, tapping the side of mine.

She frowned down at her high heels, frowned up the path once again and set off into it, frowning. Her blouse got snagged straight away by a bramble.

"Allow me," I says, stepping in and trying to unsnag the fucker. It came off easy, but I made the most of it, standing close and pulling the material away so I could get a gander inside. Fucking hell.

"Thanks," she says, pulling the blouse straight and cutting short my glimpse of heaven. "Are you alright? You look...peaky."

"Nah, I'm just a bit..."

Peaky? Randy, more like. But I couldn't give way to that just yet. I had to work on her, win her over and get her appreciating the old Royston Blake magic. Be a fuck of a lot easier if I'd drove her out here in my old Capri instead of the Vauxhall wossname I'd had to swipe off a bird who were getting out of it in the supermarket car park back there, but needs must. And how were I to know there were a babby in the back?

"Whoops, looks like little Vectra's awake," says Kerry, looking over at the car, where the wailing had started up again. "She really is a sweet little baby. I wouldn't have bothered you today if I'd known you were a full-time dad."

"Nah, it's alright," I says, looking over there meself and rubbing me chin. I still weren't sure how to play that angle. The babby had helped win Kerry over a bit, true enough, but I could see one or two problems looming on the horizon, what with the mum making all that racket back there and running after the car and calling the coppers, like as not. Luckily I'd got Kerry to wait for us over by the arcade, and she didn't hear none of it. "Erm, I think she's just a bit hot or summat. Reckon I ought to open a window?"

"Well, you know your own baby, but I'd say she wants changing. Or maybe she's hungry. Anyway, I'll leave you to it. And thanks for the lift. Is there a bus that comes by here?"

"You ain't going in that wood on your tod," I says.

"Why not? I need to find my father-in-law. If here's where he was last seen, here's where I look. I've got to say, though, you told me you knew exactly where he was. This isn't that exact, is it?"

"Nah, it's…Look, I'm coming with yers."

"Don't be silly—you've got Vectra."

"She can come and all. It'll be alright, honest. Look, I know she stinks a bit, but if we gets too many flies following us, I'll just light a fag. They hate fag smoke, flies does."

"You can't do that."

"I can—look, I got four left." I popped one out and lit it. "Fancy one?" They was only Silk Cut, mind. I found em in the Vauxhall.

"Hmm…" she says, taking one. "I didn't have you down as a low-tar man."

"I'm on a diet," I says, lighting her up and stepping a bit closer. I could see me lighting her up in other ways before long. All it had took was a fag and a babby, and finally she were thawing out.

"Tell you what," she says, stepping away slightly. You couldn't blame her for wanting to preserve appearances, class bird like her. "You go and change Vectra, I'll try Jock again on his mobile."

"I didn't see no mobiles on him when I seen him."

"He didn't like to use it—said it made him vulnerable to vampire attacks. I told you he was living in a fantasy world."

"Aye, well," I says, smoking and looking back at the motor. "Look, can you change the youngun? Only I gotta go for a bit of a dump meself." Which were true—I couldn't recall the last time I'd curled one out. Seemed like a week or so.

"Oh, uh…" she says, looking all flustered like I'd put her on the spot. "I don't know if I know how to—"

"For fuck sake," I says, stepping foot to foot. I had a bit of a turtle head situation going on down there just now. "How hard can it be? All you gotta do is, erm…"

I left her to it and pegged it into the wilderness. I couldn't hold on no more—that turtle were getting well brave, I fucking tell yer. Half a minute more and he'd be out of his arse-shaped shell and rattling around in Jock's trousers. Mind you, he seemed to be retreating a bit now, or staying put at least with his shoulders coming through but not his arms. I think it were the motion of my arse cheeks rubbing upon each other as I sprinted down the trail. Sure enough, when I finally ran out of puff after about forty yard and pulled up, holding on a tree, the exodus were on again. He were like Harry Houdini, that fucking turtle. I yanked down me strides and squatted, making sure to aim him over the gulley a bit, cos I'd be coming along here with Kerry just now, leading her to the battered and busted corpse of her old feller and standing by with me comforting arms. Last thing you needs in a seduction scenario is a massive shite in the path.

"Ahhh," I says. Cos sometimes you just got to express yourself, ain't you? With a range of sounds, via both ends. Mind you, there was some odd noises coming out the back bit just then. You had your usual ones, which was like someone playing a trombone while driving a tractor, but also a new one that were more like a blackbird or summat, one of them singing ones you gets in the morning and what wakes you up with their fucking racket.

Cheep-cheep, it were going, or whatever. Maybe it weren't a turtle after all but a canary. I'd been through quite a few eggs of late, it had to be said. *Cheep-cheep…cheep-cheep…cheep—*

"Fuck," I says. Cos I recognised the sound now. A phone.

A mobile fucking blower.

Down in the gulley, which seemed about the spot I'd waved goodbye to Jock the night prior. Only there were summat about it, this cheeping and whatevering. It were…

It were getting louder. *Nearer.* Then it stopped.

"Och, what is it?" says a voice about ten feet under my bare arse.

20

I dunno if you've seen *First Blood*.

In it, right, Rocky Balboa is getting chased all over the woss-name by the coppers, who told him to fuck off out of town at the start, but he didn't feel like it or summat. There's two matters there I want to talk about.

First off, why have they always got things arsewise in America? In Mangel, they comes after you if you tries to *leave* town, not stay in it. We are all leaves on the same tree, and if one falls off they all might fall off, and the tree will die. Personally I'd be happy if Mangel carked it, being as I'm sick of the fucking place. But no one else thinks that way. So why do the coppers in America get fucked off when a new leaf tries to join? They should be happy for their tree, shouldn't they? Especially when that leaf is the heavy-weight world champion.

Second off, I were starting to feel like Rambo. I were hounded, everyone coming at us from all sides and trying to corner us. I dipped sideways and into some bushes, pulling me strides up a bit as I went. I were like a ninja, silent and fast and deadly, but not wearing one of them black outfits with the mask like they does. And not looking Chinese or whatever. I were looking more like Rambo, actually, with the long hair and shite. Except my long hair were more like the mullet in the arcade back there in *Rocky III*. That's how I felt, anyhow. I realise it weren't real and that in reality I just looked like Clint Eastwood's head on the body of Ivan Drago. I yanked me anorak off.

"What? No, I'm no interested in a new fuckin' kitchen. How did yis get this number?"

Jock, who were only about ten yard to me right and down a bit, paused just then and started yakking to Kerry on the blower, who'd finally got through to him, so it seemed. I wished I could concentrate on what he were saying, but I were a ninja, weren't I? I had to focus on all the ninja things, like vibrations in the air, and...and putting me lughole to the ground. That's ninjas, ennit? Also I couldn't understand what he were saying, cos I were Chinese. Aye, I know I said I weren't just now, but I changed me mind, alright? I remembered about Bruce Lee.

"I dinnae give a fuckin' shite aboot special rates for the self-employed caterer, I'm no interested. Now fuck off, before I... What the fuck did youse just say to me, ye wee bastart?"

I still couldn't get me swede around Jock being alive. It were fucking miles down that gulley, I could now see when I looked over me shoulder and had a glance. One wrong foot and I'd be heading that way meself, and there were no way I'd survive that kind of fall, let alone climb back up and have a row with my daughter-in-law on the blower. Mind you, it were a bit odd, weren't it? Didn't he just call her a bastard? That ain't normal between father and daughter-in-law. I mean, a feller don't call a bird a bastard, do he, even if he's rowing with her? He calls her a bitch or a slag or summat.

Which meant it couldn't be her on the blower. And I might be in the clear. So long as I could get to Jock before he spilled the beans to her about last night.

"Ye cheeky wee fuckin' bampot!" he yells. "If ah had yis here with me the noo, ah'd...hello? Hello? Fuckin'..."

I looked behind us again, clocking Jock's mobile flying into the gulley. Five or so seconds later I heard a faint *plop* as it hit bottom. That were one thing out the way—least she couldn't get him via that no more. Now, if I could just shimmy over there a bit and get him in a headlock, I'd be—

"*Aaarrgh.*"

That were me that time, letting rip with a manly bellow as the bush I were hanging onto gave way and I went backwards, casting about for a grip on summat and finding fuck all. *Well, that's it from me*, I recall thinking as I fell to my certain demise. I've had a good run, doing a lot of good in the world and saving many a life and ending some bad ones (and not many good ones by accident at all), but here's the feller calling me boat in. "*Get the fuck in with that boat!*" he were shouting, waving his flag about. "*You've been out there nearly forty fucking year. Now get the fuck in and let someone else have a go, you selfish cunt.*" And I couldn't even ignore him this time, like I had done them other times when cunts had shot at us or swung chainsaws at us or tricked us into overdosing on wossnames. This time he'd got us good and proper. He had a rope tied to the boat, and he were reeling us in nice and steady and no getting out of it. Mind you, I'd break his fucking face when I touched shore. Didn't he just call us a cunt? Also I had unfinished business, didn't I?

I touched shore.

It weren't like you'd expect. You'd imagine carking it to be quite painful, wouldn't you? Or at least feel a bit different, like you're floating up to the clouds or summat. But this were not that at all. This were more like getting snatched out of the sky by a very fat bloke who stinks.

I clenched me fist and went to swing it. I put all me weight and strength behind it, aiming to demolish the fucker's face beyond repair. Cos this were the feller on the shore, weren't it? This were the big one in the clouds who'd called time on us before I'd been united with my vibrating diamond.

"Royston, wid yis…what are yis doing, Royston?"

"Wha? I thought…Eh?"

"It's me, yer pal Jock. What are yis trying to slap Jock fer, eh?"

"But I thought you was…What d'you mean 'slap'? Woss you sayin'?"

"Youse need to tread more careful, Royston. This slope here it's fuckin' treacherous. Me, I wis only saved by that wee conker tree doon there."

"What conker tree?"

"It's no there no more. The main part o' the tree went oan doon to the bottom, but I managed tae hang on to the jagged stump. Eight or nine fuckin' hours I wis clinging there, trying tae claw mah way back tae safety. I tell yis, ah'm a lucky man, Royston. Och, can youse smell sumthin'?"

"Er…"

"If ah'm no mistaken, that pong there is human faeces."

"Erm, Jock, you know you says you had a bit of a fall here last night? Well, do you recall how—"

"Fall?" he blares, eyes blazing at us like them of an owl behind his undamaged bifocals. Mind you, they was at least an inch thick, so I couldn't see how anyone could damage em. "Ah widnae call it a fall, Royston. Wid youse? Wid yis really call what happened tae me a fall? You know whit ah'd call it? A fuckin' *assassination* attempt."

Shite. Fuck and shite.

"By them fuckin' vampires."

"Ah…right…"

"Yis seem surprised."

"Me? Nah, I'm just…I reckon yer on the right lines there, Jock. Vampires, yeah."

"Ah must say, Royston, ah'm surprised that yis are agreeing with me. Surprised and heartened. Yis widnae believe the opposition ah've had from the toon at large. And when we joined forces yesterday, ah truly thought we wis all set for the big push towards total vampire eradication, ye know? But then youse changed yis tune. Youse turned oan me, ye wee fuckin'…"

"Jock, I swear I…I mean, I might of wavered a mite, but later on I got to thinking about it and—"

"What the fuck is that reek? Has some wee dirty bastart been using this vicinity for a cludge?"

Before I could ask him what a cludge were he reached inside his pants and pulled out a manky half-bottle of Bell's. He twisted off the lid and upturned it in his mouth, Adam's apple going up and down until the filthy thing were empty. "See this stuff?" he says, lobbing it behind him. "That's what saved me. That and the fuckin' tree doon there. It's like garlic, see—vampires cannae take it. From now oan, yis and me have got to keep oor bloodstreams topped up wi Bell's at all times. Reet?"

"Aye, reet. I mean…"

He got another half-bottle from his pants and held it out to us. The glass were smudged so bad with his sweat and fuck-knowed-what-else, you couldn't hardly see the hard stuff inside. Straightaway a fly landed on it and started licking or laying eggs or whatever. "Go oan—drink up."

"Yeah, it's just that I ain't feeling too—"

"*Drink up.*"

"Aye." I twisted the cap off and took a sip. For fuck sake.

He nodded and went on up towards the path, leaving us dizzy and feeling a bit sick from the filth on the bottle and that were now on my lips. Or maybe it were the sheer speed at which events was turning. Or maybe it were the smell of the cack I'd done up there.

"Oh shite," he says, "ah've gone and stepped in it noo."

I took a massive pull from the bottle. "Them *fuckin'* badgers," I shouts, following behind him.

IMMIGRANT DRUG THREAT

Editorial by Malcolm Pigg

Despite claims by the Mangel Constabulary that "there are no drugs in this town," it does not take much probing to find otherwise. My younger sources swear blind that street drugs such as Plasma and Joey can be bought openly at various pubs in the town centre and suburban areas, as well as nightclubs and even fast-food concessions. A slightly more thorough probe uncovers a more unpleasant truth: this problem is yet again spiraling out of control.

Five years ago Police Chief Cadwallader announced stringent measures to fight the drug craze that afflicted our youth at that time. The "Say No to Joe" campaign focused on education in schools and leafleting around town. After only four months, police declared that drug-related crime had dwindled to nothing, and the war on drugs had been won. But all they had done was drive the market underground, forcing the dealers to get smarter and the users to duck into the shadows.

Since then illegal drug activity has ticked over, serviced by a small gang of local dealers who never allowed the market to grow to levels that would attract attention. But at some point in the last year, that all changed. Gone are those local dealers, their thrones usurped by a new band of criminals whose methods are as ruthless as their hair is greasy.

A visit to our municipal library shows up a few interesting facts about Estravia. Over the past two hundred years, this former communist country has seen no less than eleven bloody regime changes, each one featuring the same ritual humiliation, whereby the former head of state is paraded through the streets of the capital on the back of a cart, strung up like a hammock between two stout posts. Usually that deposed leader is dead at this stage, but on a few occasions he has been kept alive to suffer the final stage of his public ousting: having his genitals removed and subsequently bleeding to death.

For our own sakes and those of our children, we should pray that no regime change takes place in our town.

21

Course I were sorted now. On the vibrating diamond front, I'm on about.

Not only were I getting Kerry reunited with her wayward old man, but he were alive as well. One minute he were a mangled corpse lying in a ditch, next he were ticking and breathing, if a bit scratched and bruised and half cut from the hard stuff he'd been supping. When you looked at it like that, you could see that I'd saved him, really. I'd saved Jock's life. And I were banking on his in-law seeing it that way. Mind you, I couldn't see why she wouldn't. It's fucking logic, ennit?

"Nah, it isnae a vampire, honest," I says to Jock. "Fuckin' *hell*, look how you got us talking now. Can't you speak proper, fuck sake?"

"Ah'm sorry, Royston. It's the way I am. Yis cannae change what yis are."

Mind you, there were still some risk involved here. He'd tried killing her yesterday, and if it weren't for me he would have, sticking it under the rib cage and angling it upwards. But Kerry looked so different now. Out with the clumpy gyppo hair and dirty togs, in with the lipstick and cleavage and nice shiny barnet done up like a bird's ought to be. She'd gone from ugly ducking to...erm, beautiful duckling, or summat, and I couldn't picture a world where a feller wouldn't want her as his daughter-in-law. Mind you, that weren't how I wanted her.

"Look, this surprise I got," I says, "it's defo someone you likes. Just keep an open swede and remember how there's folks out there who gives a toss about you. Don't fret over it."

"Ah'm no frettin', Royston, I just cannae take nae more chances. These bastarts are oan tae me, are they no? It's no often a person survives an assassination attempt from a pack ae them cunts. They'll be doubling their efforts noo, youse mark my words."

"Just fuckin' relax. Would I let you down, Jock? *Would* I?"

He grabbed an arm and wheeled us around. At first I thought he'd suddenly remembered the truth about the gulley business and my part in it and wanted his own back. Then I clocked the look in his eyes, which was gazing into mine. I've only seen that look once before—in the eyes of my own infant lad, Little Royston. It's a look of total trust and adoration. Thinking about it, I don't reckon I ever actually met Little Royston before the witch got her, me being in Parpham when he were borned. But I'd shut me peepers and imagined holding him many a time, and here's the look I got off him on each of them occasions. Then I'd put him down somewhere and fuck off down the pub, cos he'd started wailing or shit his pants or summat.

"Ah want youse to know sumthin right here and noo," says Jock after a few seconds of that look, eyes getting a bit moist. I hoped to fuck he weren't gonna start wailing. Or shit his pants. "Youse and me, we've been through a lot, have we no? Yesterday, eradicating that one in the hearse and chasing doon the female one in the Hoose o' Despair, ah feel that we bonded a bit. Do youse feel it?"

"Hoose of Despair?"

"Aye, it's what ah call it—that place behind the canal."

"The fuck's a hoose?"

"No, ah mean…look what I'm saying is that ah'm considering you as fully onboard noo. I know ah can trust yis, Royston. From noo oan, far as ah'm concerned, your mooth speaks only gospel. So if yis say there's a nice surprise waiting on us up there by the road, ah'm with yis."

"Good. For fuck sake."

"Ah'm gettin' quite excited, actually."

"So you fuckin' ought to be," I says, setting off again. I knew Kerry'd still be there and that she wouldn't abandon little Vectra nor swipe my new motor and leave us out here to fend for my own arse, but I didn't want to keep her waiting too long. Birds can be a right pain when you gets em itchy. Mind you, it's a good way of setting em up for a shag and all. But that could wait. Not too long, mind—my bollocks felt like a couple of grapefruits in a balloon. Jock went down.

"What the…" I says, turning about and clocking him scurrying behind an old oak tree. "Jock, what's the fuckin' problem now?"

"Blue light," he whispers, beckoning us over. "I swear ah just seen some blue light up theer. Ah'm no going up theer."

"Eh? But…"

"Blue light signifies vampire activity, Royston. Didnae youse ken that? Ah'm gonna have tae educate yis."

Vampire activity? He were mental, Jock were. Mind you, I could soon see what he were on about when I walked on a bit and looked through the trees: blue flashing lights, up by the road. No doubt about it. "It's coppers," I said.

"Keep yis voice doon," he says, still not coming out. "Vampires have got supersensitive hear—"

"It's fuckin' *coppers*, for fuck sake. Can't you hear their radios and that? And look, you can see the edge of one of their vans up there. *Shite*."

"It's no what yis think, Royston. Polis they may appear tae be, but it's vampires in disguise. Ah know how them cunts work."

"*Fuckin'* shite," I says again. Cos it *were* shite, weren't it? Soon as the coppers gets involved, shite is what everything turns to.

"No, it's alreet, Royston," Jock were saying, unscrewing another half-bottle. Fuck knows how many of them he were packing in his pants. "See, ah've got a couple o' wooden stakes here in mah poke. We just need tae—"

"Look, just hang back here a min, right?" I says. "I'm off up there for a scout. I don't come back in five, fuck off without us, right? And, I dunno, keep yer eyes peeled for vampires or summat."

He started protesting, but I hared off up the path, keeping low and getting that Rambo feeling again, which were easy cos I were still dressed like him. Best bit were that I seemed to have stowed my monkey wrench in the back pocket of Jock's trousers. I got it out and clamped it between me gnashers, which allowed us to use my paws for sweeping the undergrowth aside as I ploughed silently through it.

"*Aaah*, you fucker," I says, sweeping some stingers aside. They was all over this bit, and no way were I going through em with me top off and some of them nettles reaching me nipples. Mind you, I were close enough to see what were going on roadside now. And it weren't healthy.

Not for Kerry anyhow.

She were getting led into the back of a squad car just then, cuffed and none too happy about it. In another motor you could see Vectra, a WPC holding her just then and copping an earful of lairy babby. I didn't blame the little lass—you should have seen the way the copper were holding her. If I had her, she'd be quiet and kipping in no time. Everyone knows you're meant to give em a nip of whisky. Only a tiny bit, mind. No more than five or six capfuls.

I got my bottle out and took about twenty capfuls, without actually using the cap.

Thinking about it, and with the whisky warming me cockles and the bottle empty, this weren't so bad. Alright, so the vibrating diamond of my life were in a bit of shite at the minute, but I felt sure I could yank her out of the cells with a word in certain ears— namely them of Nathan the barman. I still weren't sure how that worked, but Nathan just seemed to pull strings and make shite happen, no matter how high up them strings went and who were on the other end of em. And on the Jock front, I were shet of him now. I could just leave him back there behind the oak tree, stake held aloft and a gallon of whisky sloshing around in his grots and guts. I could have done that from the start, really, saving meself a lot of grief. But my swede hadn't been straight yesterday, and now it were. Plus there were summat about that fat Scottish cunt that I just couldn't turn me back on, not when he were in front of us and making us feel soz for him. It were like he were my little brother, a little boy lost in a big modern world, and I had to look out for him else he'd be crushed 'neath the wheels of—I dunno—a bus or summat. And it hadn't turned out so bad anyhow. If I hadn't have joined up with Jock, I wouldn't have met Kerry. It were all about her now.

And clearing her of a crime she never committed.

I closed me peepers and pictured her there in the cells, sitting all lonely and scaredy. Then the door swings open and I'm there, a massive silhouette in the doorway, couple of dozen coppers lying broken on the floor behind us. I'd sweep her up in me arms and carry her off into the night then find a nice comfy spot in the grass somewhere and shag her. You pictures it then you does it—that's the way it works with men of action like meself. I opened my eyes. I clenched me fists. I filled my lungs with air. It stank a bit.

"Thought ah'd lost yis back there," says Jock, pulling alongside.

For fuck *sake*.

WOMAN ARRESTED
FOR CHILD SNATCHING

A local woman has been arrested for kidnapping a 12-month-old baby from a town centre supermarket car park. Kerry Barwell, of Norbert Green, stole a Vauxhall Vectra containing the baby at 3:00 p.m. The infant was recovered an hour later when the car was spotted by police in the Hurk Wood area to the north of Mangel. Barwell, 22, was also found nearby and was apprehended after a short pursuit. Though unharmed, the baby was hungry and needed its nappy changed. "We made her do it, the Barwell woman," said the arresting officer, PC Tom Mard. "We didn't have any WPCs available at first, and none of the lads fancied doing it. Part of her rehabilitation, you could call it. I call it punishment."

The baby has been returned to its mother. However, the mother was then arrested for leaving an infant unattended in a car, so the baby had to be taken into foster care. "Also she was driving that Vectra without an MOT, so we got her for that as well. She'll be in for a long while I should imagine. If anyone is interested in fostering a little one, get in touch with social."

22

It had been a long old while since I'd been on a bus.

I weren't sure, but I seemed to recall the last occasion had featured me having a little scrap with a lad. A grown lad, I'm on about, not a youngun. Royston Blake do not fight younguns—let's be straight on that. For starters, any youngun has a pop at me, I finish it fucking sharpish, well before it moves into fight territory. And if it's me starting on them, you can bet your motor it'll be a one-punch job. I can't get low enough to head-butt em, see.

But I'm on about the lad, the bum-fluff merchant I'd had a ding-dong with back then. Actually, fuck him—I ain't wasting me puff on little fucksticks like him. All I wanted to say, if you'd just fucking give us chance, were that there was no lads on this here bus that me and Jock was on, heading back towards Mangel from Hurk Wood. No folk at all under the age of eighteen, nor even near it. Only the one or two old fuckers you always gets on buses, hogging the worst seats and spoiling the atmosphere with their silences and their not causing no trouble and their polite thank-yous to the driver when they gets off.

"Thank you," says one of em as she gets off.

"Fuckin' old bitch," I says under me breath. Old folks is well annoying, but you don't like to offend em, does you? I'm well brung up, me.

"I heard that," she says, pausing as she stepped down.

"Heard what?"

"What you just called me."

"Go on then—what were it?"

"I'm not lowering myself to repeating words like that."

"No? You can lower yerself to suck this, then, you fuckin' old slag. Now fuck off out of my bus."

She glared at us for half a second or so, but you could see the fight had gone out of her and she'd be backing down. That's another thing about old folk—they're fucking cowards. I flicked her a V out the window as the bus pulled away. Then I put myself away and did me flies up. Or Jock's flies, getting technical about it, me still wearing his manky slacks. Not for much longer though. Soon I'd be home, and I'd put some proper smart kit on and set about springing Kerry out of jail. I might even don me court suit, seeing as I'd be in for some legal wrangling like as not. Kerry were in deep shite, when you thought about it. I mean, swiping someone's babby? What kind of barmy cow does that? It's like swiping someone's leaky bag of shite that won't stop making a load of racket. In fact, it *is* that. And were I really up for getting involved with a bird who's prepared to do that, and therefore off her rocker?

Aye, I were, I realised as I closed my eyes and pictured what I'd glimpsed down her top back there. And I'd help her. Together we'd work out what were wrong with her swede and find a way to sort it. But no matter what it were, she weren't having the bad stuff. Not like they got me on. No matter how fucked up a person is in the head, there's never a just cause for pumping that shite inside em. Better to just lobotomise em, like they tried on me. Might work on her.

It were my stop next. Fuck knowed where Jock were headed, but he'd fell akip anyhow and I were hoping to leave him be. Worst case, he'd end up at the main bus depot, and there was some skips you could doss in down there, if he were skint and not wanting to go home like I reckoned him to be. I left a bit of cash on the back seat next to him and rung the bell. Then I changed me mind and picked up the cash—I weren't a fucking charity, were I? I popped the ten pence back in my pocket and went up front, when the bus stopped.

"Ta," I says to the driver as I walked past him. Fuck knows why though, cos I'd paid me fare. Weren't like I were hitching a lift. And he were one of them Egyptians anyhow, like the ones in the bedsits where I lived, so he ought to think himself fucking fortunate to have a job at all.

He nodded at us, saying, "You are wanted man."

"You fuckin' what?" I says, turning back to him and with me hackles rising a bit. But I were off the bus by then, and the door were closing behind us. I banged it with me fist, shouting at him to open up and what the fuck were he on about, me being wanted? But he just smiled through the grease-smeared glass and pulled away. I ran alongside for a bit, trying to catch his eye, but he weren't having none of it. Then I ran into a fucking lamp post and had to stop for a bit and get meself together.

"Are you alright?" someone were saying to us a bit later. I'd got my nose under control with a hanky by then. Still couldn't find two of me teeth, mind.

"Eh?" I says, peering up at the blurred shape stood before us. I still couldn't see proper, but I got the impression of a feller. Sounded like one and all. Feller in a wide-rimmed hat but with one side of it bent up. I peered a bit harder, wondering if it were Clint Eastwood. Nah—no fucking way would Clint let his cowboy hat go like that.

"Do you want me to call an ambulance?" says he. There were summat a mite foreign about his voice, and also familiar. I wondered if he were another of them Egyptians. Or Scottish.

I took my hanky away and squinted at it—seemed to be clearing up nicely. Plenty of blood coming out still, but no bits of bone in it now. "Do you know what I'd really like?" I says, fishing for another hanky, cos mine had got well sodden. There weren't one. It were a fucking miracle I'd found any hankies at all in Jock's strides. Who the fuck carries hankies, for fuck sake? This one had been a bit crispy in places, mind. "See, it ain't possible, what I'd really like," I went on. "Cos what I'd really like, see, is for you to walk behind yerself and kick yerself up the fuckin' arse."

"Ah, but it is not necessary to walk behind oneself to achieve that. The same can be accomplished merely by—"

"Is you thick or summat?" I says, raising me voice a mite now. "Fuck off."

"Your vehemence is admirable, Highlander," he says. I could place his voice now: he sounded like Sean Connery. Looked like him and all. I think it *were* him. "However, there are better ways to expend your energies than abusing old women on buses and being hostile to those who come to your aid. In considering the properties of the common lamp post, for example. Tall and slender, the lamp post nevertheless is as rigid and immovable as a granite outcrop. At least it is to those who approach the world as does a mere mortal."

"What the…Who the fuck do you…"

I gave up trying to find the right words and lashed out, doling the kind of blow to the guts that would surely have brung about major organ failure if it had landed. But it never. Fuck knows quite how, but the fucker weren't occupying the same space no more. I spun around, blinking hard and thinking about summat he'd mentioned there.

"Hang on," I says. "What did you just call me?"

You heard it and all, right? Hadn't he just called us the Highlander?

"*Oi!*" I hollers, losing it now and quite rightly so. The number three cause of aggro in the Mangel area—after eye contact, pint spillage, and looking at birds who ain't yours—is calling former head doormen Highlanders and then fucking off, no matter if you appear to be Sean Connery or what. Cos this one were nowhere to be clocked. Somehow, and with my peepers now working twenty-twenty and me scanning a full rotation of 180 degrees, he'd fucked off.

I trudged home, trying to put the episode out of my head. Some things you just have to, don't you? Everyone gets them things. I'm on about the things you know don't belong in your swede, the ones that some fucked-up part of your brain has cooked up, using rotten bits of scran gathered here and there over the years. I'd had enough of them bits. From now on, Royston Blake were getting his shite together big time. Starting with finding a proper set of togs to wear. And wiping some of the blood off meself. My nostrils had caked up now, and no more was coming out, but it were all over me chest and guts.

I looked down at it as I went in the front door of my building, flexing my abs and wondering why I couldn't see em. Mind you, I do have a very hairy body. No matter how ripped you is, like me, the hair's always gonna take the edge off that. But it don't take the edge off where it counts—getting shite done and pinging swedes.

Someone pinged me swede. I went down.

23

I blames it on them fucking strides.

If I'd have been wearing my own strides, instead of Jock's manky ones that was about ten times too big for us around the middle, I'd have got away. I'd have scrambled clear and gained the stairs, where I would have got on me feet again and started looking at this situation. I'd have asked meself who this cunt were who'd just pinged my head, and I'd have found the answer to be the one from the kitchen last night who'd been chopping squid. I'd have noted the short length of pipe he'd just opened my scalp up with, a bit over the right ear. Then I'd have laughed in his fucking face and waded in, annihilating the fucker with me bare paws. But I weren't able to do none of that, cos I were wearing Jock's strides.

Which fell down a bit and got caught up around my ankles.

"Get the fuck off us, you fuckin' arse bandits!" I were shouting, trying to hoick them up again as Squid and his mate got a foot each and dragged us into a room off the main hall. Then I clocked the looks in their eyes and the bad atmosphere of the new room I were in, and I left off the strides and started kicking out at their faces.

"You not fight," says the non-Squid one. It were the other from yesterday, the one who'd slit my throat in the kitchen and looked just like the corpse from the hearse, except with a better haircut and not so many scars and pockmarks. He adjusted his grip on my foot, planted his own behind my knee and twisted sideways. Hard.

"*Aaarrrggh*," I says. Cos the corpse one were busting me fucking pin here. "*Aaa—*"

I hadn't noticed Squid let go, but he had. He came behind us and taped up my cakehole, cutting short my yell of pain.

"You not scream also. Scream is for woman. Not even boy scream. Only weak boy who must be slaughter. I slaughter you. Here, in this place of dark and not happy."

I suddenly recalled that my other pin were free now and swung it at him. He fielded it on the arse cheek then planted his other foot on that ankle and pushed my legs wide. I felt my pelvis go, but I didn't know what to do. I hadn't come across this type of fighting before. It were like I were an Action Man and he were trying to pull us apart, and I couldn't do a fucking thing about it. Then I recalled that my hands was free and that Squid were behind us somewhere. I craned my neck round and saw his ankle not two foot away. I reached for it. I were gonna reel it in and bite a chunk out of it, then he'd start screaming like weak boy who must be slaughter, or whatever, and his mate would have to let go me pins and help him. But it didn't happen like that. How it happened, right, is that he slipped a fucking manacle around my wrist.

Manacles was another thing I hadn't ever come across before. I'd seen many a handcuff, mind you, and the clamp of this were wider than that and not so smooth around the edges, meaning it stung like billy-o when he pulled the chain taut. He slipped one around the other wrist. Around that time I noticed what Corpse had done to my ankles.

He'd manacled them and all.

"This is way must be," he says, pulling up the slack on that side. "You have fuck with family. When man fuck with family, he must be chain. Like wild boar."

He leaned back. Squid were leaning back and all, meaning I were yanked taut meself now like a fucking hammock. Corpse looped the chain around a hook in the wall and let go, clenching and unclenching his paws. Squid must have done the same behind us, cos I were more or less swinging in the air now, two Egyptian cunts stood on either side of us and me wrists and ankles knacking like you'd not believe. And I couldn't even complain about it cos of the gaffer tape.

"Now you shut face and listen," says Corpse, out of breath now. At least there were that. "In one minute I remove tape from mouth, and you say where is Martynas. You say nothing else and make no shout. Only where is my brother. If you not do this, you die. Like wild boar."

There were a bed to the side of him. It weren't square but long and oblong like normal beds. Fuck knows who'd started that square-bed rumour. I think it were you, weren't it? What a fucking stupid thing to suggest. Who the fuck sleeps in square beds? Anyhow, Corpse reached down behind this normal-shaped bed and pulled summat out. It were wrapped in a faded orange towel with oil stains on it. He pulled the towel off and held the thing out before him.

Straightaway I took a dislike to it.

"This special knife," he says, twisting it and flashing it around in the scant light.

Don't tell us—it's for cuttin' up wild boar, I might have said if my gob weren't taped shut.

"Is special knife for cutting man. In my country, we kill the bad man like this…"

He held the knife in two hands and lunged forwards, going down on one knee and driving the blade forwards and down. If some poor cunt had been there in front of him, their solar plexus would have been feeling it just now. For a bit. Then they would have carked it. He got on his feet again.

"But you," he says, "you we not kill. You tell us where is Martynas and you walk away with only the cut and bruise. You not tell, we kill. We kill you like wild boar."

He came over and whipped the gaffer tape off my face, taking a few hundred bristles and some skin with it.

"First off," I says, gulping for puff and ignoring the pain, "first off, right…you let us go now and say a proper soz to us, I won't bear no grudge against you. You know what a grudge is? Means when you got a grudge with someone about summat. And I ain't got one with you pair o'…fellers. I knows yer only Egyptians, see, and that you dunno the rules of the road yet. See, you gotta understand who's who in this town, who's a community pillar and who's a…a…barmy old dosser or summat. And Royston Blake is the latter o' them two. Erm, latter means the first one, right?"

They looked at each other, seeming a bit confused by that one. Mind you, they barely fucking spoke English, did they? Then Corpse nodded at Squid, who taped my mouth up again.

"I see you not cut," says the latter. Or the former. I don't fucking know, do I? Corpse, anyhow, pointing at my tadger with his big knife. Jock's trousers was gathered around my knees, and I were a bit exposed I now realised. "I see you have foreskin. But is better without, yes?"

"*Mmmmmph*," I says. "*Fnngg mmmp mmmmmph.*"

"You hear man, Myko?" he says to Squid. "Man say he like to be cut. He not want foreskin. Is better without, yes?"

"Yes," says Squid, rubbing his paws together, like as not thinking about what kind of national dish he could make out of my end piece.

"OK, you hold, I cut. Yes?"

"Yes." Squid came forwards, reaching out for us. I thought he were gonna grab us with his bare paws, which would have been bad enough. Then I noticed the pair of pliers he were holding.

"*Mmmmmmmmmmmmppphhh.*"

He lunged. The pliers snapped shut as he made a play for my tadger, but I were rocking the hammock a bit now and managed to turn my loinage away from him and keep it like so, anchoring meself with a hip to the carpet. Mind you, Corpse were on that side with his knife.

"You let Myko pull," he says. "If not pull, can be accident. Man have accident, is hard for him in life. You let Myko pull now, yes? With plier."

I weren't really listening to him. I were in my head, trying to get the opening bit of "Eye of the Tiger" by Survivor started. But I couldn't hear them guitar sounds, no matter how hard I harked. "*Mmph,*" I says, trying to do em meself. "*Mmph mmph mmph. Mmph mmph…*"

Corpse turned away and reached in his back pocket.

Fucking hell, I thought, it's only gone and worked. Not like I'd pictured it, mind. I'd been aiming to rile meself into a feat of superhuman strength, smashing them manacles and killing these two fuckers dead like Ivan Drago done to Apollo Creed (rest him in peace). But the music seemed to have done the trick on its tod, knocking the Egyptians back and making em change their ways. Then I noticed the mobile blower Corpse were holding and the bleeping sound it had been making.

"Yes?" he says into it. "Who is? No, *you.* Who *you* is?"

I could hear someone shouting from the other end. Fuck knowed who it were, all I gave a toss about were how long they'd keep it up for and thereby help us to keep my tadger intact a bit longer. But it turned out to be about two seconds.

"You stay," says Corpse, stowing his phone and pointing at us. "You try struggle free, you make worse for self, yes?"

He went out the door, yanking Squid with him and slamming it behind him. I found myself wondering who that caller might have been, cos I could have sweared I recognised that drone on the other end, like a bluebottle caught in a light bulb. But I couldn't fret over that just now. I had to seize the fucking moment. I had to grasp this opportunity that providence had bestowed upon us and bust meself free from the chains.

I pulled arms down and legs up, using my rock hard abs to tug the hooks out of the walls, or whatever them chains was tethered to. I thought about Rocky Balboa. I thought about him in the Rocky films and also the Rambo ones, where he's up against it and looking like there's no hope...and yet he still comes out on top, no matter who or what is stood before him. Also *Over the Top*, where Rocky's an arm-wrestling truck driver. For some reason I found that one the most inspiring of all, and I pictured meself in a massive arm-wrestling contest against the wall hook, the two of us locked in an epic struggle between good and evil. I were on the side of good, just to clarify.

But evil won.

I didn't have it in us.

I felt meself drifting into one, not turning lairy but the opposite, the place where Rocky gets his swede in *Rocky III* when he don't believe in himself no more and reckons Clubber Lang is harder than him. It ain't often I gets like that, but I'd done it a couple of times of late, thinking back over old times and not seeing how I could get em back again. Often as not a couple of bottles of whisky will bring you out of it, but I didn't have them here. And even if I did, I couldn't get me paws free. I looked over at the window, thinking how shite life could get and how thirsty I were. On top of that, it were starting to piss down a bit outside. I sometimes wonder about that, if it's me controlling the world with my feelings and wossnames. I fucking swear the sun always shines when I'm in a good one. And when I'm feeling chilly in the winter, you can fucking bank on it there's a few snowflakes in the air, expressing my chilliness. But I don't recall ever making faces appear at the window and try and jemmy the fucker up with a tyre iron. Especially not ones with a tight black hood over em, except for the eyes, like a ninja. Mind you, there's always a first time.

The ninja got the iron in and forced up the window, letting in a gust of my *Rocky III* mood and himself. Saying that, I weren't feeling *Rocky III* no more. I were feeling *2001: A Space Odyssey*. As in "I dunno what the fuck's going on here, but it might turn out good." He went over to the door, moving fast and silent and like he were made of balsa wood and harked at it for a second or two, hearing a bit of clatter downstairs and some foreign shouting. Then he came to me and got some bolt cutters out.

Bearing in mind I still had me tackle out, you can see why I started kicking up a fuss at that point. But he sailed straight past that area and clamped the cutters around the chain, slicing through it like a vet cutting the cord on a newborn lamb. But an unusual vet, cos he had a throwing star tucked behind his right ear. My arse and a leg dumped on the carpet, along with a couple of yard of chain. Like a newborn lamb that weighs nineteen stone and some metal afterbirth. I were gonna say summat about that and ask him about the throwing star and how they gets em so accurate when he cut my other leg free and went behind us.

Couple of minutes and I were stood tall, rubbing me wrists and ankles where he'd just got the manacles off. The ninja were by the door again, not harking at it this time but fucking with the lock, sticking summat in it and making little clicking noises. Around the time I opened me mouth to voice my concerns about all this, he opened the door and stood aside, ushering us out.

"Erm," I says in the corridor now and turning back to him. But the door clicked shut in me face. I went to bang on it, halting me fist just in time as I heard two pairs of foreign pins bombing back up the stairs and Blakeward.

I bombed up some stairs of me own.

Inside my bedsit now and panting, I noticed I were holding summat. It were the throwing star, except instead of the hard metal I'd always thought em to be made of it were made from some kind of lightweight material, almost like cardboard. I turned it over, panting quite hard and wondering what the fuck. On the back it said, scrawled in red ink that seemed to me like blood:

YOU OWES ME FOR THAT. SO GET DOWN THE PAUL PRY FLAMING SHARPISH.
YOUR FRIEND AND ALLY,
NATHAN

CLUB FALL
MAN—FOREIGNERS RELEASED

All eleven Estravians arrested for the murder of tragic club fall man Scott McCrae have been released. It is believed that the foreign nationals all had alibis.

"We're not confirming that these people had alibis, no," said Inspector Stephen Jones when questioned on this. "What we will say is that each one of them was able to prove that he was somewhere else at the time of McCrae's death, so we had to release them."

When it was pointed out that this was what is usually meant by an alibi, Jones went on: "Oh, is it? I thought an alibi was when someone has got white hair, really pale skin, and pink eyes. And you get dogs born like that as well. My auntie's got an Alsatian like it. It's a what? Are you sure? Tom, can you get that checked? And I don't want any more slip ups, alright?"

Waving away the deluge of questions from the gathered media, Jones said: "Look, I've got a prepared statement here, and I'll read it to you, but that's your lot. I've got a job to do, and we're understaffed, so, erm…Eleven Estravian nationals, all of them members of the Gustas family, have been released from custody. These foreigners— six men, two women, and three children—were all asleep in their homes at the time. At the time when McCrae died, I'm saying, not when they were released. Obviously they were in the police cells when they were released, pending co...What's this word here say, Tom?"

"Corroboration."

"Pending collaboration of these albinos. One of them was held for a further six hours due to violent and disrespectful behaviour towards a police officer, but we decided to let him go in the end because he needed his nappy changed. As a result of this, the death of Scott McCrae is no longer being treated as suspicious. As a result of the albinos, not the dirty nappy. The dirty nappy has no bearing on the legal side of things. The Gustas family have been referred to the "Welcome to Mangel" campaign so that they can learn all about how to treat police officers and local people with respect and not bawl and shout at them and pretend to cry for hours upon end."

24

Comes a time in each man's life when he knows it's got to end.

My time came about half an hour after the last bit, me lying pitwise and watching a spider up on the ceiling, listening out for them foreigners below and not hearing much from them for ten minutes or so. And when I says things have got to end, I ain't on about the events of the past couple of days, the shoving and tugging and rumbling and what have you. All that shite were par for the course, and I quite enjoyed it, except where pliers was involved. Anything worth doing, you got to shed some blood for it. Your own blood and that of other folks, else you ain't showing like you really wants it. And if there's one thing I really wanted more than ever now, it were that expensive caravan holiday.

I could picture it now—me at the wheel of the hearse, Kerry by my side passing us sarnies, cans of lager, and little smiles. And fags. I'd be pointing out features of the landscape that were rushing by. She'd be appreciating my knowledge, enjoying my jokes, and laughing in that way of hers that sounds like the gentle tinkling of a crystal glass when you drops it, spilling sparkling wine all over the place and firing little bastard shards all around that you forgets about and treads on a couple of weeks later, cutting your feet to fuck and swearing like billy-o. But in a good way.

Again, I ain't saying none of them things had to end. All that—it's the good stuff. I felt like I were getting somewhere with it, moving steady towards a goal, clearing shite up for folks along the way and making my prize all the more sweeter once I got to it. But one particular thing did have to end, like I says, and here were the moment.

I'm on about my appearance.

I were in my room. The door were gone, like you knows, as were the back of the wardrobe that Bean had helpfully put there to fill the space. And it were the same as a door anyhow, cos you just had to step through the wardrobe and push the doors open and swing em shut behind you. I were stood in front of them doors, looking at meself in the long mirrors on em. For fuck's fucking sake, I were thinking…how had it got so bad? And it weren't just the trousers, which didn't even stay up no more.

I stepped out of em, half expecting em to scurry across the Axminster and escape out the window. Now I could get a proper look at meself—and I found it hard to ignore the toll all them hard years had took on my body, the effects of not eating right and the damage inflicted by cunts in the last couple of days.

And I'll tell you summat: I looked alright.

Aye, my throat sported a cut going right across from lug to lug nigh on. And I had a couple of fat lips and an even more squashed hooter from the lamp post just now. And my arms was scratched to fuck from brambles and shite in Hurk Wood and falling down that gulley and getting caught by Jock. And there were a gaffer tape-shaped area of stubble and skin missing from me face. Plus I had dried blood all down my front and on me face still. But it were all in a good way, you know? Overall, appraising meself in the merciless light of that morning, or whatever fucking time of day it were, I thought I looked the business. And I'm coming back to the Rambo thing here.

Also Jean Claude Van Damme in *Cyborg*. The bit where he gets crucified.

Saying that, I did need a shower. To highest heaven I did stink, plus the blood were starting to flake all over the shop and rain down in little burgundy bits that looked like fish food. And that made us think of the koi carp—the ones in the pond behind the nice big house I had earmarked for meself, with gravel crunching in the drive and a couple of younguns tumbling about on the lawn. You don't get none of that shite from *Cyborg* and *Rambo*. You wants the finer things in life, you got to dress the part.

I'm talking community pillar.

I opened the wardrobe doors and peeped out into the world at large. Bathroom were down there on the first floor, but I didn't fancy venturing that way just now, not with them two cunts with the pliers and the knife. Not that I were afraid of em, just gearing meself up into pillaring mode, which is a lot calmer and more respectable than I'd have to be if I bumped into Squid and Corpse again and had to ping their swedes. So I shut the doors and went to the little sink I had in my room.

I got a dirty T-shirt and wet it then started wiping all the shite off my chest and everywhere. But that made it worser, so I just sprayed some deodorant under me pits and brushed me gnashers. The toothpaste were empty, so I had to use soap. And I ain't sure if the spray can had some left in it or was just pumping out gas. Smelled alright, mind. So I sprayed some in my mouth and all. I finished up by flaking off as much blood as I could and splashing on some aftershave where it counted. I used a lot of it and got meself way wetter than I'd aimed, but sometimes you cannot take shortcuts.

I stood savouring the tingle of the Hai Karate as it dried on my skin, looking at my face in the small mirror above the sink and wondering how it could be, how I'd ended up living in this fucking dump when I deserved so much better. You only had to see the cuts and the scars and the lines around my eyes to know all about the efforts I'd made over the years, the work I'd put in to haul meself up the ladder, only to have some wanker plant a boot in me fucking face. But you've got to take em as they comes, don't you? Everyone has a path mapped through life, and mine just happened to pass through the town dump, taking the long route through it and looping around a few times, coming back on itself. But I weren't lost in that dump, no fucking way. Sometime soon I'd be breaking out and hitting the fucking boulevard. And then they'd know.

Finally, and with my scrotum all dry now but still tingling with the Hai Karate, I pulled on me pillaring kit.

25

"I see," says Nathan, clocking us with a raised eyebrow. "Bit of a burgundy theme, is it?"

I looked down at meself: leather suit and tie, slip-on shoes, white socks. I'd only worn this getup on two other occasions, them being a wedding and a funeral. Of my wife. Both times. "Fuck you on about?" I says. "These slip-ons is grey."

"Aye, but not much else is. I've not seen so much red leather since I had to go in that abattoir the one time. Them places don't agree with me. I can't abide to see beasts suffering, Blakey. And your suit puts us in mind of it." He got a bag of pork scratchings off the rack and popped a handful, shaking his head.

"That ain't my fuckin' problem," I says. "You wanted us here, I'm here. I'm wearing me pillaring suit."

"I can see that."

"Eh? Don't you wanna know what pillaring is?"

"I knows what pillaring is."

"But…oh, aye."

Took us by surprise nigh on every time it did, Nathan's ability to look in a person's mind and see what he's thinking. I pictured a scene whereby Nathan's getting buggered by a billy goat, just to fuck him off.

"Well, I did think I knew what pillaring were," he says after a few strokes from the goat. "You sayin' it means summat different, now?"

"Erm, no…I were just, erm…"

"And that's what your burgundy suit's for, is it? Creeping up on billy goats and inducing the poor things to mount you?"

"No, I'm just…fuck sake, Nathe, I'm just havin' a laugh."

"The name's Nath*an*—that's two syllables, not one. How'd you like it if I called you Royst?"

I felt me hackles rise at that, but I did me best to smooth em down again. He had a point. And besides, it had got his mind off the billy goat thing. Folks like Nathan, it ain't good to fuck em off for too long. He had power, see. And that's why I were here.

"In actual fact, you're here because I summoned you," he says, putting a pint before us on the bar top, "after having your crown jewels saved from them two undesirables."

"Aye, I meant to ask you about that. Who the fuck were the ninja one? Were that you?"

"My ninja days is over, Blakey. Can't bend me knees to the same degree no more, see."

"Nah, I meant did you send him? And were that a proper throwing star? Cos it seemed like it were made of cardboard. That some kind of special metal from the future, is it? Or summat?"

"Where am I gonna get metal from the future? It's plain old card. I had Margaret cut it out of a pack of Lambert & Butler. Done the trick, though, didn't it?"

"I don't think it would have, actually. Lob that at an enemy and they'll fuckin' laugh at yers. If it reaches em. Wind'll take it, like as not."

"I said it done the trick, which were to get your attention and bring you here. Job done, I says. Now, let's get down to—"

Charlie Williams

"Can I just have a little word first? See, there's this friend o' mine who is in jail right now, and…well, she's more a lover than a friend, really. I mean, I ain't shagged her yet, but she's definitely—"

"Friend of his, he says! You're on about that flamin' Barwell dolly bird, ain't you? If you've not had relations with her yet, I'd strongly advise keeping it that way. It don't do to dip yer spoon in bad tea."

"Fuck you on about?"

"That's your eternal problem, Blake, ennit? Wilful ignorance."

"I fuckin' swear it ain't wilful, Nathan. Erm…eh?"

"That surgical procedure I just saved you from, back at that doss-house you calls home—reckon that were easy, does you?"

"Course I don't. But if there's one feller who could do it, it's—"

"Muggins, aye. And how do you reckon muggins gets things o' that nature done, eh? Reckon I got a magic wand? I ain't, Blake. What I got is *knowledge*. 'There is no precious metal in the world worth more than knowledge.' Know who said that, does you?"

"Aye. You."

"How the hell did you know that?"

"I just heard yer."

"No, I meant—"

"Look, Nathan, I know there's ins and outs and what-have-yous, but I don't give a toss about none of that. All I knows is that Kerry is in a fuckin' tight spot, and it were me put her there. A babby were involved, see, and—"

"Aye, and that infant is safe and rosy now with a nice foster family, no flamin' thanks to you. Little Josie her name is."

"Nah, this one were called Vectra…and I accidentally, erm…"

I stopped there cos I became aware of the silence that had befell the place, despite there being twenty or so other punters filtered in since I'd arrived. So far as I knowed, this were a record headcount for the Paul Pry. It ain't a popular place, and Nathan, who ain't ever been inclined to make it so by way of pricing nor music nor not being such a miserable cunt, stood behind the bar with his massive moustache and his hairy arms, so this turnout here came as a surprise. Not as much as the silence, though. And what went with it.

I'm on about the staring.

I felt my face getting warm. You would and all if you had forty-seven eyes burning a hole in your face just then, counting the two extras who'd just come in, and Frank Percival, who only had one eye at that time. And Old Mr. Fillery, who were completely blind. Couldn't see Gromer, mind, the miserable cunt from the offie down Cutler Road. Nor Alvin. For some reason I thought he'd be amongst this lot, and he weren't. "Fuck you cunts lookin' at?" I says to em.

"Don't offend em, Blake," says Nathan behind my back. "This here band of honest citizens don't deserve your abuse. They're your supporters, these are. They've come here tonight on account of you, and the efforts you made."

I couldn't face em no more. I'm all for having supporters, but I didn't like the looks in their eyes. Even the one or two birds who was there. And one of em were Margaret Hurge anyhow, whose face you could make a decent pair of heavy-duty boots out of. I turned around and picked me pint up. "That's fuckin' rosy and that," I says to Nathan, taking a big gulp, "but...*pleurgh*...fuck's that?"

"It's cola. And try not to spit it out over my bar."

"Fuckin' *coke*? You gone barmy or summat?"

"I've a very good reason for it, Blake. It's on account of your work in this town not being done. These lot here knows it, and I knows it. Everyone knows it but you. And I'm about to tell you it."

"Giz summat proper to drink and I'll hark."

"Not until—"

"Fuck *sake*!" I yells, nearly smashing the pint of coke on the counter. Actually, I did smash it. But I felt I could push things just now. It were a feeling I'd known before, and it were to do with holding all the cards. Wished I knowed what them cards was, mind you.

"King of spades," says Nathan, plonking a half pint before us this time. "That's the service you done for this town, although you didn't quite see it through to the end on this occasion. But these here good citizens have come down here to thank you for your efforts."

I looked over me shoulder. "I don't see none of em thankin' us."

"Oh, they are. In their hearts they are. It's because of the king of spades."

"The fuck is this king o' spades bollocks?"

"I'm on about the outsider, Blake. I'm talking about the one who brings chaos to our town. He cometh not from our shores, this one don't. From a faraway soil he did spring, and in that land he should have stayed. But him and his ilk looked across the water and did see the land o' milk and honey we got here, and that they did covet. Actually, there ain't much honey since Des Mallett's bees all went stinger up. And Clapton Dairy ain't bottled a decent pint since—"

"Yer digressin', Nathan!" shouts Margaret Hurge.

"I'll digress all I likes!"

"Just saying. Time is a factor here."

Nathan shook his head and went on. "Then they came, the outsiders did. On boats they journeyed, on horses and carts and even by foot, bare and stinking and dyed with the hue of that faraway field from whence they did spring, 'cross sea, over border, and through, erm…"

"Cat flap," I says.

"What?"

"Through the cat flap, ennit? People don't reckon a person can get through em, but I seen it done, I swear. Me and Fin, we robbed loads of—"

"I don't give a polecat's arse gland about you and your tales of thievin'! I'm on about the *invaders*, Blake. I speak of him who came first, the fountainhead who opened the floodgates to every shiftless Turk, Ay-rab, and infidel to follow in his flamin' wake."

I finished off my half pint. I were quite impressed with how long I'd dragged that one out. "Nathan," I says, examining the empty, "there's two matters I still ain't sure about here. One is why the fuck you just made me drink a half pint. Two is the fact I quite liked it, drinking lager in a thing that size. Seemed a nice size of container, I gotta say, and I'm surprised at that in a good way. Three is what the fuck is you on about?"

"He's talkin' about immigrants!" shouts Hurge. "You daft prick."

I spun and gave her a look. If she weren't a bird, I'd have staved her fuckin' cheekbones in at that moment. *Maybe I could do that anyway*, I recall thinking. I mean, you ain't meant to touch a bird in anger and that, but how cast-iron can a rule be? Plus I'd be doing women in general a favour, raising their average attractiveness by knocking a bad one out. I started getting off me stool.

So did a feller towards the back, mirroring us exactly.

He were positioned between Terrence Blandish and John Fairway from the twenty-four-hour garage up the top of Clench Road. I stood and gave him my professional once-over, sizing him up for

1. drunkenness,
2. potential weapons,
3. asking for it, and
4. previous.

But I couldn't manage that last one, which involved trying to recognise him. A doorman must never forget a face, else he won't know when he's rubbing up against some cunt he banned only a couple of weeks prior, thereby failing to dole out the fixed penalty for trying to skirt around that, which is getting knocked out and dumped over the wall behind the car park. I could see them around him as clear as you like, and some of em much clearer than that (Hurge), but not this one. He were like a shadow, though the wall-mounted lights tinged his shaggy hair orange round the edges, like he were on fire.

I sat back upon the stool, keeping me peepers on cunty over there as he done same, perching on a high barstool like I were, judging by the way his head stayed higher than them sat around. Or perhaps he were parked on a table. You weren't allowed to do that.

"Hoy," I says over me shoulder to Nathan, sliding the half-pint glass to him at the same time, "him over yonder, the fucker who's like a shadow, he's sat on the fuckin'—"

"That 'fucker,' as you calls him, is none of the sort," he says.

"Who the fuck is he, then?"

"He ain't a *he* as such."

"What, he's a she?"

"No, a golem."

"Oh," I says, looking at the golem. "Eh?"

CHILD SNATCHER
INVESTIGATED FOR
ESTRAVIAN MURDER

A woman arrested yesterday for child snatching has been charged with the murder of asylum seeker Martynas Gustas.

"We found splinters in Kerry Barwell's hands," said Inspector Stephen Jones, investigating. "These splinters were in keeping with the kind you would get from killing someone with a sharp piece of wood. So we're looking into it."

Police had previously believed that Gustas was killed during an attempted burglary at Scott McCrae's home, where the body was found, but further investigation has blown the case wide open. "I wouldn't say that," said Jones. "It's just these splinters, really. Then we found a link between Barwell and McCrae, which set off the alarm bells. From what we can see, the two were going out together. Or had done at one time. This sort of thing rarely turns out to be coincidence."

Asked why Kerry Barwell had not been questioned earlier about the deaths of Gustas and McCrae, Jones said: "What we are dealing with here is a woman who is very good at covering her tracks. We found no evidence of her at McCrae's residence, although one of the lads was sure he saw a pair of knickers lying on the floor that might have been hers. However, those knickers disappeared. If anyone out there finds a pair of knickers, white with red dots on them, please contact Mangel police."

Meanwhile, Barwell has been released on bail. "We just don't have enough evidence to hold her. Until you can link them with a specific crime, splinters are just splinters. We can't do a thing without the murder weapon. Or the murdered body. If it hadn't gone missing, trust me, that woman would be halfway to jail by now. So if anyone finds a corpse, a bloody stake, or a pair of knickers, please let us know."

26

"That's right, a golem," says Nathan, pouring a glass of sherry for no one in particular.

He poured it slow, about as slow as a barman can pour, measuring his words by the drops. "Made of the very clay from under our feet, he is. And when I says under our feet, I mean literally so. We got an access point down there in the cellar, and one or two of the lads scooped out a decent load of homegrown Mangel clay for him. Flamin' hard graft it were, scrapin' them raw materials out. Many a bead o' sweat were shed and quite a few profane words uttered, but we done it. After nineteen weeks of hard graft, we had ourselves a whole man-worth of rough clay. That's when Old Mr. Fillery stepped in."

"What's that?" says a reedy voice behind us.

"I'm just sayin' about the work you done, Mr. Fillery, turning your ornamental figurine skills to the shaping of Igor here, using only your hands and without the aid of eyesight."

"No, I meant what's that foul odour? I got heightened powers of smell, you realise, whoever done that."

I kept me swede down, me being the one who'd just dropped a silent one. It were a fucking bad one too, the kind you can actually see on a bright day. Mind you, it were dark in here.

"And then came Margaret Hurge," says Nathan, not even batting a nostril. "It were her job to fashion a full head of hair for him, using only cuttings off the floor of her hairdressin' parlour."

"Studio."

"What's that, Marge?"

"It's a studio, not a parlour. And I'm absolutely disgusted, whoever made that smell. You ought to be ashamed of yourself. And you ought to see a doctor."

"Right you are, Marge. Then came—"

"And they was specially harvested strands, not sweepings off my floor."

"For the love of the gods, Marge! I'm trying to summarise here! After he were finished in body, the final task came to me. This were the big one: bringing him to life. It were my tongue what incanted the words that gave him voice, my breath what filled his lungs, my fingers lifting his eyelids and giving him vision. Actually, it were me thumbs, cos his lids was a bit stiff. But you see the point I'm making, don't you, Blake? There were many stages in the making of Igor, if you factor in the garments, footwear, even a bit of makeup at times to make him presentable to the public in daylight. And each of them stages were carried out by a craftsman or tradesman from this very town. He is a hundred percent homegrown is Igor. He is the true son of this town, and he serves it like none before him. What do you make of that, eh?"

"That sherry yer drinkin'?" I says after a bit.

"Aye."

"Fuck sake."

"Got summat to say, have you?"

"I ain't got fuck all to say about sherry. It's a fuckin' birds' drink. *Old* birds and all, like Marg—"

"I meant about the golem, you big clot. Do you not marvel at his strength, his presence, his...*purity*?"

I glanced over me shoulder. "Looks like a cunt to me."

"A flamin'..." Nathan looked like his swede were set to burst for a minute or so, and then he calmed down. "Oh, I see. Playin' it cool, is it? I ought to have expected it from you. But the truth is that you're ruffled, ain't you? Igor here is a threat to you, I can see. Not only can he do everything that you does, but—"

"He can't do fuckin' *shite* that I does!" I yells, jumping up and kicking me stool over. It pinged off the far wall, and one of the legs came off. Served it right, the fucking twat. "What can he do that I can do, eh? I mean, can he, erm..."

"See what I mean, Blake? You can't think of one special talent o' yours that he—"

"No, I can, I'm just takin' a moment to...*doorin'*. Aye, I'd like to see him stood on the door at Hoppers of a night, letting in them who's—"

"Hoppers ain't there no more, Blakey. You knows that."

"Aye, but he could door somewhere else, couldn't he, if he had the bollocks? But he ain't, so—"

"Rockefellers."

"Eh?"

"We had him performing doorman duties at Rockefellers the other night, standing in for the usual feller who were sick. The evening passed without incident. No scraps, no drama. Every potential flare-up were nipped in the bud by Igor here, see. And he don't even have to speak, though he can. All he needs is his presence."

"He...But...you had a fuckin' *clay model* keeping door at Rockefellers?"

"Like I says, usual man were off. Manager there were casting about for stand-ins. Thought I'd put forwards Igor here. Bit of a risk, I'll grant that, but I knew he'd come through. He has the spirit of this town in his belly, see. People feel it and don't question it. Fifty pound, we got, for that night's work. That's more for the war chest."

I wanted to sit down again, and wished I hadn't bust that stool now. I grabbed another one, but it weren't as high, and my chin only came up to the rim of the bar top now. But I didn't care. I had to think. I had to get me swede straight.

"You're asking yerself why?" Nathan were saying. Using his mouth or inside my head, I weren't sure. But they was his words, no doubt about em. "Why have they gone and raised a golem, you're asking? And why do I feel like they're pitching it against me, getting it doing the job I used to do and even making it follow me out to Hurk Wood last night? And then they've got it cleaning up after me, rescuing me from my own cock-ups, like when I got strung up by them outsiders just now?"

"Bollocks were that him," I blares, jumping up again. "Him back there in the Egyptians' place, he were a ninja. This cunt here is more like a fuckin' scarecrow."

"The golem can assume many forms, Blake. He can pass silent through the shadows like the ninja you've already met. He can float through the air like a sparrow hawk, eye trained upon his prey down below and ready to swoop. He can surge through the water like a pike, teeth sharp and primed to bite the toe of some bloody fool who's splashing around up on the surface, despite all them NO SWIMMING signs they put up along the Clunge last year."

"It's the currents you got to watch out for," says John Fairway. "Looks calm up top but there's current underneath."

"Aye," someone else says. "But will they listen? Younguns around here thinks they knows it all."

"I blames the foreign ones."

"Aye, me and all."

"You know what they caught em doing? Taking swans from the river and roasting em. Roasting our swans!"

"You lot shut your flamin' holes!" shouts Nathan, face nigh on the colour of my leather suit. "I'm on about Igor and the many forms he can take as and when required. But he has a resting shape, Blake, the one he was borned into. That shape is you, Blake. That golem, though he be called Igor, he has been shaped in your selfsame image. Do you know how I sparked life into him? With your blood, Blake. Blood off one o' them syringes they been sticking into you, then dropping on the floor and leaving for any Tom, Dick, or Alvin to pick up and bring to me. He is Royston Blake, in proportion, temperament, and everything about him—except the hair, which Marge got a bit carried away with, I'll grant."

"It's a good style. Nowadays, men can wear their hair long without fear of—"

"Not now, Marge! I don't expect you to understand why we done it, Blake, but I'll tell you anyway. It's because you're worn out. For years you've done your bit, keeping a lid on this town and ensuring its flame burns strong, despite the wind and the rain that bloweth in from the outside and tryeth to extinguish it. You have done Mangel proud, Blake. But now...well, we've got a new challenge, ain't we? We're being invaded. They're coming from all over, taking what's ours and destroying our community. And you done your bit, I don't deny that. But now the real work starts, the job of fighting back. And it's more than you can do, Blake. It's time to hand over the reins, metaphorically speaking, to Igor."

You know when you get punched in the upper arm really hard, and it goes numb for a bit and like you can't move it much? That's how my head were at that minute. I had a dead head, filled with fog and heat and a swarm of bees, though I couldn't see none of em individually. But through it all I could feel summat coming. And it's a good thing I'm on about here, a thing that were gonna help us and get that dead arm popping jabs again. Summat that could prove that Nathan were just spouting bollocks, and that cunty back there weren't a golem at all. Then it came to us.

"Piss!" I shouted, spraying a bit of spit over Nathan, though I hadn't meant to.

Nathan wiped the flob off his shirt, taking it quite well, considering. "That all you got in response, is it? A profane word?"

"Nah, I mean…cunty over there, can he piss?"

"Course not. How can a clay man urinate? And his name's Igor, not—"

"I rest my fuckin' case. You said just now that it were him tracking us up in Hurk Wood, but I found his bonfire, didn't I? And he'd put it out by pissin' on it. How you gonna explain that, eh?"

"I dunno what you're angling at there, Blakey, but that weren't Igor. No, Igor here don't need bonfires to keep warm. He's tough, see? Remember how you was once tough? Igor's far beyond that. He's brings a whole new level of toughness to this town, Blake. Finally Mangel has a true a champion, a hero who will eradicate the evil that cometh from outside. Future generations will revere him. '*Igor*,' they will sing in schools. '*Igor were the one who got the parasites off our tree, and the leaves stayed on, and the tree went on living*.' Might need to jog the words around a bit and put some rhymes in, but that is what they'll sing. And the next verse will be about his doorman skills. '*He guarded Rockefellers like a knight in shining armour from days of yore, keeping trouble to a minimum and—'*

"Yeah?" I blares, getting up again. I tried booting the stool again, but it were jammed under the bar rail, and I hurt me foot. "Like a knight in days of shining armour, is he? How'd he be when it all kicks off, though, eh? How fuckin' wossname would he be when some pissed-up fucker comes at him with a bottle? Or what if you got a gang o' fifteen…nah, *twenty* lads, right, all underage but they wants in anyhow, and what they do is they *swarm* you, trying to slip past on either side and some crawling under your fuckin' feet? What'd cunty over there do *then*, eh? See, it ain't about the wossname. It ain't about the other thing neither, the, erm… the other wossname. What it's about is *experience*. I got it, see, and cunty ain't. That's what separates him from me. That's what separates the boys from the wossnames. Me, I'm a wossname."

I sat back down, glad I hadn't bust the stool this time. I were breathing hard, watching Nathan out the corner of my eye as he thought about it, rubbing down his tash and looking from me to Cunty and back to me again.

"Alright," he announces after a while, "I've made me decision, ladies and gents. I'm putting Igor on standby for this one. Blake, I'm giving you this mission. But we're counting on you, right?"

I tried to hold back the smile, but I couldn't.

"I won't let you down," I says, clenching me fist. "Erm, what mission?"

"It's a simple one," he says, stopping in front of us and plonking two hairy arms atop the bar. "What I wants you to do is eradicate the fountainhead."

27

I were walking down by the river, just taking a few minutes to reflect on things and enjoy the moment. Royston Blake were back, weren't he? They can come, the pretenders can, but they ain't getting shet of old Blakey. Not while I'm still drawing puff they ain't. Not even the ones that is made of clay.

Nathan knowed that in his heart, but he just needed reminding. And I didn't mind being the one who done that for him. It does you good to stand up for yourself now and then, put your false modesty aside and shout about how good you is and how you're still the best. Except most people ain't the best, is they? Only Royston Blake. Cos there can be only one. I turned about, feeling like someone were stood behind us and about to say summat.

But there were no one.

I looked out on the water, thinking about what I had to do. It were fucking complicated, this mission that Nathan had set us, but a piece of piss compared to some of the things I'd done over the years. What he wanted us to do, right, were to go down a certain place at a certain time, heavily armed, and there I would find the fountainhead. And by that he don't mean a bloke with a fountain on his head, you twat. What he means is...hang on, let us try and find his precise words...Here it is: "I don't mean a feller with a fountain on his head, you twat." Erm, not that bit...Hang on, here it is: "Yer fountainhead, as defined by them who spake of him in olden times, is the one from whom others ensue. Destroy him and the whole evil hoose of cards will collapse."

"Hoose?"

"House."

"Aye, but you says—"

"I said *house*. Now stop debating and get to work, otherwise there's another here who'll be only too eager."

I had all kinds of questions at the time, but I couldn't put my finger on none of them. And it weren't like I could turn him down anyhow. This were my chance, weren't it? My chance to show Nathan and everyone else in this town how much of a hero I am. My chance to achieve immortality, as Nathan had termed it a little bit later. "See that statue of Igor down the High Street?" he'd said, whispering so the golem couldn't hear. "You pull this off right, and they'll tear that thing down."

He'd just spilled for us the details of my mission, and they was swirling around in me swede, making it ache like no other. But still I hung on his every word and took it all in. I had to.

I were the man of the moment.

"They'll smash that statue up and dump it in the skip and make another one. 'Royston Roger Blake,' it will say underneath. 'Him who saved this town from invaders, and to who we shall always be grateful and sing hymns about at school.'"

"Can I have another bit?" I'd said at the time.

"Eh? What?"

"I just want it to mention summat about me, you know? Summat that gives an idea about who the true Royston Blake were and what he stood for in his life."

"It's quite plain what you stands for, so long as you does like I says and don't leave no loose ends. You stands for the pure, untainted sap that runneth through the veins of this, our tree."

"Aye, but I thought they could put summat about *me*, you know? Some of the motors I'd drove over the years, for example. And what I looked like. Tell em I were the spit of Clint Eastwood, right, but with the body of—"

"Aye, I've heard it before—Ivan Dingo out of one of your flamin' boxing films."

"No, that's just it, Nathe." I gave him a moment to correct us on the Nathe thing, but he never. I liked the way things stood now—me in charge, him keeping his hairy top lip buttoned. "I've changed me mind about my body being like Ivan Drago. See, when you look at *Rocky IV*, he's a bit lanky, ain't he? I'm more built than that, know what I mean?"

"So who shall I say, then?"

"Arnold Schwarzenegger."

Nathan shook his head and got a pen and paper out. "How'd you spell that?"

"How the fuck should I know? Make sure it's him in *Terminator* and not *Conan*. I don't want people thinking I'm an arse bandit."

"No...arse...bandit..." he says, scribbling. "Right, so you wants the body on your statue to look like this Arnold, and the head—"

"Nah, I want it to actually *say* it. 'Here lies Royston Blake,' I want it to say. Don't put the Roger—I hates that name. 'He had the swede of Clint Eastwood and the body of Arnold Schwarzenegger in *Terminator*. He drove a Ford Capri 2.8i, gold with a black vinyl roof, VGC, but he also drove some other choice motors such as...'"

I stopped there. I mean, at the time I'd gone on for quite a while, getting Nathan to write out a couple of pages of this pure gold, but I stopped going through it again in my head, standing as I were down by the river, watching a large bird float past on the water and trying to work out if it were a goose or a swan, cos they all looks the same these days. But that ain't why I stopped.

I stopped cos of the cunt pointing a gun at me.

On the other bank he were, trying to hide in the bushes and branches, but his telescopic lens gave him away, flashing sunlight right in me peepers. I hated it when they done that. Lad at school tried shining his watch in my eye one time in a sums lesson, thinking I wouldn't know where it were coming from and that he'd get away with it. I dragged him out from behind his desk and started punching him, but he were clever and knowed how to cover up, and all I could get were the back bit of his swede, and it hurt me knuckles after a while. So I started on his ribs, getting a bit more joy there and feeling some give, even though he were curled up like a stillborn kitten. After that I got his arm and spread it out, aiming to stamp on his wrist and thereby crush that fucking watch that he'd been having such a laugh with. That's when I noticed that the teacher were holding us back, and also the one from next door had come in and were trying to get us in a headlock. I think I were about nine at the time.

I threw em both off and went for the lad again, but he'd took his chance and made a break for the door. I ran down the other aisle and kicked the door shut just as he got a couple of fingers through the gap and started screaming when he realised they was now bust. I opened the door to get the fingers free, and then got him on his back and held him down with a knee on each shoulder. I can't recall what came next, cos some other cunt shone a watch in me eyes from another part of the classroom, and I went after him, and the darkness came down.

But I didn't have none of that in me swede as I stood on the riverbank, getting it in the eye from across the way. I didn't have nothing at all on me mind, cos the darkness were coming down all over again, and I were pegging it into the water, diving forwards and giving it the front crawl like Tarzan. It's a funny thing, the darkness. It's there, and you're diving into it, and you can't stop it. You don't wanna stop it neither, even though a little part of your head says, *Here we fucking go again. Don't you ever learn? There is only one place this will lead and that is into a shite pool even deeper than the ones you already dived into these past couple of days. Days? Years, more like. So, once—just for fuckin' once in your life—why not try and fight it? Why not hold back and count to ten, and then see if you feel the same way?*

It ain't often I heard that voice. And I knowed it were right and that things would be better, and I'd be a proper community pillar instead of a shite one if only I grabbed them words and harked them, claiming em as me own and turning over a new leaf. But still I ignored em. Still I ploughed on into the dark, swirling around in it and punching at fuck all and feeling the air sucked out of me lungs, and I can't breathe. For fuck sake, I can't breathe.

28

"Promise me."

I got cast-iron guts, me.

In all the long years I'd been drinking, not once had I surrendered to the upwards onslaught of vom. Not hardly ever at all, anyhow. And certainly never while on duty keeping door at Hoppers. Only the once, when I'd had a bad pint that would have felled a fucking elephant. And I done me best to clean it up, finding an old bit of tissue in me pocket and wiping down her chest with it. Weren't my fault the lass had been passing by at the moment of upchuck, were it? Weren't hers neither, but she never seen it like that. She took it well fucking personal, and no amount of trying to get it out of her cleavage with me fingers were making a difference for her. So it served her right when another surge came, hitting her facewise this time like a water cannon.

"I said promise me."

"Eh? Wha? Fuh…"

"Promise me you won't hurt me."

"Hurt? What? Hey, weren't my fault she got whiplash from it and cracked that bone in her arse from falling upon it. Any sensible person would have ducked, clockin' honk spewing from a man's mouth right at em. Mind you, I had to ban her, didn't I?

Charlie Williams

Can't have folks causing fuss outside Hoppers. And I had to make an example of her boyfriend. Way he were trying to help her up, it were like he were makin' us look bad, you know? Anything shy of a power slap and I'd of been lettin' me whole profession down. Weren't my fault the motor were coming."

"What the hell are you on about?"

"Wha? Eh? Who the fuck is…Shite."

"*Promise* me. Promise or I'll shoot."

I rubbed me eyes and had a peep. It were Kerry, although I didn't recognise her at first. She weren't back to the gyppo look like when I'd first seen her, but she weren't the beauty queen I'd gave a bit of black pud to and took out to Hurk Wood neither. Mind you, a lot had happened to her since then, like as not. And she were pointing a fucking rifle at me.

"Now *you* listen to *me*," I says in a calming voice. Like Mel Gibson in *Lethal Weapon* when he's atop that high building with the feller who's set on jumping off. "Put the gun—"

"Promise me!"

"Eh? What?"

"Promise you won't hurt me. Don't even touch me."

"I won't touch yers, fuck sake. Not unless you wants—"

"Swear on your life!"

"*Alright*, for fuck. Erm…" I put a paw on me ticker. It were beating hard under me soaking wet leather. "I, Royston Roger Blake, do hereby…nah, leave out the Roger bit, alright? I do hereby and solemnly take you to be my lawful wedded wife, to have and, erm…"

She raised the gun and went to fire. "I'll be doing you a favour," she says.

"No, I mean…fuck sake, Blakey, *come on*…"

160

I punched me swede a few times, trying to get it moving. It's like going down the gym—you have to warm large muscles up before doing feats. It's also like shagging in that respect. "I promises not to hurt you, right? I will not harm a fuckin' hair on your barnet. Now put the gun down, right? That's it, nice and easy. Blakey ain't gonna hurt no one. 'Specially not you, for fuck sake. Tell you what, you looks marvelous today. I loves what you done to your hair. That plant thing you got there on the side, it sets it all off real fuckin' spesh."

What I were doing here is lulling her into a false wossname of…I were just lulling her, basically, telling her all the nice bird things and creeping out my left arm the whole while, getting set to spring it and knock the rifle and her sideways. On the way down she'd fire it harmless into the mud, and I'd land atop her and shush into her ear until she stopped struggling. Then, I dunno, maybe it'd turn into summat sexy. It had to sooner or later. Me and Kel: I had not one doubt in me swede that we was made for each other, her being my vibrating diamond and me her…I dunno, it's a thought, ennit? What were I to her? Cos I had to be summat, didn't I? Mind you, she didn't know it yet. I could tell that from the way she jerked the barrel out and twocked us on the left ear.

"Try anything like that again and I'm firing for real," she says. "I'm gonna speak and you're gonna listen, right?"

I were on my arse again, rubbing me lug. "Like what?" I says, a hint of whinge in me voice perhaps. Mind you, it were well fucking justified. "I never even—"

"Number one: I just saved your life," she says, keeping the gun trained between me eyes while I got up again. "Maybe I shouldn't have. Maybe I should have just let you drown. And by the way, if you're wearing a leather suit, maybe think about taking it off before going for a swim. Um, that's a *nice* suit, by the way. Come in other colours, does it? Number two: I thought you were gonna help me. I came to you in good faith. I didn't ask anything of you except your help in finding Jock, who you should know full well is a sick man. But you…Jesus, do you even *know* what you did? Stealing that baby and then setting me up so it looked like—"

She stopped there, cos I snatched the gun from straight out of her hand, swinging it round like a gunslinger and pointing it at her head. "Right," I says, aiming to give her a talking to about pointing guns at folks. It don't matter how diamond-shaped she were and how much she vibrated, she could have blew me fucking swede off there. Or at least put a bad dent in it. But I didn't know what to say. How do you slag off the one you love, when you only just started loving her and all you wanna do is make her feel the same and realise that she's your vibrating diamond and you're summat to her as well, although you dunno what it is yet? Plus she were soaking wet, I just noticed, her black blouse clinging to her upper regions like nothing in the world has got a right to cling to another couple of things, not unless they want to get Royston Blake stirring and adjusting himself. And she were beautiful, weren't she? I'm on about the eyes. There were summat in em that, I dunno…It were both innocent and gagging for it at the same time. They was eyes that I felt like I could tell anything to but didn't have to, cos she knew it already. They was eyes that I couldn't put a bullet between, not even for a million fags, even though I were fucking gasping just then.

Plus she'd just started crying.

I ain't got many things I can't do, but one of em is topping birds who is shedding tears. I just never been able to bring meself to. Not more than a couple times anyhow.

She flopped down on the riverbank and gave full vent to her sobbing. I would have shushed her up for fear some cunt might hear us and stick their hooter in, but I had a good view down her top from here, and her shoulders was heaving up and down in time with the sobs, making certain parts move in a special way. Sometimes you just got to stop for a moment and appreciate Mother Nature in all her glory. Both of em.

"Look," I says, sitting down next to her after the special movement had died down. "That bollocks back there—Vectra and that—I swear it weren't planned. The whole thing were a complete—"

"You kidnapped a baby, Royston! How can that not be planned? What did you think would happen if you kidnap a baby? Of course the police came after us. And you made it so I was there when they did. Shit, Royston, why didn't you just tell me you didn't want to help me? Why did you have to do that?"

"No, no, you got it all wrong. See, erm, this Vectra, she's…"

"What?"

"Hang on, I'm just trying to…"

"Trying to make something up. Yeah, save it for the—"

"*No*! See, what it is, right, is that Vectra—"

"She's not even called Vectra! Her name's Josie, and her mum *spat* in my face. Do you understand that, Royston? Can you stop lying and scheming for long enough to imagine what it was like for me? That poor woman believed I stole her child. She probably always will believe it!"

"No, I'm not lying. Alright, so her real name's Josie, but… look, I'm her real dad. I shagged the mum a while back, and she had the sprog, and we'd sort of drifted apart by then, and I didn't know about it. But I found out alright. And when I did, I went right round her place and told her to name the youngun Vectra, after, erm…"

"Royston, the car you stole was a Vauxhall Vectra. Do you seriously expect me to believe you didn't just make it up on the spur of—"

"Yeah, and that were my motor, weren't it? Think about it—I went out with that bird for a bit, and she pumped one for us, so it stands to fuckin' reason I might let her keep my wheels. I mean, it's a family motor, your Vectra is. Actually, it's more your executive—"

"Crap."

"It ain't crap, Kel. None of it is. It's easy to lie, I knows that. And I have lied in me time, just like every other cunt has. I bet even you lied once or twice, and that's me saying that as a person with a very high opinion of yers, even though I only met you the twice, and you was a vampire the first time. And the second time I landed you in jail. But, erm…what were I saying?"

I don't reckon she were harking us no more anyhow. But she weren't crying neither, which were a good sign. Nor lairy and breathing hard, which were an even better sign. Once a bird has gone through the lairy and crying stages, the next bit is always shagging, so long as you plays your cards right. Every fucking time. You just watch. Only watch for a bit, mind. A feller and a bird has got to have some privacy. I sat down next to her, making sure there was no contact yet, not even hip to hip.

This is what I were saying about playing your cards right.

"Least they let you go, though, eh?" I says, peeping in her handbag, which were on the ground beside her. I noticed there was some fags in it and that they was JPS. Pretty fucking impressive, I thought. "I mean, you've proved to em yer innocent, so—"

"I didn't prove anything, Royston. Those bastards don't listen to a word you say."

"They are fucking cunts. I can vouch for that."

"I'd still be in there now if...well..."

"What?"

My mind were getting going. If she didn't know why they let her go, I might be able to snatch some more ground here and make out it were me who'd sprung her. She'd swallowed everything I'd come out with so far, and you got to push while the pushing's good. Plus I needed a tiny bit more bargaining power here. There were still some frost on the turkey, and I felt that the only way to thaw it were a bit of knight in shining armour. Or shining burgundy leather, in my case.

"You know," I says, easing the jacket off. It were nigh on welded to us, soaking wet like it were. And stinking. "Sometimes, when yer stuck in jail, it takes a man to get you out. And I'm on about a special type of feller here, one who is a community pillar and is a bit like Rambo when required but with the head of—"

"I had to do things."

"Eh?"

"To get out. The fucking bastards in there, they only let me go because I...I did stuff. Favours, you know? Sick, perverted..." She started crying again.

"Hey," I says, putting a strong yet gentle arm around her. "Don't think about it. You're safe now."

"But...they were *sick*, Royston, and...well, they..."

"Shh...you don't have to talk about it." I put my head against hers and stroked her hair. Some powerful, dark feelings was coming through on my part, but I needed to put em off for a minute. "Did they, erm..."

She stopped sobbing and looked at me, big brown eyes all glistening and hurt. "Did they what?"

"Did they, you know, get you to suck em off?"

"I thought you said I don't have to talk about—"

"No, you're right," I says, standing up and letting them dark feelings come through. They was stronger than I thought, and I found meself balling a fist tighter than any I'd ever known—so tight I sunk two or three fingernails quite deep in my paw. It stung like fuck, but in a good way. You gets to feeling like this, you welcomes it. You feel more alive and human than at any other time. Also like the Incredible Hulk. I slammed that fist into the nearest tree, picturing a fucking police helmet atop it. I kept punching, knocking shite out of that poor tree and trying to get the helmet off. The darkness were shutting us down, I could feel it. I knew it weren't the right time, but the things she'd said…them fucking bastards, making her do…

"*Royston.*"

But it didn't go completely dark. I were in the lockup garage of darkness, but the up-and-under door hadn't shut proper, letting in a chink of light. Not that Kerry were a Chink, although she did have black hair like a Chinese bird, and she were well slim but with quite big tits. And she chased the darkness off with them tits. She took her wet top off, threw her arms around us, and made the world light again, sucking the aggro from my veins and bringing us back to calm like no one had ever been able to. I grabbed her head and went to kiss her.

"Wait," she says, pushing us back.

I looked down at her and raised me paws to her chest, but she shooed them off and all.

"Not yet," she says.

"Fuck's you on about?" I says. "I'm here. You're here. No one's looking, and you're my vibrating—"

"I need you to prove yourself to me."

"Eh?"

"I need you to show that you're a man. A real man. It's old fashioned, I know, but…just trust me. I need proof."

"Fuck sake," I says, undoing me belt.

"No, not like that."

She bent down and started rummaging in her handbag. I watched her slender back and the tits jiggling about under it as she yanked bits and bobs hither and thither. It were hard to think how someone so frail had pulled us from the River Clunge and saved my life, but she had. I'd saved hers, and now she'd done the same. Whatever she wanted, I'd give it to her.

She stood up and held out a bit of wood. It were like an off-cutting from a joiner's shop, all rough around the sides and sharp fuckers sticking out. "Then hold this. Hold it tight."

"Eh?"

"Do you want me?"

"Course I do, but—"

"Then hold it. Hold it tight like it's my soul, and you're protecting it from evil forces that are trying to steal it away."

"But…" I shrugged and grabbed the wood, shutting my eyes and reflecting how birds can be fucking odd at times, but it's alright, cos she's got her top off and her nipples is like rubber bullets. She started pulling, representing them evil forces, like as not. I pulled back, which were a piece of piss for me, being as I'm Royston Blake, and there ain't no one stronger. Then she started yanking it, tugging like a robber after an old dear's handbag. I gritted me gnashers, feeling the splinters go in but not making no sound. She wanted it and here it were, a real man, knacking like billy-o but able to convert the pain into summat else, summat that weren't so bad.

At some point she stopped tugging. I let go the wood but it stuck to me palm, dripping with blood and half its grain embedded under my skin. I flicked it off and pushed her back. She bit me face and scratched my back, and I rammed her so hard I thought I might snap her pelvis but didn't. Seemed like all afternoon we went at it on that riverbank, rolling over on them nettles and not knowing what the fuck else were happening in the world besides the thing we had going.

Afterwards I lay back on the mud and flattened nettles, smoking one of her JPS and looking into the sky. There were a lot going on up there, dark clouds gathering like they does at certain times, threatening to piss down on the lot of us, fucking up all our plans and making us look like little insects that you can tread upon and kill. I looked up at that sky and felt all this, but in a good way. It were like I had everything that mattered here, right next to us under me arm, and I didn't give a flying wank if it all ended right now. Cos I had my vibrating diamond, and I realised now what I were to her.

I were her joker.

29

Stinging nettles I can take, but me paws knacked summat chronic.

"Why the splinters though, for fuck?" I says, licking em and blowing on em but not having no effect upon em. "Why not just stub fags out on each other, like normal couples do?"

She thought about it for a bit, slipping into her damp bra and reaching up behind her to do the strap. "I'm not normal," she says, sort of smiling but not. "Nor are you."

It were my time to think about that. "Woss you trying to say?" I says.

"We're just not. Like attracts like. Based on the couple of minutes we've just spent here, I think we've proved the attraction part."

"Couple of minutes?" I looked at me watch, but it had stopped. I stared at it for a while, wondering when that had happened and casting me swede back further and further through time, realising that I hadn't looked at it in years.

"Ouch," she says, trying to pull summat out of her back.

I went over and had a look, finding it to be a thorn. I pulled it out then ran me fingers across the red bumpy marks around her shoulder blades and spine where the nettles had done their bit. She shivered, and I could tell it were a good kind of shivering. Or vibrating. Then she slipped her blouse on. "I've got a confession to make," she says, not turning round.

I hate this, when birds have got summat to say and they know you won't like it, so they looks away and pretends to be interested in summat over there, although you can feel their eyes craning sideways and wondering how it's going down in the Blake department.

"Go on then," I says, sighing the heavy sigh of a poor old sap who's seen it and heard it all. "Who were he?"

"What? Who?"

"This other bloke. Come on, spill the fuckin' beans."

"What other bloke?"

"Oh, I mean…I were just getting ahead of meself there. Go on."

"Right, um…it's about Jock. You know I was so keen to find him earlier, even though he tried to kill me with a wooden stake yesterday? Well, it wasn't for the reasons I said. I want to find Jock because I'm fearful for my life. He's insane, but the police won't do anything about him. I think they want him to get himself killed, which would clear up a problem for them. With Jock out of the way, there's no one left to complain about the awful way they've handled Scott's death. He's confused about it now, but he'd be dangerous for them if he sobered up for long enough to look at it."

I started pulling me leather strides up. I'd only been able to get em down to me knees, damp like they was, but it were still hard to shoehorn the fuckers over me thighs. "Who's this Scott, then?" I says.

"What? But I told you—"

"Oh, s'alright, I recalls it now."

"Good. I thought for a moment there that you'd not been listening to—"

"He's the vampire, right?"

She jerked her head to me, ready to start shouting and have a pop. Then summat went click in her swede, and a smile broke out across her face. "Oh, I get it," she says, giving us a big hug. "You're joking me. Maybe you're right. Maybe I'm taking all this too seriously."

I hugged her back, wondering what the fuck she were on about. Still, a hug's a hug. Especially when you can get your paws down the back of her strides and have a feel there. She wrenched herself free and turned away, bending over. I thought it were an invitation at first then saw she were picking up the rifle. I'd forgot all about that in the heat of the wossname.

"I want you to take this," she says, handing it over.

I took it and had a feel, turning it over a couple of times. It were a good one alright, with a trigger and pointy metal tube where the bullet comes out and everything.

"Have you ever handled a gun before?"

"Me? You havin' a fuckin' laugh? Don't you fret over me." I tore me eyes off the gun and put em on her, realising summat. "You askin' me to shoot Jock, is it?"

"What? Of course not! I just…I thought you might need it more than me. If you…" She sidled up close, wrapping her fingers around mine and sliding em up and down the length of the barrel. "If you were to protect me."

She looked into my eyes and me into hers. Suddenly I recalled where I'd seen her before and why she'd looked so familiar ever since I'd first run into her, however long back that were. I'd clocked her in my house, under that selfsame roof where I'd been stripping down to me bollocks these past few months and kipping like a babby. She must have been visiting someone downstairs. Mind you, that couldn't be right—only ones down there is them fucking foreigners.

"Here, Kel," I says, aiming to ask her about that.

But she were gone.

I looked up and clocked her running off down the path, leaving us scratching me swede and pondering how the world can tilt of a sudden and everything's different. But it don't really, do it? Underneath we're the same as we always was, only we knows it a little bit more or less, depending on the shite that happens to you. And right then, hauling my arse up them fishermen's steps after Kerry and finding her to be nowhere when I reached the top, I knowed one thing: I needed scran.

I parked my arse on a nearby bench and started ferreting through me togs, seeing how much wedge I had on us. The brekkie at Burt's were three quid, which were a fucking rip-off, but if you orders a bacon butty for one fifty and wink at the bird there the right way, she'll slip a fried egg in it.

"Och, yis have done well here, Royston," says Jock, leaning over and picking up the rifle. "The vampires willnae stand a fuckin' chance against this. We'll have them bastarts eradicated in short fuckin' order, believe youse me."

He yomped off down the trail, opening up the chamber and having a look inside. He stopped and looked over his shoulder. "Are yis comin' or what?"

KERRY BARWELL:
A LIFE OFF THE RAILS

In many ways Kerry Barwell, who has been charged with the murder of an Estravian asylum seeker and known drug dealer, had the perfect upbringing. Raised in a detached house with a large garden in the leafy suburb of Danghill, Barwell had many of the privileges denied to most of the children of Mangel. Sent away to a private school in Barkettle at the age of 11, she seemed destined for great things, such as being a nurse or the manageress of a clothes shop. But all was not well behind the scenes.

According to school records, she was suspended at the age of 15 for "disrupting other students," that catch-all offense that hides a multitude of scandals and keeps parents paying their fees. But how much of that disruption was talking in class and how much was supplying classmates with soft drugs? In light of a conditional discharge she received from Barkettle police later that same year, a shrewd parent would surmise that talking in class was the lesser of the problems removed when Barwell was expelled from school later that term.

Returning to Mangel, Barwell was soon coming to the attention of our own police. "We knew what she was up to," says an insider.

"She was getting involved in the drug market in this town, setting up supply lines with contacts in Barkettle, Tuber, and even the City. But we could never charge her for anything. She never went anywhere near the actual drugs and always got others to do her dirty work—young lads like this McCrae one. And we all know how she persuaded them, don't we? The same way she persuaded police officers to conveniently lose evidence and let her go on the rare times we did get her in for something."

And how was that?

"Erm, I have no idea. End of interview."

But Barwell's grip on the local drug trade was yet to encounter its severest test. Little more than a year ago, the first wave of asylum seekers arrived from the Baltic state of Estravia. So far none of them has been linked conclusively with drug crimes. "We know they're in it, though," claims the same police source. "Remember that massive fight up at the Chequers back in April? That was them. Since then, it's been all on their terms. They've got the channels. They've got the dealers under the cosh. No one can touch them."

No one except Kerry Barwell, who found herself marginalised in a drug world that she had once controlled. Did she murder Martynas Gustas in a fit of rage, her tried and tested methods of persuasion having failed her? Was it a calculated execution designed to wrest control of the drug market back into her hands? And how does the tragic Scott McCrae fit into the picture? Only Barwell knows.

30

I love sounds.

Birds singing when you wakes up in the morning. Birds stopping singing and letting out a little squeal of mock horror when you gets in the shower with em. Birds actually screaming as you pegs it out the shower and down the stair, realising you kipped in the wrong house again. The rumble of a two-litre engine starting first time on a warm morning. The shout of the owner as you hares round the corner in his two-litre Audi, flicking a V at him. Even quiet sounds, like the faint popping of bubbles atop a freshly pulled pint of lager as you contemplates how lairy folks gets over such minor wossnames. But there is no sound I enjoys more than frying.

Especially when it's sausage, bacon, mushies, eggs, black pud, bread, baked beans, and some other bits Jock found down the bottom of his freezer.

"Do yis like yer beans burgered or au naturel?" he says, turning to us and wiping sweat off his brow with his apron.

"The fuck is 'burgered'?" I says. "Buggered, you mean? The answer to that is no, I prefer my beans not to be fucked up the arse."

"It's *burgered*. Yis get them and fry them into a patty with a cohesive ooter shell. It wis a popular dish with the lads in mah squadron. Did ah tell yis I wis in the army? Aye, ah was. That wis a fuckin' marvellous time, Royston. And ah've retained many a true pal from back then. It's through those pals that ah've built up mah stockpile."

"Stockpile o' what?"

"Provisions and materials," he says, holding up a tin of beans that I didn't recognise the brand of. "Do yis want them burgered or no?"

I thought about it. "Aye, go on then."

"Good man."

We was in his van, which were parked at that time on the bomb site down behind the Hairy Factory. It weren't really a bomb site but a bit of rubble-strewn scrub that had been like that forever, and no one had done fuck all with. I'd left the van up the street from my place, but some cunt had swiped it and had a laugh in it before dumping it here, realising like as not that it weren't good for wheelspins.

"So you just happened to be passing?" I says, chewing on a few frozen hotdog buns as a starter. "And you clocked your van here?"

"That's reet. The door wis hanging open but nae much other damage. Have youse got the keys, though?"

"Dunno," I says, trying to recall. "Might have left em back at the flat."

"I been meaning to talk tae yis aboot that," he says, ladling the meal onto two tin plates and making sure one of em had way more. I always appreciates that, when they takes into account how someone like meself needs to eat for two just to get by.

"We are talking about it," I says, clearing the mags off me lap ready for the feast. I'd been looking through some of Jock's pornos. He had some fucking good ones, I swear. Some of em I hadn't even seen before. "We been yakking on for the past ten or so minutes."

"No, we've been talking *shite* during that time, Royston. What ah'm proposing is we get doon tae fuckin' business noo, yis ken?"

I looked over me shoulder. "Who the fuck *is* this Ken feller?"

"Youse and me are set for the next phase in oor project tae eradicate vampires from this toon," he says, plonking the plate in my lap, along with a couple of dirty plastic forks. "It's time tae take out the drones. And that means surprisin' them in their nest."

"Hold up a minute there, Jock," I says. "What the fuck is you playin' at, givin' me the small portion?"

"What, the brekkie? Och, that's jist mah way. Ah'm a man of appetites, Royston. Aboot this invasion, ah plan tae—"

"For fuck sake, Jock...ain't I got an appetite and all? Look at the muscles on me, for fuck. Do you reckon I can keep em going with a fuckin' *youngun's* portion?"

"This is no mah primary concern, Royston. Yis want more, here, help yis self." He scooped some beans and a bit of bread off his plate and onto mine, making it look like we was even. "Mah thinkin' is that we've no time tae waste here. I say we go in just noo, take the fuckers by surprise and eradicate them. Ah've a decent wee cache o' stakes put by, and we can use them all. See, after this we've no need o' them. The path tae the fountainhead will be cleared, wi' nae drones in the way tae bugger things up."

"Aye, but...fuckin' hell, Jock, look how many fuckin' bangers you got! Play the fuckin' white man, eh."

Jock looked down at his plate, bothered by summat. "That's a racist phrase there, Royston."

"Eh?" I looked at his plate, trying to find the racist phrase he'd found. "Where?"

"Play the white man. Yis are implyin' there is a particular race that is inherently fairer than others, by dint o' skin tone. Me, ah've nae time for that kind o' flawed logic. Ah'm interested in the basic good that resides in every human, nae matter what the colour. And eradicatin' vampires, who are evil fuckin' wee bastarts."

I scratched my head, looking at the two bangers I had. "Right," I says, "so you ain't sharin'? How about a bit o' bacon? Come on— you got about nine rashers to my three. Ooh, I tells a lie—here's another under this fried slice."

"Royston, I'll share mah food wi' yis, no fuckin' problem, pal. But I need yis tae step up tae the plate here. Do yis agree tae mah plans, as set oot by mahself just noo?" He got a fork and impaled about three of his rashers, which were fair enough. He also snagged a nice bit o' black pud, which made it a bit too fair as far as I went, but I weren't saying nothing. I ain't thick.

"What fuckin' plans?" I says.

All the vittles except the black pud slid onto my plate, and he gripped the fork harder and held it under my chin. "Wis you no listenin' tae me?" he says, baring his yeller-and-black gnashers. "I just set oot for yis the terms and conditions ae my attack. Are yis in or no?"

If I raised my knee, I'd have that fork in Jock's face, making him think about his actions for a bit while he underwent emergency surgery to save his eyesight. But I didn't want to waste the scran, not now I had a good deal on it. Plus he were Jock, weren't he? I'd come to quite like the barmy old cunt. Folks like him, you need to watch out for em. "Aye," I says, ramming a banger sideways in me gob and chewing. "Fuckin' whatever. Jusht calm down, for fuck. And I reckon thatsh my bit o' black pud on yer fork there."

"Reet," he says, relaxing a bit. "So it is, so it is…" He tossed it onto my plate like the scran professional he were then flicked the kettle on. "Do yis want tea wi' that or what?"

31

I felt alright now.

Having a full belly helps, but it weren't only that. And not the fag, although I were enjoying that. Nor were it the fishing rod bag slung over me shoulder containing the rifle Kerry had gave us, although that do give you a nice feeling of being able to just kill people if they fucks you off. Not even were it the recent shag I'd had with Kerry, satisfying a lot of yearnings that seemed to have been building up all me life. I know I'd just met her, but it weren't like that. Sometimes you find someone and you just knows they'm meant for you, and you for them. The world has been a desolate place hitherto, a barren wasteland full up of weeds and litter and dog shite, and you're walking the lonesome trail on your tod, knowing not whither nor wherefore. And then you finds em. You find your jewel, your piece of jigsaw that slots home and makes every bit of pain and grief and aggro make sense. Then you get to shag them, and it's even better.

But like I says, this weren't what gave us an easy stride as I walked down Cutler Road, smoking a fag and scratching me knackers and doing a massive burp. It were the old tosspot walking alongside us.

Jock.

Aye, he were a fucking spanner, weren't he? And he'd been a bit lairy to us just then, threatening us with the black pud and making demands. But we was mates now, me and Jock was. He were well older than meself and not so much of a community pillar, but I got on alright with him. We'd had a laugh together these past couple o' days, knocking back the Bell's and playing vampire bounty hunters or whatever. Plus I'd learned to understand what he were trying to say, most of the time. I felt like Tarzan again, talking to monkeys and giraffes and that.

"You know what I could eat right now?" I says. Cos I found I could say any old thing to him, which is the mark of being proper mates. "A fuckin' Bounty bar is what I could eat. You know them? Choc round the edge and some sort o' white bollocks in the middle."

"Coconut."

"Nah, it ain't coconut."

"Aye, it is."

"Honest, Jock, it ain't. This stuff is like rice that has been cooked too long. Sort o' sticky and white but with quite a nice taste."

"That taste is coconut, Royston. Read the wrapper next time yis buy one."

"Jock, you're startin' to piss us off now. It *ain't* coconut, get it? And I don't buy em anyhow. It ain't worth buying em. Little things like that, I just swipe em."

"Yis are a thief, Royston? Ah'm disappointed, I must say."

"Nah, I ain't a fuckin' thief. I gets em from Gromer's offie just along here. He don't mind."

"Hmm, seems a wee bit unorthodox tae me. Are yis sure this Gromer chap is aware o' these wee acquisitions o' yours?"

"Aye, he knows. Come on, I'll show yers. Do you fancy one?"

"I dinnae like coconut."

"It ain't coconut."

"Look, youse go oan and get yis Boonty bar. I'll wait here and finalise mah plans. Ah've a wee bit o' refinement tae apply to em, ah must admit."

"You want a Mars or summat? They got Milky Ways as well. You can eat them between meals without fuckin' up yer appetite, or summat. I had about fifteen the one time, and it didn't affect it at all. I think they'm made of air."

"Nothin' for me, thanks. Youse go oan."

I went in the shop. I knew he were just being polite and perhaps a bit embarrassed cos he were such a fat get, but I didn't wanna argue it no more. We was friends now, and it don't do to have too many rows. I'd just get him summat light, like a couple of Yorkies or summat. Aye, he'd like that—Yorkies is made in York, which is the capital of Scotland. Next to burgers and hotdogs, you can't get a more Scottish type of scran.

"Ah," says Gromer, clocking us through his watery eyes. He were an old codger now and about thirty year beyond his sell-by date, along with every other piece of mank in his shop. "If it ain't Mr. Blake, the so-called saviour of our community. I must say, Mr. Saviour, you don't come across like much of a messiah to me. Do you know what you seem like to me? A mental case, that's what. And don't think I don't notice."

I stopped. I were up by the till now, where he had the sweets. My arm were reaching out to a Yorkie for Jock, but I held it steady. "Notice what?" I says.

"*Notice what*, he says. Are you takin' me for a moron?"

"Erm...what's that over there?"

"Where?"

"That on the ceiling there. You got subsidence?"

"What?"

He looked up in the corner. There was no crack there but he didn't know that, him with his shite eyesight. I lifted a few Yorkies for Jock and some Bounty bars for me. You have to get ten or so, cos they only puts two in the wrapper, and they ain't much bigger than Maltesers.

"I can't see a thing. Are you sure?"

"Aye, I'm sure," I says, lifting a couple of Turkish Delights while I were at it. I fucking hates em meself, but you never know when you'll bump into a bird who is hungry. "There's a crack right there."

"Where?"

"Top o' yer legs," I says, pocketing the lot. Piece of fucking piss. "Stretches right round to the bottom of yer back. It's what you talks out of, you dozy fucking spaz."

"What?" He looked confused now. Oh, he didn't half.

But Blakey were here to clarify. I felt like lamping him, so lairy did I feel of a sudden, thanks to him and his sharp tongue. But you have to look after old folks, not lamp them. Even ones who are cunts, like Gromer here. "Shall I tell you what you are, you spindly old shit stain?" I says instead. Cos I'd held me tongue as yet, and I felt like unleashing it. "What you is, right, is a…erm…" For some reason I couldn't think of no words strong enough, and it gave him a moment to recover his wits.

"Like I says," he says, smirking now, "don't think I don't notice."

I let me arms hang to me sides, covering up my bulging pockets.

"Not that, you flamin' halfwit. You think I cares about a few sweets going missing? I get that every day from the dozen or so other juveniles who comes in here. I'm on about your dirty little secret."

"What dirty fuckin' secret?"

"You want us to say it?"

"There ain't no dirty secrets about me."

"Oh, aye? What about the one where you're mentally handicapped, in actual fact? The one where you have to take medication every flamin' day just to stop yourself from going off on one? It ain't even a secret—every flamin' person knows it. Do you know what, Royston Blake? I actually stood up for you. 'We'll use the soft one, old Blakey,' is what Nathan says. 'Let the dangerous one do the purging, the shedding of impure blood, then get Blakey for the clean-up job. The dangerous one is himself impure and must also be cast out. Preferably by one whose insane ramblings will fall upon deaf ears on account of him being a well-known nutter.' Do you know what my reply was to that? I said leave the soft one alone. Soft folks needs helping, not exploiting. We ought to get a professional in for the purging. Like Alvin."

I've always been in two minds about old people. On the one hand, I'm thinking how we ought to look after em and respect em, no matter what kinds of cunts they been when they was younger. Even convicted murderers and that. They ain't a threat to no one no more, they've like as not calmed down a mite in old age, and they're paying for their sins just by being old and weak and fucking useless. But it were the other hand what won out here, so much so that it kicked shite out of the first one and left it for dead down an alley, emptying his wallet first and gobbing in his fucking face. On this hand, a cunt is a cunt, no matter what the age. I dropped my head on Gromer.

Fucking hell, I thought, closing me eyes and leaning against the wall, that hit the fucking spot. I opened em and had a look at him and didn't feel so nice no more. So I shut em again and felt my way out of the shop, getting that marvellous feeling back as I shuffled along. Outside I edged along the path a bit, brushing a hand along the shop front, aiming for where I'd left Jock applying his wee bit of refinement to his plans, or whatever. I found him straight off and held on to his lapel while I fished out his Yorkies from my pocket. Funny, I hadn't noticed his anorak having lapels before.

"Royston Blake, I am arresting you," he says.

I opened my eyes and felt bad again. Not only were it not Jock, but it were a copper. On top of that, it were Jonah, the shitest copper in Copperdom. "Aye," I says, ignoring him. I were looking around for Jock and couldn't see him nowhere. "Just fuck off, eh."

"You ain't getting away so easy this time, Blake. We got incontrovertible."

"It ain't my concern if you can't hold your shite, I got places to go. So get out my face, you little shite ranger."

"This is all going down as evidence, Blakey," he says, nodding at another rozzer stood behind him who were jotting it down.

"How'd you spell *ranger*?" that other copper says.

"You ain't getting out o' this one," says Jonah, ignoring him and giving me his undivided. "I'm sending you down for life."

"Fuck's you on about?" I says, finally clocking onto what he were saying. I peered through the shop window. "I only butted him a bit." Gromer were staggering onto his feet again, using the counter. Fair play to the fucker—I'd gave him the full weight of my swede.

"Butted who?" says Jonah, trying to gander where I were gandering. "You hurt someone in there as well, have you?"

"Erm, I thought, erm…"

He kept trying to peer through the glass, no matter how much I kept moving in front of him, so I shoved past him and pegged it instead. I dunno why I didn't do that in the first place. The thing about coppers in Mangel is they don't hold no authority. Mangel is one of them towns what looks after itself, via pillars like meself who keeps the community ticking straight and narrow, and if you don't fancy getting arrested, you don't have to. That's how come I'd never got incarcerated in Mangel Jail and why I'd come to realise I were never gonna be. You don't fancy it, don't let em nab you. Pegging it down Cutler Road towards the Wall Road, I reflected on that simple message and how it had passed so many by, Mangel Jail being full to bursting, so I'd heard. Maybe I could get a job with the council, going round all the freelancers and telling em that there is another way, a path through life that is infinitely more rewarding, and saves the taxpayer a load of wedge—you just have to tell the coppers to fuck off and peg it. I were still thinking about that when I ran into the roadblock.

"Didn't you hear him?" says Police Chief Cadwallader, doing summat with my arm that made us go facedown on the tarmac with his knee pegged in the small of me back, although no part of my back were small, in actual fact. "You deaf or summat? He says you are under arrest. For murder."

32

Copper station had moved since I'd last been in it. They had a big posh place now on that road going down to Ditchcroft, all glass and pillars and shite to make em feel important. But they weren't important, coppers in Mangel weren't, and I took this opportunity to tell em that. But not in so many words.

"You can eff and blind all you likes," Jonah says in reply, strolling behind while four of his largest grunts struggled to get us through the back door and down the corridor. And me wearing cuffs and all. Plus my back were knacked from the chief's twenty-odd stone bearing down on it through his knee just now. "None o' that changes the fact we got you now, Blakey. This time you are snookered well and true."

"Am I fuck," I says, trying to turn my face so I could flob on him. But he were wise to it now and walking out of flobshot. "Coppers can't fuckin' touch us, you twat. You don't even know what's going on in this town, does yer?"

"Oh, aye? What's going on that we dunno about, then? What's this big secret?"

"It ain't secrets, you dozy fuckin' shitstick. All you gotta do is open yer eyes and take the fuckin' tit off yer head."

"In case you ain't noticed, I no longer wears the constable's helmet. I'm an inspector now, as well you knows."

"Funny, I still sees a tit."

"Come on, tell us one thing we ain't aware of."

"You don't even wanna know."

"Nah, come on," he says, getting the grunts to stop a min. "You brung this up, so you can lift the scales from our eyes."

"I'll fuckin' blacken your eyes, you piece o' fuckin'—"

"You dunno, does you? You're as blind as you says we are. Royston Blake, the big fuckin' local character, and he don't even know what's going on under his own—"

"Vampires!" I blares, getting him with some spit this time, although I hadn't meant to. Glad I did, mind. "Seventy-five percent of folks in this town is fuckin' vampires. How about that, eh? How's that make you feel, not even knowing that?"

About so high, judging by his reaction. His eyes went all anguished and he put a paw to his mouth, covering up the frown of defeat that had no doubt took up residence there. But I weren't finished with him. When you got your opponent against the ropes, and especially if he is a copper, it is your solemn duty to break his fucking face.

"And what about the golem, eh?" I says. "Bet you don't even know what one o' them is, does yer?"

"I do," says one of the grunts, putting a paw up like the four-eyed little spod at the front of the classroom. "It is a mythological creature from Jewish folklore. The golem can be constructed from clay and given life via magic. The stories go that he was used by the Jews against their oppressors, but he got out of hand and turned against his own."

"What happened then, Tom?" says the other grunt.

"Well, Wayne, they had to get the magic man back, didn't they? He had to put a magic mark on the golem's head, which killed him."

"Ah right, so it turned out OK, then?"

"Yeah. Most people were alright in the end."

"Good. I likes happy endings."

"And me."

"What the fuck is you two on about?" I shouts. "That ain't what a fuckin' golem is."

"Oh yeah?" says the second grunt. "What is it, then?"

"It's a…a fuckin'…and there's other shite happening, shite you dunno about. Like, erm…"

"If you're gonna mention the werewolves, we knows about them," says grunt number one. "Caught one last night, didn't we? Up at Hurk Wood. There's loads up there. Apparently there's a ready supply of food up there for them."

"Is that so, Tom?"

"Yes it is, Wayne. But not like you'd think. See, most people think a werewolf can only eat live flesh, but they can eat *dead* flesh too, even flesh that has been dead a long while. So they feast on all the zombies up there."

"That's a flippin' good idea for em, Tom."

"Yep. But it won't last, see. They've already reduced the Hurk Wood zombie population by 50 percent. So it's little more than a temporary solution for them."

"Ah, right."

"And you know where they'll come looking then, don't you?"

"Shite."

"Exactly."

"What's we gonna do, Tom?"

"Wayne, I honestly don't know. It worries me."

I couldn't believe what were happening here. My life gets turned around by a Scottish burger van man, I falls in love with the vibrating diamond of my dreams, gets arrested for a murder I didn't commit—and I don't even know who I'm meant to have murdered—and now I'm stood in a brightly lit corridor in the copper station, listening to all this. "For fuck's fuckin' sake," I says, losing me rag. "There's a bunch of fuckin' *werewolves* planning on eatin' us, and all you cunts can do is shrug about it? It's *your* job to fuckin' *stop* em, you useless pieces of fuckin' shite."

I knew I'd got to em there, cos they all looked from one to the other for a moment, realising the gravity of the situation and what their responsibilities was. Then they burst out laughing. Right in my face, so I could smell the cheese and onion sarnies they'd had for lunch.

I let em do it for a bit. They was enjoying emselves, fucking around with old Blakey and getting a bellyful of mirth at his expense. That's what they thought, anyhow. But it was them who were paying here. You get Blakey into the mood I were headed for, with the darkness coming down and thoughts of what they'd done to Kerry flooding back into me swede, and you got to pay. But you can't afford it. No one can afford the fee I got for em.

I started tugging at the handcuffs.

MAN ARRESTED FOR
IMMIGRANT BURGLAR MURDER

A Mangel man has been arrested for the murder of Martynas Gus-
tas, an Estravian asylum seeker. Royston Blake, of the DSS hostel in
Cartridge Way, was picked up by police as he left Gromer Wines in
Cutler Road, following an anonymous tip-off.

"People often belittle circumstantial evidence," said arresting
officer Inspector Stephen Jones, "but sometimes there is just so much
of it that you can't ignore it. The main thing here is that we have
received reports that Blake was seen fornicating in public with Kerry
Barwell, who was also romantically linked with both dead men, we
believe. Our theory is that Blake had been seeing Barwell for some
time, became insanely jealous of his love rivals, and killed at least
one of them in a fit of rage. With a piece of wood.

"Then there are the splinters. Blake's hands are literally riddled
with the things, as would be those of any man who had rammed a
sharp piece of wood into the body of an adult male. Coincidence?
Possibly, but not when you put it next to Blake's criminal record. I
won't bore you with the details—we all know what Blake has been
charged with in the past and what he has slithered out of due to
whatever loophole or stroke of good luck. But his good luck was our

bad luck. Again and again he got out of it and went free to commit more crimes. Martynas Gustas, that innocent man who just wanted to bring up his family in our good and tolerant town, paid the ultimate price for that."

The corpse of Gustas, however, remains at large. "It is true that we cannot conclusively link Blake with the murder of Gustas using the usual forensic means, but sometimes you don't need forensic evidence. Sometimes, like in this case here, you don't need to do any sums to know that two and two is four. Saying that, we wouldn't mind getting that corpse back. If everyone out there could have a look in their sheds and under their hedges and the like, and keep their noses peeled for any rotting flesh odours, all of us on the force would appreciate it."

Asked if Blake is being detained in police custody, Jones said: "You see, it's more complicated than that. I want the public to have every confidence that we intend to place Blake in custody and keep him there—forever, if we get our way. But we've, erm…"

The rest of Jones's sentence was not picked up by the PA system. Asked to repeat it, he said: "I said we've lost him, OK? Happy now? You bloody reporters, all you care about is results, isn't it? All you want to see is criminals getting arrested and safely brought to justice without escaping or endangering innocent members of the public. Well, I'm here to tell you that there's a bigger picture at work here. There's forces at work, evil influences that are out to thwart our actions and scupper the public interests."

Asked to explain more about these "evil influences," or at least expand on the circumstances that led to Blake escaping, Jones hastily gathered his papers and left the stage, tripping on a cable as he went.

Kerry Barwell, who had previously been linked with Gustas's murder, has been cleared of all charges.

33

First thing I thought when I came to, slumped against a dustbin down an alley up the top of Clench Road, near where I used to live, were that I were having a wank.

My paw were clutching summat that felt like my tadger, and it were well fucking hard and out in the open air. Then I noticed that I weren't getting no feeling from it, and that it might be someone else's cock and not my own, and I let go sharpish, balling me fists and getting ready to punch some arse bandit's jaw off for taking advantage of my unconscious hand. Then I opened my eyes and realised that it weren't a tadger at all.

But a truncheon.

I picked it up again, turning it over and feeling the weight of it and chucking it and catching it, all the while trying to remember. Shite had come to pass, I knowed that much. Darkness had come down upon my swede, and folks had suffered. I looked at my knuckles and saw the scratches and bruising there, but didn't feel it. I never felt pain in that area. I noticed the pair of silver bangles on my wrists, a bit of chain hanging off each, representing the custody I'd escaped from by use of brute force alone. And the darkness. I'd never understood that shite. I didn't want to neither. But I felt like I was gonna.

I had a go at tugging off the bust handcuffs. It hurt like billy-o, but I kept on yanking anyhow, feeling like it were doing us some good. Or at least getting the balance back where it ought to be. When my wrists started bleeding, I stopped, feeling much better. I got up and stretched and yawned like I were at home and it were time to wake up and go to work. It were, in a way. I couldn't for the life of us recall what, but I knowed I had shite to do. Major shite, with folks depending on us and wrongs waiting to get righted. I slipped the truncheon down the inside of me leather and started walking. I knowed it would come to us in a bit.

It were a nice morning. Or evening, or whatever the fuck time of day it were. Air were warm, but the whole sky were one big white cloud, and you couldn't see the sun, but I knowed it were up there somewhere, between the Deblin Hills and that empty space to the east. I felt like it were spying on us, and I wanted to turn me face up to it and tell it to fuck off. But I never done that. What do you reckon I am, a fucking mental case?

But you're right, ain't you? You and them other know-alls, you been right all along. Royston Blake is tapped in the head, and the sooner he realises it, the better for every cunt hereabouts. Well, I realised it now. Fuck knows how come, but it were clear and simple like a nursery rhyme. Roses is red, violets is blue, shit stinks, and Royston Blake is mental. I went home.

I knowed it weren't my home no more and hadn't been for a couple of years, but I found meself going there anyhow.

It's an odd thing, knocking on your own door. Even odder when you clocks a shape moving inside and realises it's some-one in there, someone who don't belong. It's odder still when you notice the state of the front door and that it's got a nice coat of white paint and a brass knocker on it. Just when you reach out to knock that knocker, the door opens.

"Can I help you?" she says, looking us up and down.

I didn't say nothing. I knowed it were her house now and I were the stranger, not her. Not only were I a stranger, but I'd just got a waft coming up from below, and I think I must have pissed meself back there in the alley.

"I think I know who you are," she says, pushing the door wider and stepping aside. "You're Roy Blake, aren't you?"

"Royston."

"That's it. Royston Blake. Come in."

I stood like so for a bit, trying to look her in the eye and not being able to. She had a new carpet in the hall, and the little table I'd had there were gone. You could see through into the kitchen, and things was different there and all. I went in.

"If you sit yourself down in here, I'll make you a cup of tea," she says, leading the way into the living room. I followed her, looking at the back of her neck and considering how frail it were and how I could twist it like a chicken's. Not that I would—she were a bird, and you don't normally wring the neck of a human bird. But if she were a bloke, I could. And I would, like as not.

"You shouldn't let strange men in yer house, by the way," I says. "Not that I'm strange, but…I'm just saying, your neck is a bit like a chicken. I mean, it *ain't*, but I could twist it like one. You got a nice neck."

She rubbed her neck then clamped her arms under each other. "It's like you said, you're not a strange man."

"Aye, but it's the principle, ennit? I could be a fuckin' rapist for all you knows. There's all kind of spanners out there. I knew these two fellers once, they used to cut holes in heifers and shag the wound. They done it to a little girl and all, so I hears."

"Oh…" she says, putting a paw to her face. She were white as a bucket of milk.

"Look, I don't wanna worry you nor nothing. Them two, they ain't around no more, so you don't have to be scaredy of em. Honest, they're fuckin' dead. I killed em meself."

"Um...milk and sugar?" she says, making her way to the kitchen.

I found meself positioned ready to park my arse on a leather recliner. "Aye," I says. "Eight."

"Eight sugars?"

"Nah, make it six." I didn't want to look greedy. Not with this nice bird here. I says nice bird, but I didn't fancy her. She were like a librarian, all glasses and cardy and skirt like a kilt but not made of tartan. Unless there is a type of tartan that is just brown.

I thought about Jock for a moment then put it out of me mind and concentrated on the quality piece of furniture I were now sat in. It were well fucking comfy.

"Eh," I says to her as she came back through holding a mug with an England flag on it, "this chair is fuckin' quality, I tells yer."

"Thanks," she says, giving us the tea.

I took a sip. It were too hot. I took a few more sips and found it to be not so hot after all. "Where'd you get it?"

"Furniture Express. On the retail park."

"The what?"

"The Igor Retail Park. You know, on the new development over by Muckfield?"

"Igor fuckin' Retail Park? What the—"

"Would you like a biscuit?"

"Aye, I would, ta. Woss you got?"

"We've got...um, hang on. Let me..."

She went out again. She weren't so bad, this one weren't. She made a nice cup o' tea, and I liked what she'd done to the old place, putting some new curtains up. And getting that mold off the skirting boards down there. Actually, I couldn't find a thing she hadn't changed. And I didn't have a problem with none of it. Not even getting shet of the telly. Tellies is shite anyhow these days. Have you seen what's on em lately?

"No, I don't really watch much," she says, standing in the doorway again.

"Fuckin' hell," I says, almost spilling me tea, "is you fuckin' telepathet...I mean, telethap..." I stopped there, cos it weren't the librarian bird.

It were Rache.

"Hiya, Blakey."

"Alright, Rache. It's fuckin' nice here, ennit?"

"Yeah, she's made it very...Aren't you wondering how I found you?"

"I'm more interested in how you could read my mind just then, about watching telly."

"I didn't, Blake. You were speaking out loud."

"I fuckin' were not."

"Sorry, Blake, but you were."

"Oh. Well, how'd you find us here?"

"This was once your home. It's the obvious place to look."

"Aye, but I don't live here no more. I ain't been here in...I dunno, since they took us back into Parpham. Have you got yerself a cuppa, by the way? She makes it nice."

"You've been here, Blake. You've been here lots of times since you lost this house."

"Fuck's you on about? Why the fuck would I—"

"I dunno why, Blake. Only you know that, somewhere in your mind. But you keep coming here. Whenever there's a crisis, I suppose. That's why Myrtle lets you in."

"Who the fuck's Myrtle? What kind of a fuckin' name is Myrtle?"

"Here's your tea," says Myrtle, handing a mug to Rache and going back to the kitchen.

"Well done, Blake," says Rache.

"Woss I done now?"

"What *haven't* you done. The *police* are after you."

"Oh, aye."

"It was on the radio just now. You're wanted for murder, Blake. What the hell have you done?"

"I ain't done fuck all, Rache. It's that cunt Jonah again, sticking his hooter where it—"

"It wasn't him. It was Cadwallader."

"He's a fuckin' wanker as well."

"They're looking for you everywhere, Blake. Sooner or later they'll come here and find you. You're lucky Myrtle didn't ring them instead of me. It's only because I gave her my number last time. If he comes round, I told her, just ring me. No matter where I am or what I'm doing, I'll…"

Rache were getting a bit boring now, and I weren't really harking her. Plus me tea were finished. I were about to shout through for another cup—and ask where them fucking biscuits had got to—when the sun came out and poked through them posh curtains, which was drawn and pulled back all neat and diagonal, like a picture of a house you might draw at school if you're a fucking poof. But Myrtle were a bird, so she were alright. Fucking odd name, mind. Who the fuck has a name that rhymes with *turtle*? But I ain't on about Myrtle and her turtles and her curtains. I ain't even on about Rache, yakking on like she were over there and barely pausing to sip her tea. I'm on about the sun.

It were giving us a sign, see, using them curtains and the window frame and making a shape just like before, back in the bedsit.

A vibrating diamond of light.

I stared at it, clear and bright on the left tit of Rache's dress, right where her heart were. The top corner tipped over onto her cleavage, setting us stirring a little bit in the pants area but even more in the swede area. How could I have been so blind? I'm crashing around, getting into shite and upsetting irritating little runts like Jonah, when all the while I had someone who loved us, who looked out for my welfare and made sure I were alright. Also she were well fit, with quite big tits and an alright face. I ought to be concentrating on her, not all that other shite about eradicating vampires and destroying fountains.

"…and take you to him," says Rache, finishing up whatever she'd been saying. "He said he'd always be on hand to administer it, night and day. And if he's not, one of the orderlies will."

"Aye, whatever," I says, going over to her and grabbing her paws. "Rache, I seen the light. It's a vibrating light, and it's shaped like a diamond, and I seen it on your tits just now. Just here, look…"

"Blake, don't *poke* me like—"

"I wanna apologise to you, Rache. For all the fuss I caused and making you yomp out here after us and that."

"Well, I didn't exactly yomp. I've got a car now."

I started giving her a nice hug. "I just want you to know that—"

"Look, Blake," she says, breaking free but laughing a bit as well, "will you come with me or not? It's still only five, and I'm pretty sure he'll still be there right now."

"Aye, I'll come with you, Rache. I'll come with you anywhere."

I followed her out, thinking how I really did mean that. Wherever she wanted us to go, it were as good a place to start as any. Start my search, I'm on about. For Kerry.

"Thanks, Rache," I says, squeezing into the shotgun side of her car. "Without you, I'd still be in the dark. I'd be well and truly fucked."

"Yeah, well," she says, pulling away. "Don't mention it. You know I'd do anything for…well, no matter."

But I had to mention it, didn't I? Cos it were down to Rache, me getting set back on the path to happiness just now. Rache and her left tit.

34

Rache had a Fiesta. I wouldn't have minded if it were your RS Turbo, but it weren't. It weren't even your XR2i, which is about two seconds slower up to sixty in my experience but more reliable, and you can get em way cheaper. But no, Rache had your basic Fiesta Popular, which is about as popular as a septic bellend in my opinion. You have to shift down to second for most hills, it's got the turning arc of a twin-trailer artic, and the ride is like perching atop a fucking 150cc lawnmower.

"Look, it's just a car, OK?" she says, shifting up to third. About twenty-miles-an-hour too late, but I weren't mentioning it. "It's not even mine—I'm just borrowing it from the garage while my little Mitsubishi is in for a service."

"Who's doing it? He should have gave you summat better than this."

"Does it really matter? If it goes from *A* to *B*, who cares? I only need a car for shopping and the school run anyway, and the occasional picnic in Hurk Wood. I'm not interested in doing nought to sixty in twelve seconds, or whatever."

"Twelve seconds is shite."

"I said I'm not int—"

"And you don't wanna be taking that lad of yours out to Hurk Wood, by the way. It ain't a place for younguns. Nor birds."

Rache paused a bit before saying, "Why?"

"Rache, for fuck sake," I says, shaking me swede in disbelief. "Do you honestly not know the shite that goes on up there?"

"I've got my ideas, but maybe you should tell me. Maybe you should get all that stuff off your chest now, sort of like a confession. It could be part of the healing process."

I had a look at her. "Are you sure you wants to hear it?"

"Yep."

She had sunglasses on, and it were hard to get an idea of her mood. She looked serious, mind.

"It's fuckin' hairy stuff, some of it," I says by way of a final warning.

"I'm OK. I think I know some of it already. You hear rumours, you know?"

"Right," I says, sitting back and watching the road turn into a bridge as we went westward over the River Clunge. "On your fuckin' swede be it, mind. I ain't takin' responsibility if you can't sleep at night."

"I'm a big girl."

I looked down at her chest.

"Blake!"

"Alright, well, what it is, in a nutcase, is that…"

"Please, Blake, just say it."

"I'm searching for the right words."

"There are no right words. Just speak."

"Werewolves."

"What?"

"And zombies."

"Blake, I dunno what you—"

"The werewolves is eating the zombies, but when the zombies runs out, we're all set to get invaded by the fuckin' werewolves."

"What the hell are you on about?"

"It's fuckin' gospel truth, Rache. You know who I heard it off of? Coppers. Three coppers, one of em high up."

"What rank?"

"Hmm. I think he said he were a private investigator or summat. Anyhow, it were Jonah."

"Right, well, he's an inspector."

"Aye, that's what I says."

"No, you—"

"Plus there's a golem."

"Oh God...Blake, I dunno if I can take this."

I folded my arms and shook my head. "I told you, didn't I? I fuckin' *warned* you that it were well fuckin' scary."

"No, I mean...we'll be at the doctor's soon, and...look, Blake, you do realise who this Kerry is, don't you?"

"Don't try and change the subject, Rache."

"She's a drug dealer. She's a spoilt little rich kid who has got herself into trouble playing gangsters with the wrong people. And she's trying to set you up for a murder. You need to tell the police everything, right down to...Oh no, what's this?"

"Fuck sake, Rache, ain't you been harkin' us? You need to face up to this stuff. I ain't even mentioned about the vamp—"

"Shut *up*, will you. Look, there's summat going on up there."

"Eh?"

There were a queue of cars up ahead, and Rache pulled up behind it, crunching the gears summat chronic. We was on the main Branston Road west of Norbert Green, and I couldn't recall ever seeing a jam here.

"Someone must have crashed," she says, putting a paw to her mouth. "I really hope they're alright."

"Fuck em—they should of beed more careful."

"*Blake.* That's no way to—"

"Like fuck is it not. Some cunt prangs his motor and carks it, that's one less shite driver on the road. It's a safer place for sensible folk, like you. And meself."

"Yeah? And what if it was someone else's fault? What if someone was drunk, and—"

"For fuck sake, Rache, think about it—you drives a decent motor with a bit o' poke under the hood, you can drive yer way out of danger. I bet you he were in a Fiesta Popular, this cunt holding us up."

"You've got no compassion, Blake. No feeling for your fellow man."

"I ain't feelin' up me fellow man. What d'you reckon I am, a fuckin' shite stabber? Fellow bird, mind, I'll have a look at her."

"Can I see some ID, please?"

He were stood next to my window, jotting summat down in his notebook. I hadn't noticed him creep up. Maybe that's cos he were such a short-arse that he barely even reached above the motors in front. They must have lowered standards on the police force since I applied to it a couple of years back. He stopped jotting and peered in, looking aggro.

"I said," he says, "can I see some…fuck."

That were him recognising me when he said the bad word there. He staggered backwards. Dropping his notebook and fumbling for his truncheon. "Dave?" he shouts, not taking his eyes off us. "Dave, I got him!"

Rache held my arm.

"Please, Blake," she says. "Just stay here. Whatever happens, I promise I'll stay with you. I've always been with you, Blake. And I always will."

I looked at her. "Fuck you on about?" I says, pushing the door wide. I yanked my arm free and bailed, whisking my own truncheon out and scanning left-right. I done the lot in one fluid motion, but it went wrong at the end and I fell arsewise into the gutter, dropping my truncheon down the fucking drain. For fuck's fucking sake.

"He's down! Dave, I got the suspect down!"

The little one gave up trying to deploy his weapon and started shoeing us in the face. Hard to tell from that angle, but I reckoned he were about a size two, and that ain't enough to trouble Blakey for long. Fourth or fifth kick and I grabbed it, yanking him sideways and against Rache's Fiesta, slamming the door shut.

"Aaarrgh! Dave, I'm being assaulted by the sus—"

From my deckwise position I punched him in the bollocks, giving it my full force and lifting him right off the ground a bit. But it didn't seem to hurt him much—either he didn't have no bollocks or they was in a strange place. Like as not he didn't have none, I'd say. He planted a foot on us and got his truncheon out.

"Let him have it, Mike!" someone's hollering, pegging it towards us from the front of the jam. This were Dave, like as not. "Let him have it!"

I were trying to get up but finding it hard and not knowing why. I reached out my hands on either side, feeling the ground and a drain cover and trying to push up off it and failing.

"What?" says Short-Arse, looking down at us. "You mean the baton?"

"Aye, give him the fuckin' baton before he…Mike!"

When you're as strong as me, all it takes is a split second. That's all he'd took his eye off us for, but it were all I needed. I'd got me fingers through the drain cover and yanked it up, and I had it in two hands above me chest, ready to bench-press the fucking thing at Short-Arse. I winked at him.

"It's a bit fuckin' late for the baton, pal," I says. Then I launched the drain lid right at his face, which were only about four foot away. But the lid only went up about three of them foot, and it were straight up instead of at the required angle.

"*Blake!*" yells Rache behind us.

I craned me neck sideways so I could see her. The drain lid hit us, right on the forehead. I passed out.

35

But I only passed out for a moment.

I got up, shaking the drain-lid pain out of my head and thumping the copper in the face. Or maybe I shook the pain out of the copper's face and thumped meself in the head. Either way, the other one arrived and swung his truncheon at me, which I fielded to the side of the neck. I swung back at him, but he leaned away. I swung once more, making no mistake this time.

He leaned away again.

"Fuck *sake*," I says, turning arse and pegging it.

Everyone knows about wooden fences in Mangel. They are fucking shite, most of em put up by the Gretchum family or associates, and all it takes is a gentle summer breeze to send em horizontal. I ran right into one. My plan were to cross a couple of back gardens and get down to the left bank of the river, which were quite near here. I'd jump in it and float downstream underwater for a bit, using a straw sticking up into the air like a snorkel. Maybe I'd be able to float all the way to the ocean that way, cos I did once hear that the River Clunge leads you to it. But the fucking fence didn't budge an inch when I shouldered it, bouncing us back into the path. Trust me to find the one bit of wooden panelling in Mangel not erected by the Gretchums.

"Right, you," says the copper, catching up with us and jumping on my back. "Get down on the ground, you awkward little bugger."

Mind you, I were glad to have a robust fence to hold on to now. No matter how much he squeezed an arm round my neck and cut off the blood flow to my swede and airflow to me lungs, I weren't going down. The longer the fence held us up, the more I knowed I could handle him. Felt like a minute or so we was struggling like that for, and I could feel his panic rising towards the end. I reached round to grab his face. That's when the fucking fence decided to give way.

We both went down into the garden, him pitching forwards and doing a roly-poly onto the lawn, me landing in the fucking pond. It were a deep one and all, coming nigh on up to me chin. Then I realised I were on me knees and tried standing up. But it were slippery on the bottom, and I went arsewise again, getting proper submerged this time and hearing only bubbles all around and the intense ringing that had been in my head for a long while now. I were thrashing around, trying to get hold of summat to pull us up but only finding a bit of wood. I found a bit of pipe or summat with the other paw and traced it to its source, which were on dry land, thank fuck. That's when I started hearing the sirens.

PC Dave were still on his knees, clutching his lower back and making sounds like someone had pinged him with a lump hammer. I booted him in that area as hard as I could then disappeared up the side alley. I stopped and thought about it for a moment then went back and kicked him a few more times. He called us an awkward little bugger, didn't he? I ain't little.

Couple of minutes later, jogging along a back street now towards Lower Tick, I realised that I were still clutching that bit of wood from the pond. But it weren't a bit of wood; it were a fish.

A koi carp.

A squad car hared around the bend towards us up ahead. I pocketed the fish, dived into a hedge, and lay still, hardly making no noise at all but wishing to fuck I hadn't chose a hedge that were made of thorns.

36

Have you seen that film *Fame*?

I don't normally like films about dancing. Me, I can be a fucking amazing dancer at times. When the mood takes me, I'm a dancer in the style of Michael Jackson in that vid for "Billy Jean" where he turns into a zombie. I can do the moonwalk and everything. It's just that the mood don't take us that often. Thinking about it, I don't reckon it ever had took me, except when I got wedded and had to do a dance with Beth, the bird I had to marry on that day. She were so fucking pissed that I fell atop her, breaking a couple of her ribs, meaning I had to be gentle with one of her tits that night instead of doing it the way I likes it. I done it the way I likes it anyhow, and she fucking liked it. Not enough to keep her a one-man bird, mind. Not in the long run. But I'm on about Michael Jackson, not dead wives and former friends who are also dead.

Actually, no, I'm on about *Fame*.

You know that bit near the start, where the bird says about wanting fame and paying for it in sweat? I fucking love that bit. I ain't seen the program in nigh on donkey's years, and still I hears her say it in me swede every now and then, when I really wants summat and I'm finding it hard to get it. I really wanted Kerry, as you knows. She were vibrating, and she were my diamond. She were the missing piece in my jigsaw. Actually, thinking about it, *she* were the jigsaw and I had the missing piece, and it were right here in my trolleys. I'd tried it out, down on the riverbank earlier on, and it slotted perfect (although it were a fucking tight fit, as ever). But still I had a feeling I wouldn't be getting her. I dunno what it were about her. Maybe it were the way she spoke, which were a bit posh. Maybe it were the fact she seemed to have a couple of swede cells to rub together, meaning I'd have to up my game a bit on the chat front and wouldn't be able to get away with the usual shite I spouts and birds lap up, the fucking slags. No, Kerry weren't a slag, I could say for fucking surely. And that's perhaps why I had a feeling she couldn't be mine and that I wouldn't be able to hold her forever and put her next to my heart, making it vibrate along with hers. But then the *Fame* bird popped into me swede, and I realised it were possible.

"If you wants fame," she were saying, dressed in her leotard and looking well fucking sexy. It's the bird on the telly I'm on about, by the way, not Kerry. Mind you, they don't come sexier than our Kel. "If you wants fame," she says again, cos I'd interrupted her, "right here is where you starts paying, you bunch of lazy cunts. In sweat."

I inserted a word there, you might have noticed. She don't actually say the word *lazy*. But I realised that laziness were what it's all about, as I lay there under the hedge halfway between Norbert Green and Lower Tick, thinking about how I ought to be sitting in a nice living room in a nice house up in the Danghill district, couple of younguns playing footy on the back lawn and koi carp in the pond, instead of in my pocket. I'd be watching telly on the biggest fucking screen you ever seen, selecting a premium sports channel from the millions I had available via the satellite dish on the roof and that I'd paid for and not got off Filthy Stan down the Volley. But more than anything—more than the sprogs and the fish and the televised tractor racing—I'd have Kerry there with me. Actually, no, she'd be in the kitchen, rustling up some scran or polishing the oven or summat. But she'd be nearby. She'd be mine and she'd be vibrating and she'd be diamond-shaped, although she ain't actually that, having nice tits and hips and a thin waist, making her more of a sort of a dumbbell shape, only in a nice way.

But it were a mirage, weren't it?

I were like the feller in the desert, nigh on carking it of thirst and spying a pub in the distance with cold lager on tap. And pork scratchings. Plus pie and chips, long as you orders it before two in the afternoon. But the pub ain't there. And Kerry weren't there. She wouldn't ever be there, long as I cowered under this hedge and waited for a bunch of coppers to leave me be. I had to make an effort, didn't I? I had to toss me cards down atop the table and put me cock on the block, although the other lads I'd be playing cards with wouldn't be happy to see that, unless they'm arse bandits. I had to start paying.

In sweat.

So I pegged it.

If you wants Kerry, the *Fame* lass were saying again, *you gotta start sweating like a fucking pig, you fat bastard.*

"Fuck off!" I'm shouting, sprinting down the path. I'd done well over forty yard already, and I were still going strong. "I ain't fat."

Oh yeah? How come you can't run very fast, then?

"Fuck's you on about? I'm like a fuckin' *train* here."

A steamroller, more like. Plus you want to stop now. You really, really want to stop.

"Kiss my arse, you fuckin'…old slag…I can keep running like this for…for fuckin'…oh shite."

She were right, much as it gave us grief to admit it. I pulled up, hanging on to the back of someone's Talbot Horizon and chucking me guts. But I were sweating. She'd said about me having to pay in sweat, and the fucking stuff were pouring down me face like my head were a balloon full up of water and there were some holes in it.

Yeah, but I didn't mention puke. I didn't say, "You want fame, you'd better start paying for it in vomit," did I?

"I'm fuckin' sweatin' buckets here."

I got bad news for you: the puke cancels out the sweat. No cigar.

"No cigar? I'll ram a fuckin' cigar right up yer...*bleurgh*..."

"Keep yis fuckin' voice doon, will yis?"

I looked up, wiping sick off my chin and trying to recall if the bird from *Fame* were Scottish instead of the Australian I'd always had her down as.

"Ah'm here, ye blind wee bampot." Jock's head appeared from under the car, owl eyes staring up at us through lenses covered in grease and thumbprints. "I been waitin' oan yis, Royston. We've work tae do."

"How'd you know I'd be here?"

"I didnae. Ah just hid mahself under this car here and trusted fate tae do the rest. And fate came through for me, Royston. Youse bolting doon here, it wis meant tae be."

I puked on his face.

"Och, look what yis have...ach..."

"Soz about that, Jock," I says, grabbing him by the collar and hauling him out. "Look, Jock, I gotta ask you summat. And it's a thing of a personal nature I'm on about here, so I'm trying to be all sensitive and steppin' careful, right?"

"Aye, go on."

"You know that bird your dead lad were shaggin'?"

"Och, yis mean the harlot?"

"I wouldn't really put it like—"

"She's a vampire."

"Jock, she ain't a vampire, honest."

"Aye? And how would youse ken that?"

"Don't fuckin' bring Ken into it again."

"Come oan—ah wantae know. In what way is that...*woman* not a vampire?"

"Jock, she just ain't. Look, I might as well tell you that I'm... well, I reckon I'm in love with her. I know she were like your daughter-in-law and that, but—"

"Daughter-in-law? That wee witch showed her true colours when she got mah Scott hooked on...I mean, when she introduced him tae that pack o' bloodsuckers."

"She ain't a fuckin' vampire nor a witch, Jock, you just gotta trust us on that. See, I've really got to know her. I've shagged her and everything. She's a top girl, Jock, really down to earth and that."

"I'll flatten her."

"Don't say shite like that, Jock."

"I fuckin' swear it, Royston. I see her, ah'm comin' doon on that lass like a ton o' *shite*."

I glared at him, clenching me teeth so hard it were hurting my eyeballs. I'd been in situations like this one before, where you're well into a bird but your mate don't see it, and he's slagging her off in front of you. Them other times I'd just ping the fucker. No one talks about my bird like that—especially not pikey little cunts like whoever it were. But I'd thought about it since and come to realise that it ain't like that—he's just looking out for you, even though he's pissing you off. But I still think you should ping the fucker. And try and bust his nose and all so he remembers for next time.

But this situation were different in some key ways, I now realised. Jock had puke on his face, for starters, and I didn't want none of that on me fist.

"Listen, Royston, we've no time for this," he says. "These vampires, ah think they're ontae us. If we dinnae eradicate them right noo, I believe our chance will have come and gone, and the world will suffer at their evil hands."

"But—"

"We've got tae shift, Royston."

"Aye, I know, but—"

"Here, yis can drink some of this while we jog along."

I took the bottle of Bell's off him. "For fuck's fuckin' sake, Jock!" I yells, watching his giant arse cheeks surge up and down as he plodded down the road, holdall swinging from one hand and an open bottle in the other, hard stuff sloshing out of it.

"Aye!" he shouts. "Come oan."

I shook my head, took a big swig, and went after him.

37

"Erm, Jock, can I just ask you summat?"

He opened the holdall and started counting out the wooden stakes inside. There was eighteen, from what I could see. Plus six more half-bottles of Bell's.

"Right, that's twenty-three stakes. Youse take twelve, I'll get by on just the eleven."

"But Jock—"

"Ah'm no arguing with yis, Royston. Yis'll need that extra stake, believe youse me. Remember that I have detailed knowledge of how these beasts operate, which ah can use tae my advantage."

"I know but—"

"And drink one o' these, for fuck's sake." He handed me another half-bottle and started stowing his stakes about his person.

I necked it. "But Jock," I says, burping, "why the fuck is we outside my house?"

He stopped. "*Your* hoose?"

"No, my *house*."

"Since when wis this your hoose? It's a fuckin' vampire nest, Royston."

"It's a normal house. I got a flat there on the third floor."

"Where?"

"There, look."

"That's the second floor, Royston."

"Nah it ain't. Look—one, two, three."

"No, this one here, we call it the groond floor. That one above it is the first, and—"

"For fuck sake, I'm just saying there ain't no vampires in it. All you got in there is meself and a bunch of fuckin' Egyptians."

Jock looked sideways, moving his lips quick like he were working summat out. "*Egyptian* is another word for *vampire*, Royston. Aye, it's a classical term, from the Byzantine period. It appears throughout gothic literature from that time, translated from the ancient Latin."

"Ah, right."

"Yis are OK with that, aye?"

"Yeah, no fuckin' probs." I picked up a stake and looked it over. "Erm…"

"Reet, it's time for the big push. Fate chooses its heroes, and right noo we are the chosen ones. There's no quantifying the disastrous effects if we fuck this up, but if we get it reet—if we go in there and eradicate every last evil fuckin' bloodsucker of them— we'll be remembered forever. Wid yis like that?"

"Aye, I fuckin' would."

"Me too. They'll erect statues, Royston. One ae youse, one ae me. Just think aboot that, eh? Have a wee moment tae reflect while I, erm…" He grabbed another bottle, twisted off the cap and started sucking.

"I have thought about it, Jock. What I want, right, is the head of Clint Eastwood and the—"

"Come oan!" he blares, tossing the bottle across the street and opening the front door. The bottle smashed about two yards in front of a couple of little girls walking home from school, making them stop and look over at us. I pointed through the open door to indicate that it were Jock, not me. They still looked shite scared, so I grinned at em and gave em a friendly wave with the stake. They started screaming and ran off. Grumpy bitches.

"Jock?"

I were halfway up the first flight now, stake still held aloft in case a vampire jumped out. I must admit, I found it all a bit hard to believe. I mean, vampires living under my own roof and me not knowing about it? Mind you, I had been kipping sound every night for the past year or so. I'd led a sheltered life, thinking back on it as I went up the stair, glugging whisky. Seemed like I'd been in a coma, not thinking nor doing nothing nor feeling nothing. But I were awake now. I drank some more whisky.

"Jock, where the fuck is yer?"

He came trudging down from the third floor or the fourth floor or whatever the fuck he'd called it. All urgency gone from his movements, stake hanging limp at his side. "Ah cannae find them," he says, sitting down on the step. "Ah've searched everywhere, even in the fuckin' broom cupboard and in the attic. They've flown the roost, Royston. The wee bastarts got wise tae me."

I went up and tried sitting next to him. But I didn't fit, his arse being so wide. I sat a few stairs down from him. "I been thinkin' on it, Jock," I says, giving him my sympathetic face. "You know, I really don't reckon you got the right place. I never noticed no vampires here nor nothing like that."

He didn't seem to hear us at first then clocked us like I'd just materialised there. And he didn't look happy about it. "What are youse sneering it?" he says. "What the fuck do youse ken aboot vampires?"

"This ain't a sneer, Jock, it's my sympathetic face. And I ken more than you—"

"How did they find oot, though?" He looked up at the ceiling, trying to locate the answer there. "How did the creatures o' the night uncover mah plans? Do yis ken what ah think? Someone must have let oan tae them—that's what ah think. But who? Which wee deceitful cunt wid do a wicked thing like that?"

He seemed to find his answer on the ceiling, near the bare light bulb that hung up there. It started swinging slightly, perhaps cos of a draft coming through the little window on the landing. Or perhaps it were on account of the rage that filled Jock of a sudden.

"Come here, ye wee fuckin' snitch!" he yells, launching himself at us, stake aimed at my face.

"Eh? Me?" I says, moving aside slightly and watching him sail past. He landed about halfway down the flight, crunching a couple of stairs, then carried on, tumbling arse over tit and hitting the wall at the bottom, knocking half the plaster off it.

"Erm, you alright, Jock?"

In response he started bleeding from his head. And not moving.

"Shite," I says, going down to him. "Fuckin' shite." Mind you, I dunno why I were fretting. He tried to kill me there—did you see him? And for a crime I never even committed, I don't think. But fretting I were, kneeling by his side and giving him a little shake and getting nothing back.

"Fuckin' shite," I says, trying to recall me first aid. As a head doorman I used to take courses in it every year or so, learning about how to revive folks and stop em bleeding and that. Mind you, I never used it on the job. It were their fucking fault for getting pissed, weren't it? But it were all there in me swede. "Erm..." I says, trying to recall what to do when a person is unconscious and bleeding from the head and also making gurgling noises like a babby. "Erm...oh, aye."

I went up and got his holdall from where he'd been sat, rummaging through it for one of them bottles. Cos you had to pour liquid over the patient's face, didn't you? "Pour liquid over his face," I think the guidelines went, "and keep pouring until he wakes up. If he don't wake up, give him the kiss of life."

"Fuck!" I shouted. Not only at the thought of giving Jock a kiss, but also cos he didn't have no whisky left.

"If no whisky can be found," the guidelines went on, "use another liquid. But don't hang about—time is of the essence."

"Time is of the essence," I says, undoing me flies. "Time is of the...*ahhh*..."

Dear Sir,

"Integration is key," according to you. But integration of what? Integration of our local world with the outside? Integration of our stable community with a load of parasites, cast out from their own homelands? Integration of the pure with the impure?

There is a river that flows through our town. It flowed before we were here, and it will flow after we have gone. From outside it do flow, from high up in faraway mountains, bringing impurities into our midst and letting them swarm in its currents, rubbing up against our purity. For a while this is healthy, fertilising our seed and bringing our world unto flower. But that healthy time is limited, so the river carries the impurities out, casting them back into the wilderness from whence they did come.

There is a growing number in this town who believe that if integration is the key to anything, that thing is our own downfall. The only way for our town to survive is through the efforts of those born here, good men and women who are made of the clay that grows beneath our soil, dyed with the hue of that local field from whence they did spring. Not only do we believe this with all of our hearts, but we are taking active measures to bring it about. We aim to cast the cuckoo from our nest before he grows big.

Before our river runs red.

The Old Guard

38

"What the fuck are yis doing?"

"It's the kiss o' life, Jock."

"Is it fuck—that's a romantic kiss. Yis are tryin' tae molest me."

"Eh? Fuck off, I'm—"

"And look—yis have got yer fuckin' willy out. Help!"

"Jock, *listen*, for fuck...I've just fuckin' saved your life, mate. You was in a coma or summat, and I brung you out of it using the kiss o' life, like I says."

"Did yis truly? Ouch, mah heed..."

"Aye, you'd better not touch it. You got some blood comin' out still."

"Why am ah wet? And what's that foul odour?"

"Yeah, you don't really wanna know about that. Stage one of the first-aid process, let's call it."

"Is that so? Well then, ah won't ask. But yis have still not said why your willy is hanging there."

"Erm..."

"Och, it disnae matter. Nothing matters noo, does it? Ah've failed. The vampires have flown the nest. And it's a full moon the neet, which means vampires are able tae better cloak themselves.

We'll never find them. They'll be hiding all over, ready for their final push tae destroy us all. All ah wanted tae do wis eradicate the bastarts from this fair toon, a toon that welcomed me when I first came doon here and gave me a chance ae makin' a living. But ah couldnae even do that."

"You done what you could, Jock."

"Aye, but..." He rubbed his face. I thought it were to wipe the piss off it at first, then I noticed the little noises he were making, like a rutting sow, and I realised he were crying. Another couple of seconds and he were wailing, like a rutting sow who is really fucking distressed about summat.

I went to put a paw on his shoulder and make it all better for him, using some skills I had. I'd done a bit of nutter subduing in my time, back when I were locked up in Parpham for a crime I never committed. Actually, I did commit it, but the coppers never found out about it, and I got tossed in Parpham anyhow, cos it's a fucking asylum, not a prison. Thinking about it, maybe I had been a bit mental back then. But not half so much as some of the other spanners in there. You ought to have seen em, running around and doing shites in corners and stroking their arms like they was cats. Other ones was more quiet, less prone to span-nering about but just as fucking mental nonetheless. It's them ones I learned to work my magic on, using a little technique I developed.

Spanner whispering, I called it.

I had a 99.99 percent success rate with it, or summat near that. Even cured a mong during me peak, allowing him to leave Parpham and start a new life as a normal person, getting a job as a lollipop lady, even though he were a man. Mind you, he did look a bit like a very rough kind of lady, with that overgrown barnet of his and them tits. And he never told em different, being happy to land any job at all and not wanting to rock the boat, like as not. Got killed under a bus within a week, mind you.

I whispered in Jock's ear.

Don't really matter what the words is, just so long as you gets the tone right. And I had me tone bang on, pitching my whisper exactly halfway between Marlon Brando in *The Godfather* and a pigeon. Get the tone right, you can say whatever words comes into your swede, although I use summat motivational most times. Worked a fucking treat in Parpham.

"Had the what?" says Jock, stopping his sobbing. He examined us with his owl eyes, tears rolling from em still but not a trace of self-pity no more.

"Guts," I says. "Got the glory. Went the distance now I ain't gonna stop, just a man and his fuckin' will to survive. It's the… eye of the—"

"By fuck, Royston, ah think yis are reet."

"I knows I'm right. Them words is the truest fuckin' things ever writ down by anyone."

"I agree. Is it a poem of yoors, is it?"

"Erm…"

"Yis are a very talented man, Royston."

"Yeah, cheers."

"Mind you, it does sound like something else ah've heard along the way somewhere, if ah could just think ae it."

"It's all mine, Jock."

"Ah'm impressed. And what wis the next bit? It's the eye o' the…what?"

I had a quick think. "Wolf."

"Eye o' the wolf? That's a nice wee image. I can see how that's a thing to aspire tae, that grim determination and killer instinct yis see in a wolf's eye. But there's also a wee something else in that look, do yis no agree?"

"Aye," I says, shrugging. I weren't really harking him, cos I had some thinking of my own to do. A plan were taking shape in me swede.

"That other thing in the wolf's eye, I think I can say what it is, Royston. I think it's madness."

"Aye, whatever."

"Yis see, the wolf pursues a thing tae the grim and bitter end, I believe—his end and that of the thing, whatever it may be. But we're no like that, are we, Royston? Human beings are better than that. See, where the wolf hasnae any choice in the matter, your human being has moments where he can step back and see what it is that he's up tae. He can see his madness. And do yis ken what I'm doing right now, Royston? I'm seeing mine. I'm looking at what ah've been doing since…since Scott died, crashing aroond and trying tae find someone tae blame for it, letting folks take advantage ae mah vulnerable state and plant ideas aboot monsters in mah heed. But there isnae any such thing as monsters, is there? All we've got is human beings with problems in their heeds. Aye, it's high time I should—"

"Fuckin' shut up a min, will yers?" I says. "I'm tryin' to think."

"Och, ah'm sorry, I wis just saying that ah think I ought tae sober up noo, clean up mah act and move oan. Och, look at the damage ah've done alreedy, charging aroond like a luna—"

"Werewolves," I says. "Aye, fuckin' hell…what a fuckin' top idea. See—give yerself a moment and you can think up anything. And I've gone and come up with a way to locate all the vampires and get em eradicated *once and for fuckin' all*."

"Royston, ah'm no sure I understand."

"That's cos you're a fuckin' spanner, Jock. See, what it is…"

I laid it all out for him, telling him all the official secrets about Hurk Wood and how the werewolves would come into town looking for food when the zombies ran out. So if we could get rid of all the zombies, or make the werewolves think there ain't none left, we'd be sending em townwards. "Cos werewolves are harder than vampires, right? And they hates them, meaning they'll go for them first and eradicate them all from Mangel. Can you see it now?"

Jock spent a while staring at a mark on the wall. I'd made it meself a few month back, shifting all me gear up here and scraping fuck out of the wallpaper. But summat told us I'd be hauling it all out again soon, headed for pastures posher with a gravel drive and koi in the pond. I reached in me pocket: the carp were still there. I stroked it, telling it I'd get it in some water sharpish, don't you fret. Everyone knows you can have koi out of water for fucking hours, by the way, so don't go reporting us to the NSPCC.

"Aye," says Jock, reaching into a pocket of his own and finding not a fish there but a half-bottle of Bell's. "Aye, I can see it alright. And dinnae forget aboot the full moon the neet, meaning the wolves'll be oot and the vampires'll no be so good at hiding. It's fuckin' genius, Royston. Not only that but it is touched by the delicate hand o' serendipity, making it a hundred percent fuckin' foolproof."

He twisted off the cap, downed the bottle in one and lobbed it, hitting the mark on the wall nigh on bang on.

"Come oan, we've no time tae fritter."

39

I felt a bit like Robin Hood.

This is how he must have went about his business, I thought to meself as I pulled up on the edge of Hurk Wood in the Merc. Robbing from the rich to give to the poor, I'm on about. Not that I'd be giving this little beauty to no pikey scrounger any time sharpish, but I'd certainly robbed her off of someone rich. It were the toppest motor I'd ever drove, bar none, except for your Granada Mk. II 3-litre GL. The fucking thing dripped class out of every hole. Even the fag lighter hole, which seemed to give off a certain bluish light when you sparked your fag up.

"Are yis sure aboot this, Royston?"

"Sure? It's *my* fuckin' idea, Jock. Course I'm fuckin' sure."

"Aye, but it's only natural tae get cold feet. Especially when we've great and dangerous deeds such as these aheed o' yis."

"For fuck sake, Jock, my feet is toasty like a fuckin' spud out the microwave, and with plenty o' beans atop it. And cheese. I ain't having none o' that lettuce and shite, mind. You got any Scotch eggs?"

"Ah'm no on about food, Royston."

"Shut the fuck up, then. You got them spades?"

"Aye, ah've got the spade. What I mean is your demeanour. Yis have been different ever since we left the vampires' nest back there."

"I ain't different. How am I different?"

"Youse just seem a wee bit distant."

"Distant?" I looked around, in case I were missing summat or he were talking to someone else. But there were no one—just me and Jock, separated only by the most finely wrought hand-brake you ever seed. "Fuck you on about, distant?" I says. "I'm two fuckin' foot away from yer." I opened the door.

"Ah dinnae mean spatial distance," he says, getting out of his side with the spade and pickaxe. "Ah mean...och, just forget it."

"Forget what?"

"What ah wis sayin'. Oh, I see what yis mean—yis are pretending yis have forgot already."

"Jock, I honestly dunno what the fuck you're on about. I'm trying to concentrate on other shite here, in case you ain't noticed. *Important* shite, get it? And I wants you concentrating and all."

I popped the boot and got my gear out. We'd stopped off on the way here to pick it up. Luckily no one were in Lionel's Hardware at the time. Fucking loud burglar alarm, mind. And Jock got some glass down the back of his trolleys from the window. Served him right for being such a fat Scottish spanner.

"Are yis sure yis ken how to operate that thing?" says Jock, watching us setting up the chainsaw.

"Jock, what I dunno about chainsaws you can write on the inside of a book."

Jock thought about that. "Can yis?"

"Aye, I think so. Or summat."

I checked the petrol: half full. Enough for what we had in mind. And if I ran out, I could get Jock to suck some out of the

Merc tank. Not too much, mind—you can damage the system if the fuel gets too low. Plus he'd like as not start swallering it, the fucking pisshead. I started her up. "Fuckin' smart, eh?" I says, waving it around in front of him. I swung it a little bit close and nearly clipped him.

"Aaarrgh!" he blares, making a fucking meal out of a mountain. "For fuck's sake, yis have cut mah nose!"

"Have I fuck," I says, stopping the motor. "I were nowhere near yer."

"Yis have fuckin' cut it! *Fuck*..."

"Let's have a gander...ah, right, that's just a normal nose-bleed."

"It's a fuckin' *chainsaw bleed*, you stupid eejit!"

I paused a moment, then got the starter cord ready. "You fuckin' call us stupid again and I'll do it for real, right?"

"Yis have done it for real already!"

"Just don't call us stupid."

"Yis *are* fuckin' stupid. Yis cannae even identify a fuckin' chainsaw. That's a hedge trimmer, you fuckin' stupid eejit."

I started the motor again. I weren't standing for this. I didn't give a shite if we was acting like a partnership here, and I felt sorry for the barmy old fucker—no one talks to us like that and gets away with it. I raised the chainsaw about shoulder-high and bored down on him.

He stopped fucking around with his hooter and gave us his undivided. Behind him were a wall of thicket all clogged up and brambular, either side being his only hope of escape. And I had em both covered, me being so fast over forty yard and him fat. He started one way, I mirrored him. After a couple of them, he tried a dummy but slipped on some dog shite and went arsewise. I knelt down beside him and went to cut him in half. Summat at the back of me swede were trying to tell us to stop and have a think about this, but I couldn't hear it too well. It got drowned out by the noise of the 50cc motor.

I went down.

In a backwise direction, luckily for meself and Jock, otherwise I would have fell atop him with the chainsaw raging away between us. But it went sideways and hit the ground next to my left ear, the motor idling. "Ahh," I says. Cos summat were sticking out of me neck.

"STAY ON THE GROUND," someone were shouting through a megaphone. "WE ARE THE POLICE. DO NOT MOVE. KEEP YOUR HANDS VISIBLE."

"I'll have to move one of em, cos it ain't visible!" I shouts. "It's behind me back."

"WELL, LEAVE IT THERE!"

"But you says—"

"NEVER MIND WHAT I SAID. JUST KEEP STILL AND LESS OF THE LIP."

"I ain't lippin' yer. I gotta move me paw—I got pins and fuckin' needles in it."

"DO I LOOK LIKE I GIVE A TOSS?"

"I don't fuckin' know—I can't see yer from this angle."

"WELL..."

"Make up yer fuckin' swede."

"SHUT UP. I'M THINKIN'."

While the copper thought, Jock sprang into action. Sprang ain't the right word, picturing it in me memory, but he got up in his own time and rifled down his pants for summat. He found it after a bit and got it out.

"Fuck's that?" I says.

"It's just a wee hand grenade."

"A wee…"

He pulled the pin and lobbed the grenade at where the cunts were, dropping the pin by my feet. I watched the grenade sail through the air, then realised that the coppers weren't in that direction after all. I also noticed that it weren't a grenade sailing through the air but a pin. I looked by my feet.

"Fuck sake, Jock!"

"Och, sorry. It's a long time since ah did this."

I got the grenade and went to lob it behind us, expecting it to blow my arm off and kill us both dead. But I got it airborne, giving it a bit of spin so it'd shift faster and get as far away as poss before it went off. I'm sharp like that.

"IF THAT'S A GRENADE YOU'VE JUST THROWN AT US, I CAN TELL YOU THAT IT AIN'T GONNA DO MUCH. IT'S AN OLD ONE FROM WORLD WAR II AND—"

I hadn't ever felt a grenade go off before. Feels like a big giant kicking the ground from underneath, like he's pissed off with all the racket and giving you a polite warning before he comes up and knocks heads. It threw us up in the air a few inches or so, nigh on winding us when I touched down again. Then came the soil, loads of little bits of it raining down all over us and going in my eyes and gob. Jock were sucking my neck.

"The fuck do you think you're—"

"Keep still," he says, taking a little break. "And dinnae talk. Yis have been hit with a wee tranquiliser dart."

"Fuckin' get him out, then!"

"Ah said keep still. The more yis struggle, the more the poison will get roond yis bloodstream. Just lie back, relax and picture a nice thing. Otherwise yis will become paralysed long enough for the next wave ae polis tae pick yis up for murder." He started sucking again.

Fuck. What were happening here? One minute I got the plan of the century in the offing, next minute the shite hits the spinner, and I'm staring Mangel Jail up the fucking nozzers. But Jock were gonna sort it for us, aye. Even though I'd just been set on chainsawing him in half, he were rolling back time and making it as if that fucking spiked dart hadn't hit us. But this were my only chance, and I had to make it work, so I done like he says and pictured a nice thing. I breathed deep and relaxed my body and conjured up the nicest possible thing I could, and it were Kerry.

She had her kit off. I'd shagged her alright down by the river, and she'd kept some of it on there, us being in public and her a class bit of woman, but here she'd gone all the way, right down to actually taking off her knickers instead of me just pulling the gusset aside. I fondled her hair and let her do what she were doing, which were kissing my neck and giving us a massive love bite. I felt meself stirring. Stirring like a fucking baseball bat.

"Could yis no feel yisself up like that, Royston? Ah'm no comfortable with it."

"Eh? Get the fuck away from us, you bent fuckin' bandido."

"As I explained tae yis, ah'm—"

"Just forget it, right?" I says, getting up and adjusting meself. "I ain't paralysed. Fuck sake…"

He spat a few times and wiped his lips. "What's the matter, Royston? Yis look ashamed o' yis self."

I spun on him and thought about kicking him in the swede but noticed a cloud of dust appearing down there on the horizon, coming from town.

"That's the second wave," says Jock. "We've no time tae lose."

"Aye, but…" I looked at the dense wall of thorns we'd pulled up in front of. Seemed to stretch a hundred yard either direction without a way in. Jock started up the chainsaw.

I flinched away, thinking he were after payback for me trying to slice him just now, but he were more interested in the wall of thorns. He stuck the chainsaw into it and cut through it like it were butterscotch ice cream and the chainsaw were a red-hot knife. Fuck knows why it had to be butterscotch flavour, but that's what popped into my head. Within about ten seconds, he had an opening and a big blob of thicket lying on the dirt in front of it.

"Take off the handbrake," he says, cutting the chainsaw motor and nodding at the Merc.

"Eh?" I says. "That's fuckin' hundreds-of-pounds-worth of top-quality British engineering, that is. I ain't gonna—"

"Release the fuckin' brake or...so help me God, I'll ram this wee bad boy up yer jacksy and pick yer teeth wi' it," he says, holding up a wooden stake.

I thought about it and released the handbrake, stifling a little sob as the Merc trundled townward.

"Come oan, for fuck's sake!" he yells, sticking his head out of the hole he were now in.

I took one last look at the growing dust cloud on the horizon, and the Merc that were picking up pace towards it, and followed him.

40

"Can I ask yis sumthin?"

This were a new part of Hurk Wood. Not that they'd just created it. To look at the place, it were like it had been here since dinosaur times—oak trees getting bigger and fatter, ferns growing denser, little wossnames with red berries growing weirder, and all the while no cunt venturing in it, besides me and Jock just now. Not that I were a cunt.

"Aye," I says, sparking up a fag. "Go on, then."

"Wis yis truly oan the—"

"In English, please, for fuck's fuckin' sake."

"Right. Were youse truly on the point of quartering me with that hedge trimmer?"

"It's a fuckin' chainsaw."

"Aye, but were yis?"

Mind you, we wasn't lost. I got a feel for this place, no matter what part of it I'm in nor whether or not I been in that bit before. It were like Hurk Wood were my homeland, the place I knowed better than any other, without even having to look at a map nor grow up there. I knowed each trail through the trees, each stream, gulley, and clearing. Each place of burial.

"I don't reckon I were trying to quarter you, no," I says. "I reckon I would of just chopped yers in two."

"But why?"

"Jock, you got a lot of flesh there. It'd take fuckin' yonks to cut you in eight."

"No, I mean why would yis kill us? What have ah done tae youse?"

I sucked on the fag so hard that the tip glowed about an inch long, pointing the way forwards through the dark like a burning arrow. I felt me neck: it hurt like billy-o and were bleeding still, but I were more concerned with the fact I had Jock's spit all over the area. Made us want to vom just thinking about it.

"I dunno, Jock."

"Yis dinnae ken why yis wanted to kill us?"

"No, I mean I dunno why I wanted to kill yers."

"That's what I...look, ah'm worried about yis, Royston. A man who tries to kill another without knowing the reason, he's no a well man. Do yis mind if ah ask yis a frank question?"

"Aye, go on."

"Have yis a history o' mental illness?"

I thought about it for a moment. "Is you asking have *I* got a history of it? Or Frank?"

"Who the fuck's Frank?"

"You says you wanted to ask a question about him."

"No, I...see, this is another symptom of it, Royston. I think your heed needs looking at by a professional. It's no making the right connections, linking one meaning to another and giving yis the full picture o' the world around yis. Dinnae take this wrong, but I believe yis are *wired* wrong."

"Hark at you. I don't even fuckin' know what you're saying half the fuckin' time."

"That's another thing—yis are always sweering."

"I fuckin' ain't."

"See? Yis are sweering the whole time, and yis dinnae even fuckin' ken it."

"There you go with this Ken feller again. Who the fuck is he? Is he a mate o' Frank's or what?"

"Ah'm no trying to have a pop at yis with this, Royston, but—"

"Better fuckin' not be. I'll pop yer fuckin' teeth out."

"But ah'm just worried. Yis and me are mates, Royston. I dinnae want to see yis suffering, be it physical or mental."

I smoked the last of the fag and stubbed it underfoot, looking around. Me ears and nostrils was twitching. Also me eyelids, and me fists was clenching and unclenching. I were coming alive, that's what I were. I were in my element, senses waking up and picking out everything around.

"Will yis just promise me one thing, Royston?"

"What, fuck sake?"

"Will yis seek medical help? After we've eradicated the vampires, I mean."

"Medical help don't do a man no good, Jock. It keeps you down and stops you being what yer meant to be."

"And what are yis meant tae be?"

"Right here."

"Yis are meant tae be right here?"

"No, I mean it's right here. The spot I been looking for."

"What?" Jock went all confused, looking around him and expressing surprise at every turn. "Erm, what exactly were we... erm..."

"The plan, Jock, remember? We dig up a zombie, parade it around a bit so it gets the werewolves hungry and following, then we cart it back into town, leaving a nice trail o' zombie scent for the werewolves to follow, and Bob's yer fuckin' granddad."

"Och, of course. Look at me—ah'd forget mah ain heed if it weren't attached tae mah...erm..." He felt all around his shoulders and neck.

"It's here, Jock," I says, guiding his paws to the swede in question. "Got it now?"

"Aye, thanks, Royston. As ah wis sayin', ah'd forget mah ain—"

"Yeah, I get the fuckin' picture. Do a bit o' pickaxing here, eh. It's only about two foot down, so go easy."

"But why are yis selecting this particular spot, Royston? What makes yis think there's a zombie doon there?"

Between you and meself, it were cos this were where I buried Sal, former bird of mine who came to an early and sad demise. It weren't a proper funeral, and I didn't put up a cross nor nothing, but I were sure this were the spot. I could recall them big branches hanging down overhead as I spaded soil onto white skin, and the fallen tree over there where I'd sat and had a fag break. Or maybe it were the Muntons who I'd buried here, along with that hitman the one time. Or someone else entirely. Either way, I just knowed I'd buried someone here and that he'd do for a zombie. "I just know," I says to Jock. "I got a sixth sense."

"Sixth sense means you've a hunch, Royston. Ah'm no sure that's enough basis for me to start digging. It's too big a wood tae be relying on sixth sense."

"It's me fuckin' seventh sense, then. Just trust us, fuck sake."

"Royston, ah'm no feeling too—"

"Ooh look—sun's gone down. Vampires'll be out and about by now, drinking the blood of innocents."

"Ah'll fuckin' *eradicate* them evil bastarts!"

He attacked the ground like it were Count Dracula, and him Dr. Van Morrison, or whatever the other bloke were called—the one who kept trying to kill him, and Peter Cushion played in them films.

I wandered off for a scout around, harkening back to the start of all this, two day ago when I first got the idea of going on holiday and went looking for a hearse in that place where they keeps one. I'd been convinced that he were Count Dracula, the one I'd clocked in there and had a little standoff with, me dinking him and him going down. But I suppose it weren't. In the cold light of day, when you've stepped away from it all and let your brain kick in, you see things for what they truly is and that you was mad to believe a thing. It's like me getting the idea into my head that Jock were the Highlander. I mean, for fuck's fucking sake, a fat Scottish burger van man being an immortal superhero on the quiet? How fucking insane an idea can a man have? But I were straight on it now, at least.

It's *me* who's the Highlander.

"Greetings, Highlander."

That's why that bloke were here again, the Connery one with the funny hat who'd turned up earlier when that lamp post hit us in the face. I felt my nose. Still knacked summat chronic. Quite a few other parts of us did and all, now I came to feel em. Best not to, like as not.

"Alright, Sean," I says.

"I am not Sean Connery, though I appear to be he. This is merely the most apt guise."

"Aye, and I ain't the Highlander, though I appear to be he. This is merely the most…what were it? Summat about guys? You an arse bandit or summat?"

"I come to offer guidance, Highlander. A wise word, affably voiced, can turn a harebrained scheme into a master plan."

I felt my scalp. That hurt and all. "What kind of a scheme did you just call it?"

"A name is just a label—it is not the thing itself. The thing itself can be expressed only in terms of what it is."

"Aye, but is you sayin' I got a hairy brain or summat?"

"That is an interesting image, Highlander, but no. I came here only to make a suggestion. You have become embroiled, Highlander. Once again, others have pulled you into their orbits with their schemes and plots, spinning you around and trying to turn your heft and your brutishness to their own ends, be they nefarious or otherwise. But I will not waste my breath encouraging you to back out of said schemes. It is too late for that. Forces are at large. Planets are in motion and—"

"Fuckin' spit it out, for fuck's fuckin' sake," I says, sparking another smoke. "I ain't got all day and night. I got a zombie over yonder to dig up."

Connery took off his hat and plucked out the feather, turning it and smoothing it out between his long fingers. Then he put that feather back, checking it were secure. He put the hat back on. I weren't watching him, mind. I were looking at a toadstool at the foot of a nearby tree. It were a massive red one with white dots, like you sees certain garden gnomes sitting atop with their fishing rods. I wondered if there might be some gnomes out here. They had to have em somewhere, after all, otherwise we wouldn't have statues of em in people's gardens. Or maybe they existed once and was now extinct. But we had statues of em, so we still recalled em. That's what you needs if you wants to be recalled by folks: a statue of yourself.

"My suggestion to you is this," says the feller. "From the most hopeless course of action, from the bear trap jaws of disaster that await your inevitable tread, success may be salvaged. A ship is never lost until the last sailor jumps overboard, Highlander. Entire continents have been discovered by those who sought only survival."

"You what?" I says, cos I were still thinking about the gnomes and not paying him no heed. But when I turned, he were gone, no trace of him left besides a hint of cigarillo smoke. I finished me fag and set off back to Jock, kicking the toadstool to shite as I went past it. Gnomes are cunts anyhow. My old next-door neighbour had one and it were pulling a moonie at you. That's how they got extinct, like as not: pulling moonies at the wrong fellers. Fellers like meself who won't stand for it.

Jock were pulling summat out of a big hole in the ground when I got back to him.

It were an arm.

41

They says the hair carries on growing after a person has carked it, making them look different after you digs them up. Even dead birds, like Sal, who always had nice silky black hair on her swede and between her legs and under her pits when she let herself go. But not on her chin and tash area. Which were the first thing that told us that this zombie might not be her.

"Yis have done brilliant, Royston," says Jock, trying to sit the zombie up against a tree. "How yis knew this one would be under there, ah'll never ken. Seventh sense, did yis call it? Ah'll have tae look into that, aye, ah will."

Second thing to make us think it weren't her were the swede itself. I weren't 100 percent sure on the matter, but I could have swored I'd lopped hers off before burying her. Not on purpose, mind. A feller ought never to lop a bird's swede off on purpose, especially if she's dead—that would be an affront her memory, or summat. But Sal had been alive at the time, so it were alright. And this one here—who were without doubt a feller with shortish hair and a black beard and tash—he weren't decapitated at all.

"But, Royston, there's just the one thing ah have a problem with, if yis dinnae mind me sayin'. See, a zombie is an animated corpse, by most definitions. It is supposed tae move and walk about, is it no? This one here, he's no going anywheer."

And it weren't one of the Muntons neither, nor the hitman, nor other sundry folk I'd had to stow up here over the years, them being cunts who'd asked for it, and me not wanting to see the inside of Mangel Jail. See, each one of them had gone ground-ward in a piecemeal manner, meaning I'd chopped em up and buried em a piece hither and a piece thither then gone home for a big meal. And this one here, he had all his arms and legs and everything. And like I says, he were with head. But still there were summat familiar about him.

I crouched down and started brushing the dirt off his face, trying to get a better idea of him.

"Is that what yis have tae do?" says Jock, squatting the other side and getting to work on the dead one's cheek. "Yis have tae rub them, like when Aladdin is trying tae get the genie out ae the lamp?"

"Fuck you on about, Jock? I'm tryin' tae think here."

"Ah'm sorry, Royston, but we need tae move things along here. This corpse here disnae seem tae be a zombie."

"Zombie?"

"Aye. Remember? The plan was tae lure the werewolves back towards toon by—"

"Oh, aye…yeah, this un here is a zombie alright. He's just playin' dead."

"Is that so? But I thought zombies were deed anyhoo? So why would he have tae pretend tae be it?"

"Don't you know nuthin'? Zombies is *undead*, not dead. See?"

"Ah," says Jock, looking at the zombie with a newfound respect. "That explains it, then. Ah must say, he's a fine example of a zombie. Yis expect them tae be falling apart, worms in theer eye sockets and that."

"Aye, well, it don't always work like that," I says, getting hold of his legs and dragging him.

"Does it no?" says Jock, getting him by the wrists. The zombie were a dead weight, but we was both strong lads, me and Jock, and by the time he spoke again, we was halfway back to the Merc, walking along that path next to the gulley. "How does it work, then?"

"Never you mind," I says. Cos my thoughts was off elsewhere now, picturing the Merc and how I could customise her a bit. Window stickers, one either side at the top of the windscreen, ROYSTON and KERRY. Then I recalled how we'd waved goodbye to that motor a while back, letting off the hand brake and sending her off copperward. What a fucking waste of a beautiful motor. A felt a pang in me ticker just thinking about it, like summat had fell out of my hopes-and-dreams bag and I'd never get it back. I let go one of the zombie's ankles and felt in my pocket: the koi were still there, heart beating and gills trembling. Least I still had him. I stroked him.

"Good idea," says Jock behind us. "Let's have a wee breather."

Up ahead I could see blue flashing lights through the trees.

Loads of em.

"ROYSTON BLAKE AND JAMES McRAE," a loudspeaker blares again but with a different voice this time. "YOU ARE SUR-ROUNDED. DOWN YOUR WEAPONS AND COME OUT WITH YOUR HANDS UP."

I turned to Jock. He'd picked up the zombie and got him in a piggyback. Behind him I could see more blue light through the trees. I could see em on all sides.

"Do yis trust us?" he says, getting us by the arm.

"Eh?"

"Just answer the fuckin' question, would yis? Do yis trust us or what?"

I looked into his eyes, trying to get the measure of his mood. The zombie's head were just behind his, and both of em were looking back at us. I couldn't decide which one were uglier. "Aye," I says, "I suppose I does."

"BLAKEY," the loudspeaker were blaring in yet another different voice this time. It were a voice what got my attention, making us turn away from Jock and look up at the stars, feeling summat warm and familiar getting going somewhere within my rib cage. Also I felt meself stirring slightly in the groin area. "IT'S RACHE HERE. YOU'VE GOTTA LISTEN TO ME. PLEASE COME OUT BEFORE ANYONE ELSE GETS—"

Jock got us in a bear hug and threw me, him, and the zombie into the gulley.

ASYLUM SEEKERS TAKEN INTO POLICE PROTECTION

Following intelligence received by police, thirty-five members of the Estravian community have been rounded up into a van and taken away.

"We did it for their own good," said PC Tom Mard, officer in charge of the operation. "We have reason to believe that certain factions are intent on launching an offensive against these people, and we can't have that. If anyone is to launch an offensive around here, it is us, the police. And we will do it against anyone who breaks the law in this town."

"I'd just like to point out that no wrongdoing has been committed by these Estravians," interrupted Sergeant Lee Plim, coordinator of the "Welcome to Mangel" campaign. "Our priority is their welfare and making sure no harm comes to them. They are not being held against their will. They are at a secret location, under constant surveillance, and with sympathetic officers on hand to service their every need. Except for TV. For some reason we can't get the aerials to work at the new station, so they'll have to do without for now."

Asked who was behind this proposed "offensive," and if it was the fugitive Royston Blake, Plim remained tight-lipped. "But I will say this," he said, loosening his lips, "there are vulnerable people in this town, and I don't just mean these immigrants. I'm talking about people who have weak minds, who have had their brains softened by birth, or substance abuse, or personal tragedy, or whatever, and they are being preyed on. Certain people are using these vulnerable souls for their own ends, feeding them a lot of superstitious claptrap that is lapped up by the vulnerable ones. Because we all like to believe stuff, don't we? Everyone likes to think that impossible things exist and that magic demons and whatever are responsible for the bad luck that happens to us. But we don't need all that rubbish, is what I'm trying to say. If we want to believe in summat, we should look at ourselves. Look at one another and find the goodness that is in each of our hearts no matter what colour our skin or what kind of gibberish our tongues speak. So let's throw all the superstition out, join hands, and all march together towards a brighter future."

42

One of Jock's legs had twisted right round. It made you wince just looking at it. And harking him wail like a grief-strook wife as I tried setting it straight again made it hard for us to concentrate on the matter in hand. Surgeons don't have to put up with this shite, does they?

"Fuckin' hell," I says, nodding at summat behind him. "The fuck's that?"

"Eh?"

"Him there. It's a fuckin' vampire, ennit?"

"Wha..." he says, taking the whisky bottle away from his mouth. He'd spilt the stuff all down his top and in the water. Mind you, I didn't think he could fit any more in him. "Wheer is the wee bastart? I'll fuggn...*hic*..."

I got hold his knee again and had a go at straightening it. It cracked and crunched but got no more nearer being straight. Mind you, my distracting technique had worked a fucking treat, didn't it? "Nah," I says, "you've defo fucked yer pin. You fuckin' twat."

Not that he could hark us over his own wailing.

I had a look round, trying to find answers in the environment I found meself in. That's what you have to do when you're in a

Rambo scenario. Cos that's what this were, weren't it? Pursued by cops, hiding out in the woods, dealing with serious injuries using whatever wossnames come to paw.

"This is what they used to do in the war," I says, yanking off his belt and using it to tie the stick to his leg. "Patching folks up on the move, getting em pukka again so they can get back in the saddle and blast some more cunts. It's called field surgery."

"It's no field surgery, this is called...*hic*...this is called *torture...hic...*"

I stopped and had another glance about. "Hmm, maybe you're right," I says. "Maybe this ain't field surgery. I mean, this ain't really a *field*, is it? It's the bottom of a fuckin' gulley. The same fuckin' bastard gulley that a certain Scottish *twat* made all three of us fall into." I pulled hard on the belt, making it good and tight on his knee. Mind you, I dunno me own strength sometimes. The belt strained and stretched and finally seemed to pass right through where the knee ought to be. "You got a fuckin' strange knee," I says, scratching my head.

But Jock weren't really listening. Not that he were wailing no more neither. His eyes and gob were wide, face going a sort of beetroot and vibrating slightly.

"Fuck sake, Jock," I says, turning away. "Show some fuckin' gratitude, eh."

Unlike Jock, the zombie had come out of the fall in good nick, besides a couple of rips in his togs and a bloodless graze across his forehead. But the problem now were how to get him back to Mangel, Jock having the bust leg and me not fancying doing the carting.

At the bottom of the gulley, invisible to all who pass by on the path up top, were a fast-flowing stream, and that's what we'd fell into, Jock hitting some submerged rocks and me landing atop the zombie, which he'd still been piggybacking at the time. The stream were waist-deep in the middle section, and even a strong lad like meself had trouble standing in it and keeping still against the current. I scanned around the edges, noting the fallen logs either side and the foam and scum that had built up on a little shingle shore over there. Then I looked downstream. It were fucking dark, but the moon were out, high and full, and I could have swore I gandered summat flickering a brownish silver through the trees down that way. And there's only one thing that flickers like that.

The River Clunge.

"I got a plan," I says.

"Whu? Whussa? Ah tell yis…*hic*…tell yis what, Royston, I'll tear them fuckers apart with mah bare hands, ah will…"

"Aye, fuckin' shut up for a bit, will yers?"

"Ah'm telling yis…"

"I need yer socks."

"When ah find em, ah'll…yis need mah what?"

I yanked his trainers off him before he could do anything about it and got hold of his manky socks. Not that he had many options, being as good as crippled at the minute in terms of injuries sustained and whisky necked. But my yank were too hard, or his feet too fat, so I ended up yanking the whole of him off his rocky perch and back into the rapids.

"Fuck," I barks, letting go of him and wiping my brow for a moment. Cos he'd been a cunt to haul ashore in the first place, and now I had to do him all over. But I weren't gonna let it get me down. I were Rambo here, not the fat cunt copper in the film who were after him and kept getting foiled and even more pissed off. That's how Rambo wins, ennit? He stays calm, even when he's sewing his arm up or rooting a bullet out of his side. He keeps a

cap on his emotions and lets others lose their swedes. When all
round you is losing their swedes, make sure you don't count too
many black kettles into your broth. Not before they'm hatched,
anyhow. That's what I always says. Especially in Rambo scenarios.
I reached for Jock.

"Jock?"

I moved around a bit, casting for him but grabbing only bits
of driftwood and other floating shite. I would have shouted out
to him, but I didn't want coppers up top hearing us. Fuck it, I
thought, shrugging and turning back to the zombie. Least I had
the socks, which were the main thing. I got to work.

About half an hour later, and with me sweating like a fucking pig but not complaining about it, I had a raft. It were laid
out on the shore where I'd constructed it, using about twenty
long and sturdy bits of wood, Jock's and my socks, my shirt,
my pants, and a bit of string I'd found. Truly, it were the best
fucking raft I'd ever seed. And don't go saying it were the *only*
raft I'd ever seed, cos it weren't. I just couldn't recall them others just now. I got the zombie and set him atop it, tucking his
paws and feet under bits of wood that was sticking up here and
there. I'd thought of everything, see, which is how I knowed it
were gonna go right when I cast off and launched him into the
water.

And it did.

I stood by for a moment, watching the raft find its balance
and direction. It rotated a couple of times in the shallows and
started drifting out towards the rapid part, me shaking my head
in wonder the whole while. You plan things right and know
they'll work, but it's still a marvellous thing to see em come good.
I started off after it but stopped when summat started poking us
in the hip from behind.

I stepped forwards and lashed out behind us, thinking it were Jock or perhaps a copper come sneaking up on us, but no one were there. And the poking were still going on, more in the ribs now that I were in deeper water. I felt round there and located the poking thing to be the koi carp come back to life now in the pocket of me burgundy leather and thrashing like no other. I got him out. I held him in front of us, wanting to examine him to make sure he were alright. Against all the odds, and after me ferrying him out of the water for fuck knowed how long and getting battered all over the shop when I fell down the gulley, he were still looking good as brannie. He lay still in my paws for a moment, gills going in and out slightly, scales glinting under the moonlight like gold plate and mother of pearl. He were fucking brilliant, that koi, and he'd been mine for a while. But I had to let him go.

I lowered me paws into the stream, resting him near the top until his gills filled with water and his tail started wagging. After a bit he moved off. He swam slowly downstream, his colours visible and near the surface for fucking ages, like a pot of treasure getting carted off and me not being able to do nothing about it. But maybe I could. Hang on, what the fuck were I doing, letting him go? He were *mine*, and—

"I think ah can just about hobble along oan the one leg, now ah've got used tae it," says Jock, coming out of some trees opposite and using a branch as a crutch.

"Where the fuck have you been?" I says.

"Just in these woods here. Yis have done a good job, splinting mah leg up. Mind you, do yis think yis can make me a better crutch? This one's hurting mah underarm a wee bit."

"Aye," I says, wading over to him. "That ain't a bad idea. And perhaps I could put together some sort of cripple chair. I noticed a couple of old prams up there a bit."

"Yis mean a wheelchair? People don't use the word *cripple* nae more, Royston."

But I weren't harking him no more. I were off upstream, looking for them prams. I found one right away, with bulrushes growing up through the undercarriage. Wheels was rusted to fuck, mind. I started looking for the other.

"Could I make one last request Royston?" Jock blares after us.

"Fuck sake, Jock. I'm busy. And keep the fuckin' noise down."

"Aye, and ah'm sorry. Ah just wondered where yis have stowed the zombie. Ah cannae see him."

"He's on the fuckin' raft, for fuck. You blind or summat?"

"What raft?"

"Erm..."

43

"It's no yis fault."

There is a species of moth that you only gets in Hurk Wood.
I knows it cos they taught us it at school, alongside other shite
about all being leaves on the same tree and not being able to leave
the tree else the tree carks it. This little flying fucker, so they tells
you, relies upon that selfsame tree. See, the moth lays his eggs in
the seeds of the tree, and a caterpillar hatches and grows fat by
eating them seeds, then wraps himself up in summat and fucks
off to sleep. But it ain't a parasite. The Hurk moth, it is a friend.

"What ain't my fault?"

"The zombie. It's no your fault that yis lost the fuckin' zombie."

See, after the caterpillar hatches out of his coconut and turns
into a moth, he flies on up to the branches of that same Mangel
tree he growed up on. He's wanting to lay some eggs, thereby per-
petuating his wild oats and making sure his name lives on. But
he requires seeds to do that, so he sets about making em, going
from flower to flower and spreading pollen from one to the other.
After that, and with the tree all pregnant now and seeds growing,
the moth lays his eggs. Actually, I think it's a she, what with the

egg laying and that. Mind you, the bloke moth can't be far off, cos someone must have shagged the bird for her to be popping eggs.

"How come yer sayin' it like that, then?"

"Like what?"

"*Fuckin'*. It ain't my fault I lost the *fuckin'* zombie."

"Och, that's just mah way o' speech."

"No it ain't. It means yer pissed off."

"Why should ah be pissed off? Ah'm saying it's no your fault, so—"

"Ain't my *fuckin'* fault is what you'm sayin'."

"For fuck's sake, Royston."

"Now hark at him—he's swearin' like a fuckin' pissed-up vicar now. Jock, you got summat to say, fuckin' say the fucker, eh."

So there you have it—the moth needs the tree, and the tree needs the moth. They are different wossnames who goes about their lives in different ways, and they comes from different places originally. But they've worked out a way of living side by side. They gets along alright.

Anyhow, I'm saying all this by way of letting you know what a Hurk moth is. Cos one of the fuckers had just flown into my eye, blinding us.

"*Shite*," I says, squashing the bastard against my eyelid.

"Are yis alreet?"

"Fuck does you care? I'm fuckin' *blind* here. All you gives a shite about is fuckin' zombies and rafts."

"That zombie wis our lifeline, Royston. Withoot him, how the fuck are we going tae—"

"There *ain't no fuckin' thing as zombies*, for fuck!" I shouts, glaring at him even though one of me peepers were shredded to fuck with moth dust.

Jock opened and closed his mouth then looked away. We was coming out of the woods now, having followed the stream to where it came out in the river. I bent down at the stream edge and cupped some water, washing my eye out with it as best I could. Then I blinked a few times. I were alright now.

"Tell me this," says Jock, giving us a hand up. "If there isnae such a thing as zombies, who wis that we dug up back there and lugged doon here? Who was that yis put on a raft?"

I thought about it. "Oh, aye," I had to say finally. "I forgot about that."

"Ah thought as much. But dinnae fret over it, Royston. All of us is prone tae a weak moment now and then. The trick is tae no let the seeds o' doobt take root in yis heed. Always remember the mission. And that mission is tae purge this toon of a menace we have uncovered. Ah'm talking about eradicating vampires, Royston. Are yis with me?"

"Eh? Aye."

"Are yis *with* me?"

"I says *aye*, fuck sake."

"Good. Come oan."

"But we've lost the fuckin' zombie, Jock. That zombie were our whole plan, for fuck. Woss we meant to do now?"

"Dinnae youse fret."

"Dinner? I am fuckin' starvin', I gotta admit."

"Och, there'll be time for feastin' after the job is done, Royston. When youse and me are done, they'll be layin' on a huge banquet for us in toon hall. And after that, with oor bellies full and all vampires eradicated from the entire region, that's when the statues'll go up. Youse and me, Royston, side by side up top o' the High Street. In granite."

"But—"

"The final push, Royston," he says, setting off on the river-bank towards town. "Are yis ready for the final push or what?"

"Aye," I says, going after him. "Fuck it."

44

Took us about two hours to yomp back into town, Jock with his busted pin. We hit Ditchcroft about eleven of the evening, by my estimation, or twenty-seven hundred hours in army lingo. A good survival person, like Rambo or meself, can tell the time just by looking at the night sky, seeing which part of it is blacker than others. Also the clouds. "You got the time, Jock?" I says, wanting to have my workings-out confirmed. He had a watch, see.

"Aye. Three thirty in the wee hours."

"Bollocks is it."

"Och, it is."

"It ochin' ain't. Your ochin' watch must be busted."

"Ah'm no using mah watch. Ah can tell the time just by examining the night sky."

"Yeah, so can I. Them clouds up there, and that fuckin' dark patch over yonder—it all adds up to eleven o' fuckin' clock."

"Clouds? What the fuck are yis on aboot, Royston? All yis have tae do is look at the stars. It's no that difficult."

"Go on then—woss it say on yer watch?"

"Och, come oan, we've no need tae argue aboot this. Youse and me are oan the cusp o' great—"

"Woss the watch say?"

"For fuck's sake…it says three thirty-five. Happy?"

"See?"

"See what? Are youse bonkers or sumthin?"

"Hang on—three thirty-five? How'd you say that in army lingo?"

"Army lingo? What the fuck is—"

"You know, like thirty-eight thousand hours and that."

"Och, yis mean military time? Zero three thirty-five, we used tae say."

"Aye, that's what I meant. I only knows army time, see. When I says eleven o'clock, I meant what you just says."

"Is that so? And what did ah just say?"

"Erm, zero…zero hours and…erm…fuck, look at that."

"Don't youse try and change the fuckin' subject."

"I ain't. Jock, you'd best have a look over—"

"Ah'm no fallin' for that shite again. Youse started this, and youse can fuckin'—"

The bullet hit him right in the swede, pinging it sideways in the manner of a golf ball hit off a tee by someone fucking good at golf. Except his body stayed attached to it, yanking it off into the scrub like a bag of dirty laundry lobbed off a moving train. I went down.

"I FUCKIN' GOT HIM."

"YOU NEVER GOT HIM, JONE. YOU HIT THE SCOTCH ONE."

"I NEVER. LOOK, BLAKEY'S GONE DOWN."

"YEAH, FOR SELF-PROTECTION. THE SCOTCH ONE WENT FLYING INTO THAT BUSH THERE."

"I REALISE THAT, PLIM, BUT IT'S COS I GOT EM BOTH. IT IS POSSIBLE TO GET TWO—"

"YOU NEVER GOT EM BOTH. I WARNED YOU ABOUT THIS—YOU SHOULD OF BRUNG THE MARKSMAN. YOU'RE ALWAYS GOING OFF ON ONE, INSISTING ON DOING IT YOUR—"

"FUCK THE MARKSMAN. THIS IS *MY* KILL. I MEAN, MY...ERM..."

I were on me belly, breathing hard but trying to make it so I were a big, still thing, like a dead cow or summat. That's what good actors does in films—imagining like they'm trees or badgers or whatever, putting emselves in the swede of that thing and trying to work out what it might be feeling. A dead cow wouldn't be feeling much besides a bit of sadness, I started thinking, but by then I realised my mistake—you don't get cows down here on Ditchcroft. But it were too late—I were a cow. And if I changed into summat else now, like a couple of bags of fly-tipped rubbish, they'd fucking surely notice. I'm on about Plim and Jonah, on the megaphone across the river there, although I think it were only Jonah meant to be using it.

"ROYSTON BLAKE, YOU ARE UNDER A REST," they hollers. "YOU ARE UNDER EVEN MORE OF A REST THAT JUST NOW, UP IN HURK WOOD. THIS IS A MASSIVE REST NOW, BLAKE, AND YOU ARE SO FAR UNDER IT THAT YOU CAN'T EVEN—"

"IT DON'T MEAN THAT."

"WHAT?"

"IT'S *ARREST*, NOT—"

"WOULD YOU JUST SHUT UP? WHO'S THE INSPECTOR HERE? WHO'S THE SERGEANT?"

"RANK DON'T COME INTO IT. AN OFFICER IS ALWAYS OBLIGED TO POINT OUT POTENTIALLY DANGEROUS—"

"RANK *DO* COME INTO IT. I COULD FUCKING *FIRE* YOU RIGHT NOW, YOU LITTLE TWERP."

"LOOK, JUST LET US HAVE A GO. I'VE BEEN TRAINED IN THIS, JONE. I BEEN COMMENDED FOR MY EMPATHY SKILLS."

"EMPATHY SKILLS? WHAT GOOD IS EMPATHY SKILLS WHEN YOU GOT A MANIAC ON THE LOOSE?"

"YOU WANNA CATCH HIM, DON'T YOU?"

"YEAH, BUT—"

"YOU LET HIM GET AWAY NOW, THERE'S NO TELLIN' HOW MUCH BLOOD MIGHT GET SHED."

"GO ON THEN. BUT YOU'D BEST NOT FUCK IT UP."

"WHAT, LIKE YOU DID?"

"I NEVER FUCKED NOTHING UP. WHAT ABOUT YOU, GETTIN' THAT RACHEL BIRD INVOLVED BACK THERE IN THE WOODS? FAT LOT O' GOOD SHE DONE."

"I DUNNO ABOUT THAT. I STILL THINK SHE'S THE KEY TO HIM."

"WHAT THE FUCK ARE YOU ON ABOUT?"

"JUST GIVE US THE MEGAPHONE."

They stopped their blaring for a moment, and I took my opportunity, turning from a cow into Rambo and darting bushwise where Jock had gone. But I got it wrong and turned into an elephant by accident, not even noticing the bench there and going right over it, knacking fuck out of me shins and landing facewise in the thorns.

"Aaarrggh!" I yells.

"BLAKE? WE CAN HEAR YOU. WHERE HAVE YOU GONE? PLIM HERE HAS GOT SOME SYMPATHY FOR YER, SO—"

"EMPATHY."

"THAT'S WHAT I FUCKIN' SAID."

"NO, YOU SAID—"

Making matters worser, I couldn't find Jock. You could make out the dent in the bush where he'd hit it and everything but no sign of the fat bastard himself. A patch of grass behind it were a bit wet, mind. I took my paw out of it and held it up to the moonlight.

Red.

"Jock?" I says, looking all around.

"BLAKE?"

A bullet whizzed past my head, making a whining noise like one of them fireworks that you can launch at old people out for a walk to shit em up.

"JONAH, FOR FUCK SAKE. PUT THE GUN DOWN."

"I THINK I GOT HIM."

I scratched me swede and shook it, making sure he hadn't. Seemed fine to me. I got up and pegged it around to the other side of Ditchcroft, keeping to the ditch. I had to slow to a trot after forty yard, but that were alright, cos that ditch were full up of old bikes and shopping trolleys, and I kept stumbling over em, knacking me shins even further and also other bits, like me hips and elbows—and knee—when my foot found a massive pothole and went right in it, swallowing me pin right up to the bollocks, hurting one of em a bit.

"Fuckin' shit," I wanted to holler, but kept it in me swede. Coppers was all around, two or three posses of em, poking around Ditchcroft with their dogs and their torches.

"Did you hear that?" one of em shouts, a bit too near for my liking. "He just shouted 'fuckin' shit.'"

"Did he?"

"Yeah. You deaf or summat?"

Charlie Williams

"No, I heard it. Sounded like 'suckin' shit' to me, though."

"Why the fuck would he say 'suckin' shit'?"

"Fuck ought I to know? Maybe he's sucking some shit or sum-mat?"

I were freaking out a bit now, what with me pin stuck down the hole and waggling around in an open space down there. I hates having a bit of meself in a space I dunno what else is in. Could be anything down there, like a giant scorpion. Or a zombie. I thrashed around even harder, picturing the fucker getting hold of us by the ankle and taking a massive chomp out of my calf. But I couldn't get me pin out, no matter what. The hole seemed to be getting even bigger, soil and bits of wood under it crumbling away all the while, me sinking lower and lower like I were in quick-sand, reaching round for summat to hold on to and finding only a rusted old pogo stick jammed between a couple of bits of scaf-folding. I tried hauling meself up on it, ignoring the helicopter hovering overhead that were tracing the route of the ditch with a searchlight. In about five seconds it'd find us, and the cunt up there would have a rifle, and he'd take a potshot at us.

Unless I lobbed summat at him, like in Rambo. But what?

I yanked even harder on the pogo stick, finally getting it free. Then I recalled how I were meant to be hauling meself up on it, not shaking it loose with a view to chucking it.

I fell through the hole.

45

Felt like ages I were falling for.

Some things flashed through me swede during that time. My life, for example. But also the whole of *Rocky V*. Which were odd, cos I'd never truly liked that film. It's alright to watch a few times a year, but it ain't up there at the top of the tree in terms of film history, like the other four is, rubbing shoulders with the likes of *The Good, the Bad and the Ugly*, *Heartbreak Ridge*, and *Emmanuelle*. And that's cos Rocky himself ain't a boxer in it.

He ain't doing what he does best.

In *Rocky V*, right, Rocky has been told he can't carry on boxing, cos of his manky eye. Apollo, Clubber Lang, and Ivan Drago punched so much shite out of him that he's now got a rare eye disease that hardly no one gets. It's called triple vision, and it got going while he were fighting Drago in the previous one. "I sees three of the fuckers out there," he says to Paulie and Duke between rounds, and they tells him to hit the one in the middle. Which works, cos he wins the fight, but it ain't no way to carry on boxing. What if the other boxers gets wise to it and shuffles the cards on him so he dunno which one of the three they is? So no, boxing's over for Rocky, and he has to move out to the old slum where he came from, although it looks like a fucking nice area compared to Norbert Green. Or parts of Muckfield. But he's hit rock bottom.

And it's because he ain't boxing.

So this new boxer turns up, a young and hungry fighter with a kitbag and a top mullet hairdo, like the one in *Rocky III* in the arcade. He is called Tommy Gunn, and he wants Rocky to be his trainer. Rocky don't wanna at first, thinking that the kid is a bit of a twat and not worth the bother. But Tommy turns him around, making him see how he has got potential and ain't a twat after all. So Rocky takes him on, guiding him all the way to the world title. But somewhere along the way, Rocky has gone off the rails. He's enjoying himself, but he's turned into a bit of a cunt, and he don't even notice how Adrian and Rocky Junior is having problems of their own. And when Tommy turns on him and wants to fight him, he's hit rock bottom again.

Again, cos he ain't boxing. He ain't doing what he were borned to do.

Like I says, all this were passing through me swede as I fell down that hole in Ditchcroft, picking up cobwebs and spiders but not hitting rock bottom meself. I realised that the longer I fell, the harder it would be when I touched down, but I weren't fretting over that. I were fretting over Rocky and the problems he were having with Tommy Gunn and his family and fucking everything. I were about to cark it, like as not, but all I knowed were that I'd die in vain if I didn't sort this shite out for Rocky. I had to find out for him where he'd gone wrong and somehow tell him.

"It is not about Rocky, Highlander," says the Connery feller. He were falling right next to me, matching my pace. "It's about you. The *Rocky V* film has arisen in your mind because it has parallels with your own situation. In the travails of Rocky Balboa, there is a lesson to be learned."

"What the fuck do you know?" I says, getting a bit of dirt out of me gob. "You ain't even seen *Rocky V*."

"How do you know I haven't?"

"Cos...I dunno, I just seem to know."

"Part of me has seen it, Highlander. One facet of me has indeed wasted those particular two hours of my life."

"What the fuck's you doing down here, though?"

"Why, I'm here to guide you through your analysis of *Rocky V*, of course. This is an important moment for you."

"But..."

"Come on, you're halfway there. Rocky has ceased doing that which he does best—boxing. What is it that *you* do best, Highlander?"

"What's that got to do with shite? I ain't gone off the rails like him."

"Have you not?"

"No, I fuckin' ain't. Look at me—I finally found the love of my life, and she's gonna get wedded to us. I got a fuckin' koi carp—summat I always wanted and ain't never got me paws on. Erm..."

"You let the carp go, remember?"

"Oh, aye. Shite."

"What else have you got?"

"Look, me swede's gone blank, but it don't mean I ain't got some decent shite."

"Very well. What have you been doing these past couple of days?"

"Wossit to you?"

"Nothing at all, but it is much to you."

"I been, erm..."

"Eradicating vampires?"

"I done a bit o' that, aye. But I also been up to other shite. I shagged Kerry. Did you see that? Shagged her on the riverbank over yonder, sun blaring down upon my bare arse cheeks. Plus there's the, erm…I had a nice motor at one point."

"But mainly you've been trying to eradicate vampires."

"Maybe, aye."

"And how would you say it's gone?"

"It's gone alright, yeah."

"You've eradicated some?"

"Aye. I think."

"But you don't know, do you? The truth is you don't know what you're doing from one hour to the next. This is no way for the Highlander to live and results in disaster—as evidenced by the sizable unit of police officers, which is hunting you down as we speak, intent on bringing about your demise via a convenient stray bullet."

"Them cunts can't touch us. I got friends in this town. I got protection from high up."

"Is that so?"

"Aye, it's fuckin' so."

"Then why are you acting like one who is hounded? Is it normal for you to be hiding down a pothole in—"

"I ain't hiding, I fuckin' fell down it."

"In a meadow to the west of the town centre, suspended in midair while you discuss the trajectory of your existence with a man in a hat with a Spanish look about him, but a slight Scottish accent, who closely resembles Sean Connery?"

I scratched my head. There was some big chunks of cobweb stuck in me hair. "It do seem quite normal, thinking about it, aye."

"Hmm…"

"You got summat to say? Cos I reckon I'm about to hit dry land any minute now."

"You won't. Not until we sort this out. Time is suspended for you. The mind is a magical thing. It is blood and fibre, but it can create entire worlds for us and make anything possible. But it can go wrong, Highlander. Your brain has gone wrong."

"Has it fuck. Yours has. Wouldn't catch me wearing that hat."

"But I am a part of you, Highlander. I am the side of your brain that has not gone wrong, trying to communicate with the other, the one that has lately gained control over you."

"Bollocks. Go fuck yourse—"

I landed.

On my head.

46

But I seemed alright.

Able to open my eyes and see stuff anyhow. Or I would have seed stuff if it weren't so fucking dark down there. I felt around my arse area, and that felt alright as well. If your arse and your swede is working, you ain't doing bad in life. I got up, bumping my head on the ceiling. Except it weren't a ceiling but bare soil, and clumps of it was coming away and raining down atop us like a shitestorm. I bent low and weathered it, trying not to think about being buried alive but thinking about it anyhow. I stood up again, making more dirt come down on us and in me hair and down the back of me pants. A massive bit of rock or summat came loose and landed square between me shoulder blades, knocking us flat.

I lay still for a bit while I got me puff and composure back. Seemed like an hour or two I stayed like so, breathing and not thinking, and looking at the blackness down there. I quite liked it after a bit and wondered if I could just stay here and how life would have been if I'd been borned a worm. Or a mole. Aye, one of them little black fuckers with velvet fur and massive paws burrowing anywhere they wants to go and no one knowing about it. Soon I found meself actually turning into one, moving along through the earth and making quite a bit of progress, although

I were sort of wriggling rather than digging. I did have massive paws though, and I were using them to grab hold of roots and rocks and whatever came to em, anything so long as it were moving us upwards. Maybe I didn't really want to be a mole. Not for permanent, like. But it got us through them hours of wriggling and scraping, being a mole did. If I'd have thought of meself as a person, as a man who had somehow took a wrong turn and landed his arse so far underground that no one could even hear him, I'd have gone barmy.

My fingers wrapped around summat, and I knowed straight off it weren't rock nor root nor bone. It were a bit of wood. Upright wood made of vertical panels, with light shining out between em.

A door.

I pressed me face up against them slats, peering in and blinking against the sudden glare after so much dark. Then summat moved in the way and blocked the light, and I realised that it were someone's swede.

"About flamin' time," says Nathan.

47

After a bit they got the door open, and I clambered through and lay on the deck for a bit, gasping for air. Nathan had Alvin with him, and they was checking me vitals for signs of life while I got me puff back. And it weren't just me puff. I had to get used to being a human again instead of a mole. The way things had been going underground there, I didn't think I'd ever get out. I thought I'd waved goodbye to Blakey the man and said hello to a life of burrowing and eating worms and grubs and that. Actually, worms ain't too bad if you fries em up with a bit of lard. You can make decent bubble 'n' squeak out of em.

"What the hell are you on about?" says Nathan, satisfied that my heart were beating and moving on to other vital regions.

"I ain't on about nothing," I says, surprising meself with the sound of me own voice. Seemed like years since I'd last heard it. Sounded quite deep and commanding, I gotta say. "I'm just thinking. I can't speak, cos I gotta take it easy awhile."

"You're speakin' now," he says. "And you was speakin' just now. About burrowing and the like. What a load of cobblers."

"It's true, Nathe, I got from Ditchcroft to here just by diggin'. You won't believe what I been through, mate. The things a human being can do when he's backwise to the wall—it amazes me, Nathe, truly it do. I became a fuckin' mole down there. No shite, I actually turned into one, in me swede at least. But I needed to, didn't I? If being a mole is how to survive, a mole is what I will fuckin' be."

"A mole? That's a flamin' *tunnel*, you great twit. There's been a secret tunnel between here and there since time immemorial. It's about five-and-a-half-foot high—even you could walk through it quite comfortable, long as you stoops a mite. Only thing you had to burrow through was flippin' cobwebs."

"Oh…but…"

"But how'd I know you'd be coming through here? You knows better than to ask that, Blake."

"I weren't gonna ask that."

"That so, is it? What was you gonna ask, then?"

"Erm…"

"As I suspected."

"No, erm…me vital regions. That's what you're checkin', right? How is they? I'm feeling a bit queasy."

"Queasy in the head, you are. I ain't checkin' your vital signs— I'm going through your flamin' pockets."

"Eh? But…"

"Alv, do the honours."

I went to smack Alvin, not knowing his whereabouts just then but taking a guess. And I guessed wrong, hitting the edge of some sort of an iron cabinet and knacking my arm like billy-o. Alvin grabbed it and did summat with it, turning us on me side and putting us in pain like you wouldn't believe, so I won't bother trying to describe it. He did the same with the other one. Also my legs. When he'd finished, after about two seconds, me paws and feet was all touching one another and held together with some string.

"Alvin has been undergoing retraining," says Nathan, crouching in front of me. I couldn't see his face, but his chunky thighs was right next to my head, looking like a pair of massive sausages gone wrong and come to life. The worst part of it were that you could see where the seam was giving way underneath, his tackle threatening to come free any moment. "Unlike some, Alvin has accepted the demise of his last occupation—that being the preparation and serving of chips and kebabs—and taken on another. What is it you calls yerself now, Alv?"

"I don't like to say," says Alvin, behind me and doing summat involving chains, by the sounds of it.

"I'm sure you don't, you being so modest by nature," Nathan says. "But say it you must. As your employer I hereby orders you to do so."

"Very well, sir. I am an enforcer, sir."

"Don't say it to me. Tell it to him."

"I am an enforcer, Royston Blake."

"Fuck's this 'Royston Blake'? I'm fuckin' *Blakey*, Alv. Blakey, who's ate more kebabs from your shop than the whole of…er, where's it kebabs come from? Arabia, is it? Aye."

"Be that as it might," says Nathan, "but your 'custom' were a contributory factor to Alvin going out of business. Consume his produce you might well have done, but you never paid for a lot of it."

"You fuckin' what? I always paid him. Alv? Get over here where I can—"

"You never paid him the right amount, though, did you?"

"Eh? What right amount? Fuck is this? Is you two cunts holding me hostage cos of a couple o' pence I might of owed him?"

"Couple o' pence, he says! Alvin, tell him the true figure."

"Hang on, there ain't no way of knowing the—"

"Seven hundred and eighty-two pounds and forty-six pence."

"Seven hundred an'…Alv, you is having a fuckin' *josh*, mate."

"He ain't havin' a josh. Debt at that level ain't no joshin' matter. And he knows the exact sum on account of he's took a running tally of your little 'shortfalls' since the very first time you went in his shop, back in—"

"Did he fuck! Alv, you don't even fuckin' know when I first went in your shop."

"He do."

"Like fuckin' *shite* do he. Alv, what did I have?"

"First time you come in, you had a tray of scratchings. Five pence it come to, but you give us four. Allowing for inflation, I'm calling that a debt of ten pence by today's money."

"*Ten* fuckin' *pence*? It ain't ten, it's, erm…"

"I can get fifty pence for scratchings these days."

"No you fuckin' cannot. You ain't even got a shop."

"That ain't my fault. Boss says it's down to folks like you I ain't got the shop no more."

"Is it fuck. It's down to you and your fuckin' soggy chips. How many times I tell you that folks likes em crispy?"

"I couldn't do crispy with the fryer I had."

"That's cos you was doin' it wrong. I fuckin' told yer a *million times* how you ought to be—"

"*Be that as it might!*" blares Nathan, filling the small space with so much racket I thought the roof might cave in. And fuck knowed how far down we were here. The cellars at the Paul Pry went down a long way—so I'd learned via bitter experiences in em—but I hadn't never clocked this bit. It were well hot down here and made you wonder if you was closer to hell than the Paul Pry. "Be that as it might," he says again, quieter, "fact is that Alvin has accepted it and moved on. He has started a new chapter of his professional life and discovered new talents, such as getting from *A* to *B* silently and invisibly, and dealing with folks swiftly and without fuss. They don't even see him coming."

I started laughing.

"Summat amusing, Blake?" says Nathan. "I gotta say, it's odd how you can locate humour in the bleakest of—"

"You're telling me Alvin were that fuckin' ninja back there with them Egyptians?" I says between massive guffaws. "Bollocks were that Alvin. He can't do all that shite."

"Ninja is just one of the roles he can play, Blakey. Alvin operates like a chameleon, changing his appearance to suit the situation. Sometimes he's the ninja, sometimes he's plain old Alvin. Other times he might be a golem."

"Like fuck were that Alvin. That fuckin' golem were as big as me. Alvin's a streak of fuckin' piss."

"Quibble all you likes—Alvin has learned to do what he must in order to get the job done. Fact is, Blake, you been left behind. Some men can adapt, turning emselves into whatever is required as the times changes around em. Others can't. Them ones is made of stone, Blakey. You can try and bend em and shape em, but they just won't go. You puts em under intense heat so as to melt em, but it just turns em wrong in the core, and you can't never get em back. That's what's happened with you, Blake. You've gone wrong in the core."

I were blinking hard while he went on, trying to stop meself going blind from the sweat going in me eyes. The heat down here were fucking mental, and there were a smell like a gas fire burning full blast nearby. But why the fuck would they have a gas fire down here?

"And do you know what happens to wrong uns, eh Blake? They gets left behind. They gets crushed under the steamroller of time. But first...Alv, you ready?"

"Hang on a min."

"I ain't got all day, fer cryin' out loud!"

"Alright, I'm just…there. Ready."

"Good. As I were sayin', Blake, first we gotta do summat to prevent others from thinkin' these wrong uns is fit fer any kind of purpose. That means we gotta brand em."

"Woss you mean 'brand'?"

"You dunno what brand means?"

"Only type of brand I knows is what you does to a sheep."

"Aye, that's the type o' branding I means."

"Eh, but…Nathe, I don't under—"

"How many times I telled you not to call us Nathe? For the final time, the name's Na*than*."

Then I knowed what the smell were. It weren't a gas fire. It were metal getting heated up. That's why it were so hot in here.

"Here, you hold him steady," says Nathan. "I'll apply the brand. Right where good folks can see."

"Eh? Get the fuck…"

Alvin got us by the shoulders. There ain't many in this part of the country with shoulders big as mine, and Alvin were at the other end of that scale. But he got his fingertips into them and somehow made em go still as railway sleepers. Railway sleepers that was knacking like billy-o but also numb and weak as lambs. I were starting to see what Nathan meant about Alvin dealing with folks swiftly and without fuss. Mind you, there were fuck all stopping us from making some fuss. I opened me gob wide to do just that.

Nathan stuffed a wet bar towel in it.

"How's that, Mr. Mole?" he says, eyebrow hairs reaching out all over, like he'd plugged himself in. "Bet you wish you burrowed somewhere else now, eh?"

"Mmmmmmph," I says in reply, pushing hard on the bar towel with me tongue.

Nathan grinned and reached over to the side, coming back with a red-hot branding iron in the shape of an X. A drop of sweat oozed off the end of his nose and hit the X with a hiss, like a tiny bit of air being let out of a bike inner tube. Alvin clamped his knees either side of me swede.

"Right where folks can see," says Nathan again, leaning in with the iron and a friendly grin.

"*Mmmmmmph,*" I says again, starting to go a bit dark inside my swede. I wanted to kill him, despite the bindings of my limbs and the way Alvin were pinning us. I wanted to kill the both of em. And I knowed I could, so long as I gave meself over to the dark. You can always trust it, the darkness. It will always find a way, no matter whether you wants it to or no. You could be chained up and cast in concrete, and it'll somehow get a fist loose to ping with, or a foot to kick, or some other bit of you to do summat bad with. And that's all it needs.

I got my head free of Alvin's knees.

"*Mmmmmmph,*" I yells again, even though the towel were out of my gob now.

It were all I could think of to say.

I swung my head.

48

The darkness always wears off after a while. It's hard to tell how long sometimes, cos when it goes away, it's a different part of the day, and I'm in a different part of town. That's what happened here.

Usually you can tell where you are by the smell. Different areas have different aromas, and you learns which is which over a while. Norbert Green stinks of human shite, for example. Muckfield, dog shite. Up the posh part in Danghill, there's quite a pleasant countryside fragrance, which is mostly about cow shite. Other parts, you've got things like rubbish smells and factory smells, with a hint of unidentified shite underlying all of em. But waking up on me back in a little gravel backyard with weeds growing up out of it and clapboard fencing all around with half the claps missing, I were having trouble locating my whereabouts just now. See, there were another whiff overpowering whatever local flavour this spot had. And it were a barbeque whiff.

I got up, looking all around and holding me belly against the sheer agony of a hunger like you won't believe. If there's one thing to get me guts rumbling like a fucking earthquake, it's someone having a barbeque. And the best thing about em is they'm outside, so you can just walk up to em and help your fucking self and no cunt can call you a burglar. I went to each fence, not see-ing much scran action in either of the neighbouring gardens. These two didn't see much gardening action neither by the looks of em, being overgrown with stingers and thistles and bin bags. Some of them bags seemed ripe as a black banana, going by the flies hanging around and maggots falling out of the bottom bits ripped open by rats and the like, but I couldn't hardly smell em. No matter what way I turned, all I could detect hooterwise were that fucking barbeque.

And it were doing me swede right in.

"Who the fuck is having a barbie?" I hollers, clutching me guts again. "You don't tell us, I fuckin' swear I'll fuckin'—"

"Och, there's nae barbeque aroond here, for fuck sake," says Jock, popping up behind one of the fences with half his swede wrapped in dirty bandages. "Only alfresco catering yis'll get aroond this part is from your discarded bags o' chips and the like. And yis'll have tae pry the cats off first."

For a while I didn't know what to say. "Is you fuckin' follerin' us or what?" I says, finally coming unblocked.

"Why would yis think that, Royston?"

"Don't come thick—every fuckin' place I finds meself in, it's your swede poppin' up behind me shoulder. How is yer swede, by the way? You got shot in it, didn't yer?"

"Aye, them bastart vampire sympathisers took a wee potshot at me, but I dinnae get brung doon so easy, Royston. Yis should know me better than that. And it was jist a glancing blow anyhoo. Nae cranial damage."

"That what the doc says, is it?"

"Och no, I dinnae consort wi' them sympathising wee cunts. Ah got mah friend Pete Hedge tae look at it."

"Pete Hedge? He's a fuckin' tramp."

"Aye, that's the one. And youse can get tae fuck about me following youse, ye cheeky wee fuckin' bampot. It's *youse* following *me*. Ah know how passionate yis are aboot the eradication o' vampires, but yis have got to give us time to think. And *plan*, yis ken?"

"Why the fuck would I wanna follow a fuckin' headcase like you? I'm trying to get *away* from yer, for fuck. Since you turned up, it's been one pile o' bollocks landing atop me swede after another."

"Ah met a friend o' yours, Royston. Smashin' wee lass wi' a nice big pair o'—"

"Hang on," I says, "who's we talkin' about here?"

"Och, ah'm gettin' tae that. I just wanted tae mention her figure, which was of the kind I describe as Rubenesque."

"Fuckin' hold up a min, eh? Aye, it *do* fuckin' matter who the bird is. If it's someone I knows, I need to know who they is before you'm allowed to talk like that about her."

"Talk like what?"

"Saying that about her rubies, and that."

"Och, ah never got tae see her rubies. This one was a modest wee lass, Royston. Do yis ken what ah'm sayin' there? Ah tell yis, if I was a wee bit younger and wasnae caught up wi' the eradication o' vampires, ah widnae mind trying mah hand at—"

"Woss her name, for fuck?"

"Rachel."

"Hmm..."

"Am ah OK to talk about her figure?"

"Aye, no probs. But what did she say?"

"She seemed het up about sumthin. It wis hard tae tell what. Ah tell yis, yis cannae concentrate when yis have got a pair ae baps like that under yis nose."

"She must of said summat."

"Aye, she did, but…och, I remember it noo. She said yis have got tae give yisself up. Does that mean sumthin tae yis?"

"I think the coppers wants a word with us about summat."

"Dinnae trust them cunts. Them are on the side o' the vampire."

"I know they is. I mean, I ain't about to—"

"What have yis done to yis face?"

"Eh? What?" I felt my nose. Felt normal enough. I had a pick while I were there.

"No, here on the side o' yis foreheed. Is that a tattoo?" He poked it. I think he did anyhow, though I couldn't feel it. "Och, yis have got burned. How did yis do that?"

I had a feel, the whole cellar episode at the Paul Pry coming back to us as I explored the skin above me left eyebrow. Actually, part of the eyebrow were missing, singed off like as not, but it were in that sort of area. Like I says, it were numb just now, but I didn't reckon it'd stay that way. "The fuckin' cunts," I says.

Jock moved his face in and had a sniff. "I believe this is the source o' yis barbeque smell, Royston. Och, they've cooked part o' yis face like a burger. Who was it? Wis it vampire sympathisers?"

"Nah."

"Och, it *wis*, wasnae it? The wee fuckin'—"

"It weren't vampire wossnames, for fuck. It don't matter who it were. Fact is I got a fuckin' X on my head now, and I gotta get used it. I been thinkin', an X might not look so bad. You could make it look like part of yer hairdo. I were thinking of growing it long anyhow, so…Or you could just put another X across from it. Or loads of em, all joined up and looking like quite a nice pattern."

"It's no an X."

"Eh? Course it fuckin' is."

"It isnae an X, ah can assure yis. No just an X anyhow."

"What the fuck is it, then?"

"It's more of an adding up sign. Do yis ken what ah mean? Or a crucif…"

"For the final fuckin' time, who the fuck is this Ken bloke?"

But Jock weren't listening. He were backing away, looking at us like I'd just sprouted wings. Or fangs.

"Fuck's the matter with you?" I says, stepping towards him.

"Don't youse come near me," he says, reaching into his carrier bag.

"Eh? It's me, Jock. It's fuckin' Blakey, your partner in crime. Partner in eradish…eradiat…in gettin' shet of vampires, for fuck sake."

"Och, that's what they all say. It's them on the outside, but inside, yis are rotten. *Rotten.*"

"Fuck sake, not you and all. I just had Nathan going on about all that."

"Nathan should have known better, him of all people. It's no good fuckin' aroond with crucifixes, what yis need is one o' these."

He pulled a wooden stake out of his bag. Looking at it, I think it were more of a cricket stump, though he'd sharpened the end up. Either way, I didn't fancy having it where he wanted it planted.

"Come on, Jock," I says, batting him away, "it's a fuckin' X, I swear. Nathan were just trying to say that I'm made o' stone."

"Made o' stone? Made o' pure evil more like. Have this, yis wicked cunt."

He launched himself at us, holding out the stake like a bayonet. I tried getting out the way, but the fence were there, and I fell on it and knocked a couple of panels down, landing arsewise in the nettles. Jock fell and all, atop us and aiming to use his momentum to drive the wicket through me ribcage and out the other side. But I got me leg up and planted a boot in his guts, launching him over us like he were a pole-vaulter. I heard him crash into one of them bin bags behind us.

"Do you know what, Jock?" I says, clambering up. The back of me neck were stinging like fuck from the nettles. Funny how that gave us so much grief, but I couldn't even feel my scorched face. "Do you know, I've fuckin' had enough of you. I been going round with yers, helping you work through yer shite and pretending like vampires is real, and here's what I gets in return. I busted my arse for you, you fuckin' jock cunt. I got me face burned off and all kinds of cuts and bruises and that. Don't you reckon I deserves a bit better treatment, eh?"

The bin bag had busted on impact, and litter and dirty nappies and rotting leftovers was strewn all around, plus the things that was crawling through em and eating em. Made us a bit sick just to see it, but I held back. I were on a roll here.

"Plus, right," I goes on, "plus you wouldn't of got half so much done without me. I'm on about the planning side here, the ideas and that. Who were it who come up with the zombies and werewolves plan, eh? That almost fuckin' *worked*, that did. And if it had of, imagine how much of a fuckin' hero you'd be now, instead of a fat, fuckin' piss-soaked burger man with maggots in his hair."

He were getting up himself now, brushing the crap off him and refocusing on the task in hand, which were sticking that wicket through my heart. He got on his feet, snarling at us and showing his rotten yeller gnashers. A little centipede scuttled out of his bandages and into his gob.

"Fuck this shite," I says, going the other way at a jog. The fence on the other side went down easy and all. Must have been a Gretchum one.

"Yis can run!" he yells after us as I went round the bend out in the street, working out that we was in Norbert Green. "Yis and your ilk, yis can run but yis cannae fuckin' hide. Ah'm comin' after yis. And then ah'm comin' after the fountainheed."

"Fuck off!" I shouts back. He were still behind that house in the garden, picking maggots out of his grots, like as not. "Tell it to your mate Ken, you fuckin' cunt."

An old lady were walking by just then across the street from us, and she slowed and looked us up and down, taking the measure of us. "You look like my Bill when he came back from the war," she says, staring us straight in the eye. "But, do you know, he never really came back from that war. Not properly."

She walked on, going up to the bus stop and getting on a waiting bus as if I'd never been there. She were thinking about her Bill, like as not, and how she'd stuck by him through all the shite and not gone off and shagged no one else, even though she looked alright for an old bint. That's what it's all about, I now realised. You can fight and struggle and clamber all you likes, trying to get where you thinks you ought to be and stopping other cunts getting there first, but it ain't about that, life ain't. It's about having the right bird.

It's about finding her and keeping her and shagging her on the riverbank. It's about locating where she lives, going round there and trying to get a poke in her bed as well, because you're fucking knackered, and you could do with the cup o' tea she'd bring afterwards. Plus a few slices of toast. And a dozen or so eggs, half of em fried and the rest scrambled. Fuck it—fry all of em. And whatever else you got in yer fridge.

I ran after the bus, shouting for it to stop. It pulled up, and I went to get on, but the driver shut the door when I reached it and pulled away again, looking like he'd seen a monster. I ran after it for a bit, kicking shite out of the back and punching the window, but it got too fast and I had to stop.

Things were shite after all, weren't they? Just when you gets a glint of summat shiny and beautiful amongst all the pebbles and dust, off it goes again. Who were I kidding thinking I could locate Kerry's house and make her want to go out with us and stay with us? And who's to say she had a frying pan? I went to sit down in the gutter, feeling meself welling up with the sheer fucking exhaustion of it all. That's when I spotted her.

I spotted Kerry.

Up there in the window across the way, wearing a pink dressing gown and combing that beautiful long black hair of hers.

49

I loves it when a bird opens her front door in her dressing gown.

For a split second, you looks at each other, and it's like you're two animals. You knows she's got fuck all on beneath the terry towelling, and she knows you knows it and that you got a hard-on, and she can't do fuck all about it, cos she's opened the door to you, and she'd look rude if she shut it now. It's better when you never seen the bird before in your life, and vicey versa, but I gotta admit, it don't often lead to a shag on them times. Other times, like this one here where you knows her and is in fact in love with her and wanting to get wedded with her and move into a nice detached koi-carp house up Danghill with her, you got a far better chance of getting your oats. I noticed that her dressing gown was roughly the colour of oats, actually. Porridge ones, anyhow.

She let it drop to the floor.

Afterwards, with the two of us lying on the hall carpet, me atop her naked body with my shirt up and strides and grots down, I recalled a little look she'd gave us back there, after she'd clicked that it were me but before the oats came off. It were the look you gets on them other times, when you and the bird is strangers to each other, and she is a bit frigid. It were a look that says "What the fuck does you want? Cos I ain't available for a poke, Mister."

And I quite liked it on them other birds, cos it were like a challenge. You knows you can turn em round, and they don't know it, and it's all about getting your foot in the door and seizing your chance to work the magic, via chat or sheer handsomeness. Or giving em money, sometimes. But this look didn't work like that on Kerry's face. On Kerry, it knocked us right off me stride for a moment or two and started fucking with the very core of my wossname.

But it weren't summat I could bring up and ask her about. No matter what, a feller ain't meant to probe birds about the little looks they deals in. She won't give you a straight answer, and you comes across like a twat for asking.

"You alright?" she breathes into my right ear. It was the first words either of us had spoke.

"Woss you mean?"

"I mean…I just mean are you alright? You seem…I dunno."

"Aye, you seems I dunno and all."

"Do I?"

"Aye. When you opened the door just now, you…"

"I what?"

"Well, it were like when you never seen the bird before in your life, and vicey versa."

"What are you on about?"

"I'm just sayin'—"

"From what I remember, there was barely a few seconds between me opening the door and you putting it up me."

I'd gone limp now. I always got a little sad feeling when that happened, when you don't go hard again mere seconds after shooting your wad and with your weapon still in service. It shrivelled right back until it wouldn't even stay in. Or maybe it got shoved out. "Don't say that," I says.

"Say what?"

"About putting it up yers. I don't like birds talking like that. Not nice ones anyhow."

She slithered from under us, seeming like she were wet all over. Or slimy.

She weren't slimy. For fuck sake, Blake. *This is Kerry here.*

"What makes you think I'm a nice...*bird*, Blake?" she says, getting on her feet and slipping her dressing gown on again. She went to the front door and shut it, flicking a V at a couple of kids that had been watching us shagging from out in the street. Cheeky fuckers. Mind you, they gotta learn somehow.

My eyes followed her the whole while, looking for a sign that things was alright. I didn't understand what were going on here, I gotta admit. "But Kel, I thought we—"

"You *don't* think, though, do you? You're not capable of thought like other people are. You can't look at situations and work out what's behind them. You take people at face value, believe whatever you hear if it sounds halfway convincing, and only mistrust those who you've been trained to think of as the wrong sort. Like teenagers. Or men whose eyes meet in the middle. Or foreigners."

She pulled the cord tight around her middle. It looked like it hurt a bit. I wondered if she were doing that on purpose. She looked at us, waiting for a reply.

"Fuck's you on about?" I says. "Woss wrong with eyebrows meetin' in the middle?"

She shook her head and just looked at us, folding her arms now.

I hates that, birds folding arms on you. Even ones who I'm well into and have just shagged, like Kerry here. I can handle it normally, but not this time. This time, with the tight cord and tighter lips and my spunk dripping down her leg, like as not, I felt meself getting upset. I felt just a bit of darkness coming down. And I knowed it were wrong just now. I mean, she were a bird, and you just don't go dark on birds, does you? But she were *my* bird.

What the fuck right did my bird, who I'd yomped hither and thither for and battled coppers and bastards and monsters for, what the fuck right did *she* have to come lairy with *me*?

"Blake, let me go."

I think it were her who said that. She were the only one here with me anyhow. But I didn't know when I'd stood up and got so close to her. Or how me fingers had come to be around her throat.

"I'm…" I says, letting go and stepping back. I'm sorry, I dunno what…"

"It's alright."

"No, it ain't alright. It's very fuckin' far from—"

"Really. I understand."

"No, you fuckin' do not, Kel. See, these past couple of days, I thought you and me had got to be…I mean, I don't like to say, if it ain't so, but I were hopin'—"

"I hope it too. I feel it."

"You see? See what a fuckin' twat I am, not even realising that?"

I started pinging meself in the face, over and over until I got some fucking sense into me swede. How could I have done that just now—laid an angry paw upon her? She were Kerry, my black-haired sweetheart.

My vibrating diamond.

She came close and got an arm between my hammering right fist and my fucked face, making me hit her by accident before I stopped. I did it with the left paw instead, punching meself on the other cheek even harder now, cos I'd actually hit her. She stepped back and dropped her dressing gown again, making us stop and grab hold of her. I snogged her for a bit, standing up under the bare light bulb, groping her back and arse and trying to stick me tongue so far down her throat I could taste her heart. Me trolleys was still round my ankles, and I felt meself stirring sharpish and slipping between her thighs until we was almost doing it again. Then I heard the sirens.

Only two of em at first, blaring in time almost but not quite, so it done your swede in a bit just to hear em. Not that I gave em much heed, doing what I were doing. I had Kerry up against the wall now and her feet off the carpet, showing her what I had and what she'd be having from here on. But they kept getting nearer, them sirens.

And then another joined em.

"Are you OK?" she says, unlatching her lips from mine for a moment.

"What d'you mean?"

"It's just that you've…you know."

"You tryin' to say I can't get it up?"

"Jesus, I was just—"

"The fuck's them sirens for?" I says, parking her for a moment and going to the door. There were a window in it, but it were frosted, and I couldn't see fuck. I put me fist through it.

"Blake! What the hell are you—"

"I gotta know what them sirens is," I says quite calm, I thought. Saying that, there was more younguns gathered outside, and they scattered when my fist came through the glass. "I fuckin' hate sirens."

"So you should."

I cleared a bit more of the bust glass with me elbow and stuck me swede out, scanning left–right like a Rambo. I still were a Rambo, cos that shite never leaves you, not even when you're putting one up your bird. Or sitting in your conservatory while your koi carp plays footy on the back lawn. The sirens was getting louder. They was so fucking loud I couldn't hark meself think.

"Eh?" I says.

Cos Kerry had just said summat, hadn't she?

"I said, so you should hate sirens. These sirens, anyway. They're coming for you, Blake."

"Eh?"

"I said they're coming for you, you fucking headcase. Don't you listen to the radio? You're public enemy number one. You killed two people, Blake. You put a chair leg through a poor foreign national's heart—they found the splinters in your hand and everything. Jesus, what kind of monster are you? But that wasn't all, was it? Then you had to go and trick that lad into going up on Rockefellers roof and push him off, just because he might have been a witness. That poor, poor boy, barely twenty-one, just starting out in his dad's burger van operation. Then you somehow escaped from custody and…well, let's just say they won't like that. When they bash you with a truncheon and cuff you and spend a few minutes just kicking the crap out of you, it'll be because they wouldn't have liked that."

I turned to her. She were on the stairs, halfway up em already and set to climb higher any second, should the need crop up. But why would she want to?

"Woss the matter, Kel?"

"Kel? You really think I've liked being called Kel? You think I've enjoyed letting you do what you want with me?"

Seemed like they was right here in the house now, them sirens. They was front and rear and upstairs and every fucking place. Some of em was in my head, I swear it. I closed my eyes and opened em again, and they latched upon summat hanging on the coat pegs: a mask. A Margaret Thatcher mask, straggly yeller hair hanging off the back like melting ice cream. I knowed this meant summat. I knowed this mask were tied up with that vampire corpse somehow, but I couldn't recall how, nor work out what it all meant.

"Do you know what, Blake? That wasn't even the worst of it, having sex with you. I can get over that. What I don't think I'll ever get over, though, is your face. Your face as it is right now, with the truth fighting its way through to that dim light that shines behind it. It'll come back to me in years to come, that look will. I'll be standing at a checkout, enjoying my freedom and my sanity, and I'll remember this dumb expression on your haggard face as you realise how I've fucked you way, *way* harder than you could ever fuck me, and I'll burst out laughing. I'll piss myself, Blake."

She went a step higher, giggling like a little girl. She'd giggled like that in the caff, I thought. Hadn't she? I couldn't remember.

Already them times was slipping away, going faint like they hadn't ever truly happened. I slumped down onto my bare arse, looking at Kerry but not. She weren't really there no more. Some bird were, but it weren't my Kerry. I slipped a paw inside my pocket and felt for the koi, but it were gone. I'd thrown it all away. The front door burst open.

"*Get the fuck down*," someone were blaring. Some cunt copper with a rifle, thinking he were Rambo. I didn't have it in me just then to show him different. "*Get on your face.*"

I did like he were saying. Shames us now to say it, but I went along with his orders, flopping down on the floor with me mouth up against the carpet, sucking air through it. More of em was filing in behind us, stamping and blaring and getting handcuffs out.

And preparing to shoe fuck out of my ribs, like as not. I couldn't even be arsed to bring me elbows down.

I were too tired.

Click.

"You have the right to remain silent," the main blarer were saying. But far away, seeming like he were up the stair instead of down here. "Anything you do say—"

"What are you arresting *me* for?" Kerry's hollering, up there with the blaring copper. "It's *him* you want! It's him who—"

"*Shut yer face, slag. You're under arrest.*"

IMMIGRANT CORPSE
RECOVERED

The missing body of Estravian murder victim Martynas Gustas has been found. Eric Clapton, proprietor of Clapton & Sons Dairy, spotted it floating on a makeshift raft on the River Clunge.

"I were down by the river last night, standing in about a foot of water just off the bank, when I saw him. Floating along, he were, bore up on this raft thing made of bits of wood strung together with old items of clothing and what have you. I tell you, there were something biblical about it. I got a feeling like they would have had when they found Moses floating down the Nile in a basket. Except Moses were a baby, not a mature man. And he were alive."

Police have seized the body and delivered it to their forensics department. It is hoped that examination of the corpse will lead to the murderer being conclusively identified by matching up splinters in the fatal wound with those in suspects' hands. Mr. Clapton, meanwhile, has been commended by Police Chief Cadwallader for his vigilance and prompt action.

"I don't mind telling you," Clapton went on, "I were down by that river to end it all. Nothing I do can make this dairy work, not

even that two-for-one deal on gold top I mentioned to you the other day. But this Moses thing has shown me that I must carry on, that there is no land of milk and honey unless people have milk. And honey."

50

I couldn't recall the last time I'd rode a pushbike.

Whenever it were, it defo weren't a bike like this one. The seat were too low, the crank tiny, and me knees kept knocking the handlebars. But the youngun back there outside the house seemed quite pleased to give it up, so I weren't complaining. He seemed pleased not to get his arse broke by a kick from me, anyhow.

I were pedalling up towards the bridge, ignoring the beeps and hollering of the cars stacked behind us and trying to work out what were going on here.

They'd took her.

Them cunts had cuffed her, called her bad names, and dragged her out, chucking her in the back of their van like a pissed-up prozzie. And her screaming the whole while, kicking up a massive fuss and fighting like the raven-haired vixen she were. But there were summat off about all that fighting and screaming, as I went through it all again now, pedalling like fuck over the bridge towards town. Maybe my memory were fucked, but it seemed like she'd tossed a couple of screams at me as they hauled her past. I'd thought em cries for help at the time, but now I heard em like lairy words. Like the threats and name-callings of one person who is pissed off with another person. Mind you, I'd been slumped like a twat on the deck at the time, not protecting her like I ought to have. I deserved that name-calling, didn't I? And the spit she'd fired my way, landing plumb in me right eye.

I touched that eye now, seeing if there were any of her precious spit left. There weren't, but I found a flap of skin peeling off just above it and started pulling on it. You can't stop when you gets going on loose flaps of skin.

"Hoy, get out the fuckin' way!" someone yells behind us, following up with a couple of choice beeps of the horn.

"Fuck off!" I shouts back, slowing a bit and wanting to stop and kick the person's headlights, doors, and swede in, thinking they could address the boyfriend of Kerry like that. But I were on a mission here, weren't I? I had to keep going until I'd reached my vibrating diamond and got her free.

I had to make up for being a lazy fucking coward who'd sat by and let it all happen.

I were over the river now, freewheeling down Oldrum Road, which runs alongside it and takes you up to Ditchcroft. Summat were wrong with the back wheel, and it were hard to pick up speed, even going downhill. I had a glance back there and found the back tyre to be flat, and I couldn't fucking believe it. Why me? Why now, when I had so much to do? It were like the whole fucking world were against us—coppers and vampire hunters and even things that ain't living, like bikes.

I must have veered over to the right while I were thinking all this and looking at the tyre, cos I went right into a car coming the other way, the bike going under and me over, smashing the windscreen and continuing over the roof and falling off the back, near enough landing on me feet. I jogged on for a bit, limping slightly on both pins but not about to give way to it. If the world were against us, the world were looking at hard times coming, because Royston Blake don't get stopped.

I stopped for a moment though and rubbed me knee, looking back at that motor I'd hit. It were one of them Reliant Scimitar GTEs, with the Ford V6 and the overdrive unit as standard. The body is fibreglass, and I'd always wondered about that, but it seemed alright just now, not a dent in it, and I could still feel the give and bounce in my left hip from when I'd hit the bonnet. Nice motor.

I ran on.

Past Ditchcroft and up the hill to the new copper station. The sun were coming out overhead, and I were sweating like a bastard, pushing four times the effort into me gammy legs to make half the progress I normally would. I wanted to lie down. I wanted it so bad I could feel the want coming out the top of me swede and trickling down me face. But I never gave in to it. I could see it now, the glass shite house up on the hill, all windows and pillars and a big fuck-off sign out front saying POLICE. I slowed up opposite it, stopping behind a wall in the car park of a furniture shop. A couple of bricks was missing, and you could see the whole station from there.

I needed to be careful now, suss the situation, and work out how to play this. Cos I couldn't just smash me way in, could I? Saying that, maybe I could. When you comes up against a bully, so they says, you gotta bully em back. You gotta scare the shite out of em and make em roll over, not hide behind a fucking wall and wait for a miracle. I clenched me fists.

"Youse took yis fuckin' time," says Jock, coming out of the shadows behind us with a bazooka propped on his shoulder. "Ah been waitin' on yis here nearly five minutes."

51

"But, Jock…" I says.

"Och, what is it?" he says, fumbling with the bazooka.

"Where the fuck did you get yer hands on that?"

"On what?" he says, looking at his hands. "Och, the launcher? Ah thought ah told yis—mah old pals from the squadron. It's through them that ah built up mah stockpile ae provisions and materials."

"I thought you meant fuckin' *baked beans*."

"Aye, ah did. And a few wee other bits and bobs. Decommissioned mostly, and some ae them wis true bastarts tae recommission. So ah'm sorry, yis are empty handed for this."

I were gonna say more, but he got up on a couple of plastic milk crates and aimed at the station, one eye squeezed shut and the other glowing as owlish as ever, even through the bifocal lens on that side what were now cracked and half falling out. He fired.

"Shite," he says, reloading as the motor shop across the corner from the station exploded. "Ah tell yis, these things are fuckin' murder tae handle. Have yis ever had a crack, Royston? Yis cannae aim right." He pointed again, circling the end of the bazooka until he were happy and had it steady, then fired.

This time the station entrance exploded in a million tiny fragments, most of em in the air and raining down atop us.

"Och, it's a messy business, eradicatin' vampires," he says, reaching down for more ammo.

I had to get me shite together. I hated the coppers like any good citizen ought to, but what Jock were doing here seemed a mite strong. Especially when I scratched me swede and found it to have tiny glass fuckers all over it, which went under me fingernails and in my scalp. Mind you, it were fucking exciting, weren't it?

In front of us a Volvo skidded to a stop in the glass gravel that now covered the road. Cars was queuing behind it and doing same from the other direction, some of em trying to reverse out and slamming into the one behind. Horns was blaring like billy-o, and folks was getting out and pegging it all over, shouting and screaming and not knowing what the fuck were coming to pass.

"Get oot mah fuckin' way," says Jock, taking aim at the Volvo.

"For fuck sake, Jock," I says, grabbing his arm. I fell on him, and we both went down, him hitting the wall with part of his head and making noises like he were out of action for the minute. I got on me knees and went to pry the bazooka out of his paws. I stopped for a moment and admired it. It were just a length of green guttering, really, with bits and bobs here and there and a trigger with Jock's finger curled around it. He squeezed it.

The wall disappeared.

I fell backwards, almost doing a backflip and landing proper. I'd always fancied being able to do that but preferably not in a scenario like this, with explosions going off all over and the shite flying. And blood flowing. Not that I could see it.

I could hear it. Across the road. No one makes sounds like that when there ain't serious carnage.

I gained me feet again, feeling like I'd had to fight an army of rhinos for em. Brick dust and fuck knowed what else were filling the air, mixing with the screams and sirens and smashing of cars all over. I felt around for Jock but couldn't find him.

"Jock!" I yells. "For fuck sake, Jock. Can we just have a word?"

"Come oan!" he hollers in reply. He were far away, across the road and getting more distanter. "We've no time tae fritter wi' words!"

"But…" I had to stop and cough me guts up for a moment. I were fucking dying for a fag. But I battled through that craving and went after him, stumbling over the remains of the wall and shouldering into the side of the Volvo.

"Blake…" says the bird inside, turning her slumped head towards me with great effort. She looked like she'd just woke up. "Blake, you…"

"Fuck sake, Rache," I says. Cos it were her. "Woss you doing here?"

"I just…"

"Look, Rache, I ain't got time for it now. I knows you got problems, but I got more of em. Fuckin' trust us on that."

"But…"

She seemed alright, so I left her and went across the road to the station. But I couldn't find it. I spun all around, getting dizzy after a bit and nigh on toppling over but still couldn't find the station entrance. "Hoy!" I yells, hardly hearing me voice over the blaring. "Hoy, coppers! Where the fuck is yer?"

In reply I got a scream like no other. I turned and saw the feller who were screaming: a young copper half in uniform. The other half of his togs had been blown away, along with his legs.

"For fuck's fuckin' sake," I says, going to him. Cos you gotta, ain't you? When you're like me—a head doorman by trade even though you ain't got a position just now—you gotta look after your punters. I knelt down by him, trying to find a spot without blood but not finding it. "Are you, erm…"

He died.

I knowed it from his eyes, the light of which went out just as they was getting to focus on mine. Also cos of his guts, which was hanging out.

I got up and rubbed my head. I didn't like this. I rubbed my face as well, finding the spot that hurt the most and digging me nails right in.

"Royston!" blares Jock, not too far ahead of us. "Are yis with us or what?"

"Aye!" I shouts, going after. "I mean, I ain't, but—"

The bazooka went off again, making the ground under us shudder and me fall over.

"This is just a wee starter, Royston. When ah finds em, ah've a present for them. A big fuckin' present."

He were halfway up some stairs, paused to shout at us but getting moving again now and reloading. There was another set of stairs over the other side of the foyer where things weren't so blown up. People was pegging it down em, falling over each other and trampling and not giving a fuck other than to get outside and away. Away from Jock. A few of em was secretary types and the odd cleaner. I noticed one or two lads from around town who I knew and who'd like as not spent the night in the cells here. But most was coppers. Coppers who were shit scared. Coppers who didn't know how to deal with this.

Who the fuck *did* know how to deal with this?

"Royston!" Jock yells from the floor above. I could see him on the balcony wossname up there with his back to us, pointing his hardware at summat. "Are yis hurrying, Royston? Ah've found them. Ah've found the whole stinkin' lot ae them, all except the fountainheed. We can get her after."

"Her?"

"Och, yis *ken* it's a her. Yis have been softening her up for us and doing a fine job ae it. Ah must say though, ah did think yis were pushing it a wee bit doon by that riverbank. But yis were right—a man must do his duty. Even if it entails fornicating with a fountainheed."

I scratched my head a bit, wondering what he meant by that, then noticed he'd gone from view. I pegged it up the stair after him. I couldn't feel the pain in me knees no more, and I were nigh on sprinting, taking the steps three at a time. "Hold up a min, Jock," I says, surprising meself with how calm I sounded. "Just wait until—"

"Ah cannae wait. A couple o' them are trying tae flee. Ah cannae have that."

"Don't worry, we'll just—"

"But I *do* worry. That's what all this is for, Royston. Ah'm worrying for the human race. Ah worry aboot our youngsters and what future awaits them if these fuckin' vampires are allowed tae infiltrate our society. Ah cannae allow it, Royston. Ah'm going tae stop them."

I were at the top of the stair now, getting ready to charge at Jock and grab the bazooka off him. But he weren't aiming it. I couldn't understand why, but he were putting it down, placing it careful on the deck so it didn't go off by accident. I slowed up and watched him for a moment, trying to work it all out. In front of him were an open door, light streaming through it from outside, as well as a lot of noise. Birds wailing, younguns crying. Fellers shouting and pleading, all of it in foreign. I found meself edging close, peering round the door until I could see one or two faces with shit-scared looks upon em.

"Let me past, Royston," says Jock behind us. "Yis have done your bit. Ah can handle this from here oan. Yis have got a life tae lead."

He'd took off his anorak. Underneath he had one of them green body-warmers like farmers wears. Except farmers don't have explosives strapped all around theirs, all wired up, or a little electric device in their trembling paw.

"Is them explosives?" I says.

"Aye, they are. These are special explosives, Royston, capable o' eradicating vampires. Ah'm seeing this through now. Yis have been a great help. Goodbye."

"Jock, I don't reckon you ought to—"

"It's the only way, Royston. This is the only way tae keep the world safe and make the fuckers pay for what they did. They took away mah Scott, Royston. They took mah wee lad."

"I been meaning to have a word about that, actually, Jock. I reckon it might be more complicated than what you—"

"Don't you stand in mah way!"

"I ain't, I'm just…look, I had a lad and all, and he got took away. But it weren't vampires, Jock. It ain't just vampires who does all the takin' away of lads. Sometimes it's other things in the world that does it. Like drugs and that. And bad folks. There's fuckin' tons of bad folks in this world, Jock. And witches. My lad—Little Royston he were known as—he were snatched by an evil witch who took him up to the woods and—"

"Shut up, yis wee fuckin' bampot!" yells Jock, barging past us with his paw clutching the device. He charged into the room, screams getting louder of a sudden and folk shrinking away from him. All the while he's yelling about eradicating vampires and getting revenge for his lad and doing what's right. But it weren't, were it?

It weren't right.

I ran in after him, ramming into him and driving my legs, pushing him like he were a broke-down Vauxhall Viva on the East Bloater Road, which I'd had once. Mind you, what the fuck can you expect with a fucking Viva? They'm shite motors.

This were the last thought that went through me swede as it went through the glass behind Jock's. He were already in the air, out the smashed window, and on his merry way down to the car park round back. I remember thinking, shite, I've gone and topped Jock. I know he were trying to blow up a lot of folks, but shite, he'd become a mate of mine. We'd come to understand each other, me and Jock had.

Somehow he turned in the air before landing and clocked me straight in the eye. That's when I realised I were right next to him.

I'd gone with him out the window.

"Och…" he started to say, with a look on his face that said he were alright about it and he were letting us off the hook for it. I ain't just saying that neither. I can still picture it now, him saying "Och" and giving us that look. Then we hit tarmac.

52

"Someone's hit her!"

"Eh? What do you mean?"

"A feller just jumped out that window up there and landed on her!"

"Oh, shit…"

"Jesus Christ—there's two of em!"

"Call an ambulance."

"Call a…are you serious? Just about every fucking ambulance in the Mangel area is on its way over here right now. Have you seen the carnage out front?"

"Look—one of em's getting up!"

"No, that's not possib…Oh God, it's that bloke. That mental one."

My whole head tasted of copper. I reckon I'd busted a jaw. Plus my nose, I realised, when I touched it and it were covered in blood. Then I lifted my head off the deck and noticed it weren't my blood.

It weren't even Jock's blood.

I lifted her head out of the puddle of blood. "Kel, come on," I says, shaking her a bit. But you could see from her eyes. And the way her skull were coming away at the back.

They grabbed my arms and dragged us off. Her head dropped down on the hard stuff again with a damp thud. Jock were splayed across her middle, still wearing that body warmer with all the shite attached. His hand were still holding the device, thumb poised. He were gonna press it any second, I were thinking as they fumbled to get the cuffs on me. Then I noticed his head and saw that it had gone all the way round. Like an owl. One of the coppers pinched my skin with the cuffs, knacking it like billy-o.

I were dog-arse tired, truly I fucking were. But still the darkness, it came down.

SOMETIMES A MAN

Editorial by Malcolm Pigg

There is good in all of our hearts, so say some.

Personally I have no time for such dogma. Who says there is good in all of our hearts? Can they prove it? Can your forensics experts do an autopsy on any person, point to a bit of gristle in the cardiac area, and declare that here is good? I doubt it very much. But then, I can't conclusively deny it either. After recent events in our town—tragic events in which both the worst and best of our citizens have been revealed—I can no longer conclusively say anything.

Royston Blake is a man who many of us know from the pages of this journal over the years. He has been involved in every type of crime a man can do. He has stolen, assaulted, burglarised, vandalised, offended, abused, scandalised, and murdered. We know he did those things, convicted or otherwise, and I don't believe any court in the land is going to pull me up for printing such claims. Here is a man who is bad. Here, walking amongst us all these years, was a man whom I could point at and safely claim, "He has no good in his heart."

But I have been proven wrong.

What he did inside that police station, in the midst of all the turmoil, screaming, and flowing of much blood, was as good and decent an action as I have ever seen a man do. He single-handedly put an evil terrorist—wired up with enough explosives to blow half the town sky-high—through an inch of plate glass and sent him to his doom. Blake was prepared to die so that thirty-five anonymous foreign people might live, some of them children barely out of their nappies, and all of them bewildered and terrified. On top of all that, and in a stroke of serendipity that only extreme circumstances can engender, the resulting fall killed not only the evil McCrae, but also Kerry Barwell, who would certainly have been convicted for the murder of Martynas Gustas had she not been on the ground at that moment, trying to escape custody in all the confusion. And yet Blake survived.

Against all the odds, and due to no self-preserving effort of his own, Royston Blake held on to an eighteen-stone human bomb through a thirty-foot fall, then got up, brushed himself down and scarpered off, sporting not much more than a limp for his troubles.

"I judge this man wrong," said one of those thirty-five immigrants as they packed up, bound for new housing in Barkettle. "Before, I think him racist thug with small brain and no courage. But now I learn two thing: I learn he not racist. And I learn he have courage. Like wild boar."

I learned something too: I learned that deep in Royston Blake's chest, under the muscle and the fat and the scars and tattoos, there is a big lump of gristle that is pure, 100 percent good.

53

She found us down by the gulley.

I were trying to catch some fish at the time, using a stick I'd sharpened into a spear. I hadn't managed to get one yet, but I'd speared an old welly with a steel toe cap, which I didn't even know you could get, and it turned out to be quite useful. One of me boots were wearing out summat chronic, so I'd plonked the welly on a branch and let him dry out. Didn't fit too bad. Wrong foot, mind. I were wearing it now.

"Is that a fashion statement?" she says, trying to get nearer the water but too scared. Mind you, she were a bird. And she were wearing a skirt.

I didn't reply. I did give up on the harpooning though. Actually, it weren't harpooning, cos when you does that, it's for big fish, and they swims away, but you got em on a line now. Only fish I could see here was minnows.

"People have been looking for you," she says, crouching down.

I knowed I'd be able to see her knickers if I looked now, and she wouldn't know I'd be seeing em, but still I didn't look.

"They've been looking all week. And I don't just mean police. People have been worried, Blakey. There are people who care about you."

I noticed a minnow. I picked up the spear again.

"I care about you."

I chucked the spear, but it missed. Again.

"Fuck sake," I says.

"What have you been living on? Food, I mean."

I got out the water and started sharpening the spear with my blade. It were a good blade, and I'd been sharpening it on some rocks. I hadn't ever had it so sharp.

"You can talk now, Blake. You've already broken your silence anyway."

"I ain't."

"Yeah, you have."

"Woss I said?"

"You said 'Fuck sake.'"

Oh, aye. Shite.

"It doesn't matter. It's better to talk anyway."

"Why the fuck would I wanna talk, Rache?"

"Why not? We like talking to each other, don't we? Haven't we always had a laugh, even though things have been tough for each of us? And there are loads of others who want to talk to you now. The paper wants to talk to you, I hear. You're famous, Blake! Your picture was in the paper."

"I been in the paper before. Loads of times."

"Yeah, but this was good. They're calling you a hero. You saved people from being killed by that terrorist."

"What fuckin' terrorist?"

"The one with the burger van. Scottish one."

"Jock weren't a fuckin' terrorist, fuck sake."

"Oh yeah? What was he doing, then?"

I didn't answer.

"See? He was a racist maniac, Blake. And you stopped him. You saved children in that station, Blake."

"He were a fuckin' vampire eradicator," I says finally. "He reckoned them folks was vampires, not Egyptians."

I found meself to be breathing hard.

"But you knew they weren't, right?" she says after a bit.

I picked up the spear again. It were fucking well sharp now. So sharp it had lost its rigidity and were all floppy and useless at the end.

"OK," says Rache. "It don't matter what you thought then, when you were with him. But you know they weren't vampires now, right? I mean, are you a hundred percent sure in your mind that they weren't vampires?"

I shrugged.

"OK," she says. But I could hear her sighing. "What have you been doing up here, Blake? I mean, besides hiding from everyone and growing a massive beard? There must be a reason you came—"

"I been looking for my lad," I says. "Little Royston. He were snatched by a witch, couple o' years back now. Far as I knows it, she took him up here and has been bringing him up in these woods ever since. By my reckoning he's about eight by now. Or five, or summat. Anyhow, I knows he's here. I seen where he's been camping. He even called to me. When I were up here with Jock the one time, after I shoved him down this here gulley cos I wanted to know if he were the Highlander, Little Royston called to me. 'Daddy,' he went. Couple of times I heard it, but I never done fuck all about it. I got scared, Rache, you know? Scared o' being a dad. Anything can happen to them little buggers, and you can't stop it, can yers? They goes out into the world and encounters all kinds of shite, and some of it is bad, and you can't stop it. But I accepts that now. I'm back here for him, if he'd only fuckin' shout 'Daddy' again."

Rache went to open her mouth but never said fuck all. I looked at her for the first time, noticing that her knickers was black. I fucking love black knickers. She glanced up at the path, which were far above me. I knowed straight off that she had others up there. Coppers, like as not. "Are you gonna come with me now, Blake?"

"Nah."

"Why not? I mean, you're not in trouble or anything and—"

"I'll come in a bit, right? Keep yer fuckin' hairpiece on."

"Right, OK. You just wanna stay here for a bit, just taking it easy and—"

"Nah, fuck that," I says, picking up the spear and going in the water again.

Rache got on her feet, thinking I were going for her. Silly cow. Royston Blake do not hurt birds—not on purpose anyhow. And never ones who is Rache.

"I just gotta see someone about summat," I says, setting off downstream.

"What? But…who?"

"Fuckin' relax. I'll be back here in a min. Keep your knickers on, eh. Colour suits you, by the way." I winked at her and disappeared around the bend.

It were deeper in this part. I couldn't even recall when I'd come down here with Jock. There weren't much I could recall about any of that shite. A little ways along, there was a bank where you could climb up, using the branches of one of them big trees that grows half in the water and half out, never getting thirsty unless the stream runs dry. Behind that were a clearing in the trees, pine needles underfoot and not much sun getting through overhead. He were stood at the far end, practicing his swordplay. "Greetings, Highlander," he says as I drew near.

He were wearing his hat, but it looked different now. The feather were still in it, but it were ragged, like it had been plucked off one of them birds who gets caught up in an oil slick. Also the hat didn't turn up proper at the side, like it had got wet and not dried proper. He reached behind his back, never taking his eyes off us, and pulled out another sword from some sort of sheath he had back there.

"You have come a long way, Highlander," he says, coughing a bit. You could hear a rattle in his throat. "Your progress has been steady, and you are deep into the world you must now inhabit. You see things differently, yes? You see the skeleton in each leaf, the heart that beats within every insect. Soon you will be ready. Do you know whereof I speak, Highlander?"

I didn't answer him. I were determined not to.

And he weren't tricking us into saying "Fuck sake," neither.

"I speak of the Quickening. You will receive it, Highlander. It will come at you from behind and enter your body when you least expect it. But first…"

He lobbed the sword at us, trying to make it so I could catch it. But he done it wrong, setting it spinning a bit, so you couldn't see where the handle were. I stepped aside and let it land on the pine needles.

"But first you must learn how to use a sword."

He turned his back on us and stepped away a bit, swinging his arms and loosening his back muscles. I picked the sword up and ran at him, sweeping it through the air and towards him. He turned at the last minute, and I got him in the throat. The sword went right through and lopped his head off. His body stood like so for a couple of seconds then toppled over.

I dropped the sword and went back to Rache.

54

She were on the other bank now, the one with the path high up above it. She started to say summat, but I cut her off. "You know you was asking about vampires?" I says, sitting down next to her.

She got up, then sat down again, a little bit further off. Still quite close, mind. "Erm, yeah?"

"I just wanted to say that I knows they ain't real, right? They ain't real, and nor is that fuckin' witch what swiped Little Royston. I mean, she never swiped him. Fuck knows what happened to him, but it weren't a witch nor a vampire nor whatnot. It weren't a werewolf nor a zombie neither, cos them things don't exist. I mean, for fuck sake…I been going through a hard time, Rache. I been tapped in the head. I knows I have, but I can see it now and say it, which means I'm alright, right? Or I'm gonna be alright. All I needed were to sort some shite out, work out a few things and… You alright, Rache?"

"Yeah. I mean, go on."

"Woss you keep looking behind us for?"

"I don't. I mean…"

I turned just as a feller in green overalls slotted a needle in my arse and shot home the bad stuff.

"Shhhh…" he says as I drifted out of consciousness. "Shh, shh, shh."

Rache held my hand.

THE END

IN MEMORY OF
DAVID WILLIAMS

ABOUT THE AUTHOR

Photo by Lisa Williams

Charlie Williams was born in Worcester, England, where he still lives with his family. His novels include *Deadfolk*, *Booze and Burn*, *King of the Road*, *Stairway to Hell*, and *One Dead Hen* and have been translated into French, Spanish, Italian, and Russian.

3267590R00165

Printed in Great Britain
by Amazon.co.uk, Ltd.,
Marston Gate.